AMONG FALLEN ANGELS

TOM MORRIS

Dedication

To Gwen, whose encouragement, support, and patience enabled me to lock myself away in my home office for countless hours to write, rewrite, and otherwise work on this novel.

CHAPTER 1

November 1997

Michael D'Angelo was enjoying the scenery of Fairmount Park as he piloted the large SUV up the steep curves of Lincoln Drive. But the scenery didn't stop him from stealing a glance at his wife as she removed the pins from her formally coiffed hairstyle, letting down her shoulder-length mahogany tresses.

"You looked beautiful today, Carmella," Michael said.

"I hope I didn't look *too* good. This was supposed to be Maria's day in the spotlight." They'd just come from their baby daughter's baptism at the Cathedral of Saint Peter and Saint Paul, followed by brunch at their favorite restaurant, Francesca's, in South Philadelphia.

Michael thought back to the church with its stained-glass windows, ornate carvings of angels on the walls, and a vaulted ceiling that seemed to reach all the way to heaven. He felt proud when the priest held Maria high so the entire congregation could see her at the end of the baptism. Maria charmed the audience with a cherub-like grin.

"Victor seemed to enjoy the service," Carmella observed. "It's quite a feather in your cap that the family's boss showed up at the baptism of our daughter."

"Yeah. There were some FBI agents there as well. I guess they don't get too many chances to see Victor in public."

"I hope they were there to see Victor," Carmella added with a wrinkle in her brow. "I'm a little worried they wanted eyes on you as well. After all, you could be Victor's replacement when he steps down."

"So what if they did come to see me?"

"It worries me, Michael. I know you're an honorable man and you have dreams of changing the organization, but the rest of the world doesn't understand our way of life."

Maria and her two-year-old brother, Raphael, made gentle snoring sounds in the back seat. Carmella finished letting down her hair and put her hand on Michael's shoulder.

"Michael, promise me something."

"Sure, babe, what is it?" Michael sighed. His gut felt stiff and bloated from eating too much, and he needed a nap more than a discussion about promises.

"I want you to promise you'll keep Maria separated from the business."

"Carmella, you know I keep family and business separate."

"I really mean this. I want Maria to be raised like she's not part of what our family is involved in."

The two rode in silence until the automatic gate opened and they pulled up to their stately home featuring granite stones laid in place 150 years ago. Michael turned off the ignition and looked straight at Carmella. "I promise I'll do everything in my power to keep the business away from Maria. We'll work through this together."

Carmella leaned over and kissed Michael on the cheek.

CHAPTER 2

March 2019

Maria D'Angelo sat, fidgeting, as she waited in the office of her advisor at St. Helen's Convent in Lindenwood, Pennsylvania, not far from where she had grown up. After brushing her dark brown hair back over her shoulder, loud steps resonated from the hallway—amplified by the convent's stone floors and walls. When Sister Margaret entered the room, Maria rose so quickly she nearly lost her balance.

"Good morning, Sister Margaret," Maria said.

"Please have a seat," the sister said in a brittle, raspy voice.

Maria sat and smoothed the modest, blue pinafore dress she wore over a white button-down blouse. She joined her hands together in front of her in an almost prayerlike position as Sister Margaret placed a stack of folders on the desk and sat in a tall chair.

Sister Margaret wore small round glasses, and the wrinkles around the corners of her eyes made it look like she was squinting. As the sister shuffled through the files, Maria reached up to wipe the beads of sweat forming on her forehead. She expected she would learn at this meeting whether the convent would invite her to take preliminary vows and become a novice—a key step on the way to becoming a nun. Maria knew many young women who aspired to become nuns did not succeed. They dropped out along the way, or, for various reasons, the convent decided being a nun was not a good fit for a candidate.

The sister continued. "Maria, you've been with us for a year now. You've studied hard and passed all the tests. You've excelled at the service projects we have assigned, and you seem to get along well with the other young women training with you. But there is one thing I'd like you to help me understand."

Maria swallowed and bit her lip, not knowing what was coming next. Maria was aware of rumors surrounding her family's alleged involvement in criminal activities. She didn't believe the rumors, but she sometimes wondered about her father's long hours away from home and the tough-looking characters who sometimes came to visit. Many times she wanted to ask her father about the business, but she knew that in Italian families, the women were not supposed to question the men about their work. What if Sister Margaret asked her about this? How would she answer?

Sister Margaret closed the file in front of her and leaned forward. "Maria, you come from a wealthy family. You graduated near the top of your class at Villanova, and you're an attractive young woman. I have no doubt whatsoever that you could do anything you want. I'm sure you could have opportunities to be happily married and have your own family. Please explain to me as best you can why you want to become a nun."

Maria glanced around the room as she thought about the question. She was relieved the sister hadn't asked about the dark rumors, but she was still perplexed. She had already submitted a short essay on the same question when she applied for the program. Why was the sister asking again?

As if reading Maria's mind, the sister spoke again. "I know you wrote an essay answering this question. You said all the right things about wanting to serve God with a life dedicated to prayer, worship, and helping the poor. But I really want you to think for a moment and tell me from your heart. Why do you want to become a nun?"

After an uncomfortable pause, Sister Margaret spoke again. "Maria, please answer my question."

Maria cleared her throat. "Yes. I really meant what I said in my essay, but maybe I can explain better. When I was in eighth grade, Sister Theresa was my homeroom teacher at St. Mark's School."

"Yes, I know Sister Theresa well. I believe she gave you a glowing recommendation."

"I used to talk to her after school. As I got to know her, she became like a second mother to me. When I was having problems at school or at home, she was always there to listen to me."

"What kind of problems did you talk to her about?"

"I guess it was the usual teenage girl stuff. You know, being lonely and not always fitting in with the other girls in the class."

"You said she became like a mother to you. Did you have a bad relationship with your own mother?"

"I love my mother, but she was always at the church or off working for one of her charities. Sometimes I felt I was shuffled off to school, or to sports or other activities just to keep me occupied. A lot of the time I was lonely. It seemed like I could never get close to her. I met with Sister Theresa through my high school years, and she was always willing to listen when I needed help or advice. I still visit her when I can at the nursing home. She even counseled me about . . ." Maria paused.

"Yes, go ahead," Sister Margaret said, looking directly into Maria's eyes.

Maria took a deep breath. "When I was in my senior year at college, I was dating a guy. His name was Brian, and he was captain of the football team. I liked him a lot, but I was so busy with my classes and lacrosse that I felt overwhelmed. I also had student teaching coming up. My parents really liked Brian and felt he was a good catch. I think my mother was already getting excited about the prospect of grandchildren."

"What did Sister Theresa counsel?" Sister Margaret asked as she wrote something on one of the sheets from the file she had opened.

"She encouraged me to put the relationship on hold. She said I should focus on my studies, and if he really cared, he would wait until I was ready."

"So, did he wait?"

"No. He was heartbroken, and we ended the relationship. I haven't spoken to him since."

"Do you still think about him?"

"Of course, but not as much as I used to. I was sad for a long time, but I knew deep down it was the right decision."

The sister looked over the top of her glasses. "Are you saying your breakup led to your decision to come here?"

"No, although breaking up with Brian made it possible. After the breakup, I was feeling down, and Sister Theresa encouraged me to attend a retreat here during spring break. It was supposed to be an introduction to religious vocations in the church. She told me to come with an open mind and God would show me the way forward. I came and I really loved it. As you know, a few weeks later, I applied to come stay at the convent for a year and train to be a novice, and that's why I'm here today."

"Thank you for explaining this," the sister said, making some notes.

Maria spoke up. "I think I need to say more."

"Go ahead," the sister said, folding her hands on the desk.

"When I started here last year, I wasn't totally sure about my decision, but over the months, I became close to the sisters and the other women training for the novice program. They really became like a family to me. We worship, we pray, and we eat together. We do just about everything together. It's almost like I now have more of a family life than I ever had growing up. And there's one more thing. I think deep down I want to be like Sister Theresa. I want her joy, her wisdom, her goodness—her life. She's my inspiration."

Sister Margaret glanced at the file again and spent a few moments writing while Maria looked on, breathing deeply. "Maria, thank you for providing that background, and I appreciate your candid answer when you said you still think about your former boyfriend. I'm a little concerned about it since your breakup wasn't all that long ago," she said, raising her eyebrows. "I assume you realize there is no place for such thoughts in the religious life?" Maria looked into the sister's eyes but didn't speak. Sister Margaret continued. "What if this young man—I think you called him Brian—telephoned you and told you he missed you and wanted to see you again?"

"I'd thank him for thinking of me and I'd wish him well. I'd tell him that I've moved on to a different life," Maria said, continuing to look intently into the sister's eyes. She felt she had given a good answer, but she really had no idea what she would do if Brian reached out to her at this point.

The sister made some notes and closed her file. "I think we've discussed what I wanted to cover. Do you have any questions?"

"Does this mean I'm accepted?" Maria asked.

"I was just going to explain that I'm going to make a recommendation to the admissions committee that they accept you into the convent with the qualification that you spend the full three years in the novice program before final vows. I want you to have as much time as possible to prayerfully consider your vocation before making a final commitment. And, given what you said about the breakup with your boyfriend, we want to keep track of your progress in overcoming any enduring thoughts or feelings concerning that relationship."

Maria persisted. "So, I don't know yet if I'm accepted?"

"The committee meets in three weeks. You have a good record here and excellent credentials. Plus, your family is a generous supporter of our diocese. I don't think you'll have a problem entering the program."

Maria breathed a sigh of relief and smiled. Just this morning during the chapel service, she had looked around at the sisters and friends she had grown to love. The thought of leaving them was heart-breaking. "Thank you, Sister Margaret. Thank you so much!" she said, even as she began to realize three years was a long time. She would be almost twenty-six. Despite the sister's flattering comments about Maria being able to "do anything," she wasn't so sure. If things didn't work out at the convent, she would be in her mid-twenties without a definite career path—at a time when most of her college classmates would be established in careers. In addition, given her upbringing in a traditional Italian family, Maria had some concerns that after four years in a convent, she would have no prospect of getting married and starting her own family. But at least she was still in the program and would not need to leave her friends. She smiled and stood up, assuming the meeting was over. Sister Margaret stretched out her arm, beckoning Maria to sit back down.

"Before you go, I should tell you that we are assigning you to teach at St. Mark's School. There is an immediate opening we'd like you to fill. You'll live at the dormitory here and participate in the religious activities at the convent consistent with your responsibilities at the school. It will be a busy time for you. We'll be in touch soon to go over further details."

Not only was St. Mark's a plum assignment, but it also was the school Maria had attended, and just a short distance away in Flower Hill. "Thank you," Maria said, although she had mixed feelings. She loved St. Mark's, but she would be teaching kids from well-to-do families in the suburbs. Maria had dreamed of teaching underprivileged children in the city. Still, she reasoned, there would be plenty of time to seek a position helping less fortunate children.

CHAPTER 3

Maria left the main building of the convent and began walking toward the dormitory where nuns and the young women in training lived. Suddenly, she turned off the paved sidewalk onto a path that led to gardens and a lake, where there were benches and a picnic area for use by the nuns. The parklike setting dated back to the time when a wealthy industrialist owned the property before he donated it to the church. She enjoyed visiting this spot and sitting on one of the benches overlooking the lake. In warmer weather, she would take her shoes off, sit on the wall encircling the lake, and dangle her feet in the water. No matter what she was facing, the lake had a calming effect on her.

Maria thought about the meeting she had just left. Most of her peers at the convent were told at this meeting if they were accepted into the novice program. But Maria had to wait several more weeks for a committee decision. She also thought about the sister mentioning her parents' support for the church. If she was accepted, would it have anything to do with her family's donations? And there was the question about what she would do if Brian came back. The more she thought about this, she was even less certain she would react the way she told Sister Margaret. The sister said they were going to "keep track" of her progress in getting over Brian. What did that mean?

Maybe some quiet time sitting by the lake would help her process all these thoughts swarming around in her mind.

As Maria approached the lake, she saw someone sitting on one of the benches. As she drew near, she could see the young woman was crying, her head in her hands. Maria thought she recognized her.

"Julie? Are you okay?" she asked.

"I had my meeting with Sister Margaret this morning," she said, gasping between sobs. "She said I can't be a novice and I have to leave here by the end of the week."

"I'm so sorry," Maria said, putting her hand on Julie's shoulder. In a way, Maria wasn't surprised. Julie had struggled with the classes the young women were required to take, and Maria knew she had been to counseling for depression on several occasions.

"Could you just sit with me for a while?" Julie asked.

"Of course." Maria sat next to her and put her arm around her. The two sat together for a few minutes without speaking. As she focused on helping Julie, Maria forgot about her own problems that led her to come to the lake. After Julie had calmed down, Maria asked, "What did Sister Margaret say to you?"

"She said I failed too many of the tests we took. And there were a few times I was feeling down in the dumps and I left the convent without telling anyone. She said being a nun wasn't a good option for me."

"Well, maybe it's for the best," Maria said. "I'm sure God has a better plan for you."

"I don't think so. I have nowhere to go. I don't have any money or a job. What am I going to do?" Julie started to sob again.

Maria gently squeezed Julie's shoulder. "Maybe I can help."

"You mean you can get me back in the program?" Julie turned and stared at Maria with her puffy eyes.

"No, I can't do that. But I might be able to help you in some other ways. I can't promise anything, but give me a chance to try. We can talk again tonight. Please don't leave the convent before then."

"Thank you. You're an angel," Julie said, leaning in as she hugged Maria.

"I've got to get back to the dorm now, but we'll talk soon." Maria got up and started walking back down the path. Now she had an additional reason to call her parents.

CHAPTER 4

"Hi, Mom," Maria said after dialing her mother on the phone she kept in her apartment at the convent's dormitory. Nuns and novices were not supposed to have smartphones, but Maria had a two-year contract on hers and decided to keep it in her room.

"Maria, how are you?" Carmella asked. "I haven't heard from you in a while."

"Well, I've been busy. But I'm fine," she said. After taking a deep breath, she continued. "I've got some news."

"Good news, I hope?" Carmella said.

"Yes. I had a meeting with my advisor and she said she is going to recommend to the committee that I be accepted into the novice program."

"So, explain to me what that means."

"After they accept me, I will take preliminary vows and serve as a novice. If all goes well, they will invite me to take final vows." Maria decided not to mention that her term as a novice was likely to be three years.

"Are you happy?" Carmella asked.

"Yes. Of course," she answered. "Not only that, they're assigning me to teach at St. Mark's."

"That's wonderful. That's a great school and you'll fit right in. I assume you could live at home for that assignment?"

"Actually, I'll be living in the dorm here at the convent. Part of being a novice is joining the life at the convent. You can't be a novice and make your own living arrangements. The whole program is about getting used to life here."

"Does this mean when you take the preliminary vows, you're obligated to become a nun for life?"

"Not really. That happens when you take final vows. Part of the plan is to pray and seek discernment from God about continuing. If I decide God is leading me in a different direction, I can leave."

"So you can leave at any time if you want?" Carmella asked.

"Not exactly. I would need to tell the leaders here, and we would discuss it and pray. If we all reach the same conclusion, I can leave with the blessing of the church."

"In other words, if you just leave without going through the process, the church won't be very happy with you."

"I guess that's one way to look at it. By the way, is Dad home? I'd like him to hear the news as well."

"He's not home yet, but I'm expecting him soon. I'll tell him all about it."

Maria wanted to hear her father's reaction to her expected acceptance into the novice program—she sensed her mother wasn't totally enthusiastic. What Carmella said next confirmed her suspicions.

"Well, Maria, that's quite some news. I'm sure you'll give this a lot of thought. I just want you to be happy. I hope you remember that you can teach kids in school, even Catholic schools, without committing to be a nun for life."

"I know. I've given it a lot of thought and prayer and I think I'm where God wants me to be right now." There was silence on the phone for a few moments. "Oh," Maria continued, "I've got a friend at the convent named Julie. She's really nice, but she wasn't accepted into the program. Now she's in a bind since she has to leave and she won't have a job or anywhere to go. I was wondering if Uncle Joey might have any job openings?"

"I don't know. I'll ask your father. I know Joey has several other restaurants in the city besides Francesca's. It's nice that you're trying to help a friend. I think Joey may even have some apartments available."

◆　◆　◆

Michael returned home a few minutes after Carmella and Maria ended their call.

"You look perplexed," Michael said as Carmella poured a glass of merlot in the kitchen.

"Maria just called. They're accepting her into the novice program."

"I thought she was accepted a year ago."

"No, that was just a year to experience life in the convent. Now, she's going to take preliminary vows. It's like going to the next level."

"So how many more levels are there?" Michael asked, picking up the wine bottle to pour himself a glass.

"Just one. Then she'll take final vows and she'll be a nun for life," Carmella said, topping off her glass of wine.

"Can she drop out after taking vows—I mean the preliminary ones?"

"Of course, but she would need to go through a procedure to stay in the good graces of the church. She'd need to convince them it's not her calling."

"I'm a little surprised. I thought this was just a phase that she'd grow out of," Michael said with a sigh. "Do you think she'll really go through with it?"

"She seems sincere about it, and quite frankly, I'm a little worried."

"Well, we decided early on to keep her separated from the family's business. Maybe we were a little *too* successful."

"I'm worried about where this could lead," Carmella said. "She's been a good girl, better than we could have ever hoped for."

"So what are you worried about?"

"Well, for starters," Carmella said, staring intently into Michael's eyes, "you've done a great job keeping our family's activities under the radar. But how long is that going to last?"

"What do you mean?" Michael asked.

"Suppose the news reporters find out. I can see it now on page one of the *Philadelphia Inquirer*: 'Daughter of Mafia Boss Enters Convent.' Not only would it destroy what we've done keeping her separated from the family business, she'd be very hurt and embarrassed. I wish we could find a way to stop it."

"I know some people I could talk to at the diocese. I'm sure they could figure out a way to ease her out of the program," Michael said.

"If she ever found out we got her removed, she'd never forgive us."

Michael took a long swig from his wineglass, looked at his wife, then up toward the ceiling with a troubled expression.

"Please, Michael. Don't do anything we'll regret," Carmella said, knowing Michael had a talent for working behind the scenes without leaving footprints. "Have some faith in her. She'll find her way."

Michael drained his glass of wine. "As always, my dear, I'll defer to your wisdom."

"There was some good news in all this—they're assigning Maria to teach at St. Mark's," Carmella said, smiling.

"Yeah, I told my contacts that it would be nice to keep her close by and in a good environment."

"So you were behind the assignment?"

"I just told you what I told them."

"I guess all our support to the church paid off. By the way, Maria has a girlfriend who was not accepted in the program and has nowhere to go. She doesn't have any job prospects either. She asked if Joey might have something."

"I'll call Joey tonight and get him to give this young girl a job and an apartment. How does that saying go? 'I'll make him an offer he can't refuse.' Maybe we can show Maria that you don't need to be a nun to help people."

"Thank you, Michael. I'm sure Maria will be very happy we could help her friend."

CHAPTER 5

A few weeks after Maria's meeting with Sister Margaret, she found herself in the office of the headmaster of St. Mark's School. As Maria glanced through a large window looking out on a well-manicured soccer field, a tall man with dark wavy hair and horn-rimmed glasses strode in and stood behind a large desk in front of a wall lined with bookshelves.

"Welcome to St. Mark's. Or maybe I should say welcome back since I know you attended here. I'm Tom Jenkins," he said with a cheerful smile as he reached across the desk to shake Maria's hand.

"Yes, I'm happy to be here," she said.

It was about four o'clock in the afternoon and the school was nearly empty. "I assume the sisters at the convent explained to you the reason for the vacancy here."

"Yes," she said. Not all teachers were nuns at the school, and Maria was aware that the sixth-grade teacher had left for maternity leave.

"Mrs. Kozinski is a great teacher, and I'm sure she left everything well-organized. In case you didn't know, her maternity leave is eight weeks. When that's finished, there will only be a few weeks left in the school year, so we'll need you to stay until the summer break starts."

"That's fine," she said. "So I assume I'll start teaching right away?"

"Tomorrow is an in-service day and there won't be any classes. You can come in and get organized to start the next day. I know that's not much time, but again, I'm sure Mrs. K., as we call her, left detailed instructions so you can hit the ground running."

Maria wondered how it would be to jump into the middle of a school year with a bunch of sixth graders. She had done some substitute teaching in sixth-grade classes over the past year and she expected a baptism by fire.

As if reading her mind, the headmaster continued. "Don't worry about this class. It's one of our best. Just take everything in stride, and I'm sure you'll do fine. If you need anything, I'll be here to help. In fact, I'll come into the class Thursday morning when you start and introduce you."

"Thanks. That will be great."

"So, why don't I give you the quick tour of the school—I know you're familiar with it, but we've made some improvements that you'll want to see. Then, I'll show you your classroom."

After touring the rest of the school, Mr. Jenkins led Maria down a hallway she had walked many times when she attended. When the two entered the room where Maria would be teaching, she stopped dead in her tracks with a lump in her throat. "Isn't this the eighth-grade class?" she asked.

"You've got a good memory. This was indeed the eighth-grade class, but when we expanded the school, we had to move things around."

"This was Sister Theresa's room."

"Yes. She retired about six or seven years ago, just before I came on board. Did you know her?"

"She was my homeroom teacher in eighth grade, and I had several classes with her right here. She and I became close." Maria stared around the room. She could hardly believe she was in Sister Theresa's old classroom. "This brings back so many memories."

"Good ones I hope?" the headmaster asked with a grin.

"Very much so. I still see Sister Theresa. I visited her in the nursing home just a few weeks ago." Maria could hardly believe her good fortune. She could almost sense Sister Theresa's spirit lingering in the room. *Is this a sign from God?* she wondered. Suddenly, Maria's misgivings about teaching at St. Mark's were gone.

CHAPTER 6

After the tour, Maria left St. Mark's in the new Honda Accord her father had bought her for her commute. He had offered her a fancy SUV, but after Maria emphatically objected, they agreed on the Honda. Even that seemed extravagant to Maria—she still had the nicest car in the parking lot at the convent. She needed to hurry—missing dinner wasn't a problem, but she needed to be at the convent for vespers, a service of evening prayer that occurred shortly after dinner. She drove about ten minutes south toward Erdenheim, where she pulled up to a large brick building known as St. Jude's Home. It was a facility operated by the diocese that offered assisted living and nursing home care. Maria walked briskly to the front entrance and signed in at the reception area in the lobby, greeting the woman at the front desk.

"Hi, Shirley. I'm just here for a quick visit," she said.

"As always, it's a pleasure to have you come by," Shirley said with a smile.

Maria took the elevator to the third floor and continued down the hallway to a door that was partially closed. The stale smell of a nursing home permeated the air—a combination of disinfectant and the bodily smells of the aged. Maria entered the dimly lit room, and what she saw shocked her. Sister Theresa was sitting in a wheelchair.

She was pale and appeared to have lost ten pounds since Maria's last visit several weeks ago.

Sister Theresa smiled and beckoned Maria to sit in one of the chairs by her bed. "Hello, my darling," she said, coughing.

The coughing fit continued, and Theresa reached for a tissue on a little table near her wheelchair.

"Would you mind handing me that cup of water?" she asked, pointing to a table on the other side of the bed. Maria recalled that the sister seemed hoarse on her last visit, but it was worse now. The sister took a sip through the straw but seemed to struggle to swallow.

"Are you not feeling well?" Maria asked.

"I had trouble swallowing so they sent the doctor in and they took me for some tests. I've also had this cough I can't seem to get rid of. They said I've got a cancerous thing growing on my esophagus."

Maria wrinkled her brows and pinched the skin of her neck. "You'll be okay, won't you?"

"They said it's too far along to operate and they don't think I'm strong enough for radiation. But I'm in God's hands, so I guess I'm okay."

Maria's eyes teared up as she realized Sister Theresa was very ill. "Is there anything I can do for you?"

"Just sit with me for a bit. The nurse is coming in a few minutes to check on me." After coughing into a tissue, the sister continued. "So, tell me how things are going at the convent."

"I had my meeting with Sister Margaret, and she's going to recommend to the committee that they accept me into the novice program."

"That's ridiculous. I don't understand why they need to send this to the committee. They don't get many candidates as good as you."

"She said I'd need to spend the full three years as a novice. They want to make sure I'm over my relationship with Brian."

"Oh yes, Brian. We talked about him when you were in college. I can't believe they're still talking about that."

"Well, I guess it's my fault. I told them my story about joining the convent and I mentioned Brian."

"Well, that's water under the bridge. They shouldn't hold your position hostage to that."

"But let me skip to the good news. I'm assigned to teach at St. Mark's at least until the end of the year, and I'm in your old classroom!"

"That's amazing! There's no one I'd rather have take care of my old classroom," the sister said with a big grin. "You know I taught in that room for more than twenty years."

Just then a nurse and an orderly came in. "Sister Theresa, time for your checkup," the nurse said as the orderly positioned himself behind the wheelchair. "Time to say goodbye to your visitor!"

"Can't you just check me here?" she said.

"No, we need to take a chest x-ray." The home had limited medical facilities, but they had an x-ray machine.

Theresa turned to Maria. "Thank you, dear, for coming in. It's always the high point of my day." She tried hard to swallow and continued. "Just be careful with Sister Margaret. She means well, but she can be a bit heavy-handed. Try to keep on her good side."

"I will," Maria said. She leaned over and hugged the sister, who seemed like skin and bones, and kissed her on the forehead. "Take care, Sister Theresa. I hope you're feeling better soon."

As Maria walked down the hallway, tears started streaming down her face. *Sister Theresa is dying. What will I do without her?*

CHAPTER 7

"Hi, Dad," Raphael said after placing a call to a special burner phone his father used with business associates.

"Raph. What can I do for you?"

"Tessa's birthday is coming up soon."

"Oh yes, thanks for reminding me. What kind of birthday present do you think she would like?"

"Well, she's only three years old, so I don't think she's very particular. But the reason I'm calling is we're going to have a little cookout for her birthday and would like to invite you and a few family members and friends."

His father paused, then answered, "Of course. But why don't you let us have it at our house? We have a lot more space, and we can handle security a lot better."

"I guess that sounds good." Raphael sighed, suggesting he knew it was no use arguing with his father. "We were going to do it next Friday evening. Is that too soon?"

"It shouldn't be a problem," Michael answered, knowing he could line up a caterer and security guards at the snap of his fingers. "I'll ask your mother to help with the planning. She's very good at it, as you know." That was an understatement. Carmella would not only set up a great barbecue, but she'd probably have clowns and pony rides for the kids.

"Great. I'll ask Rose to get with Mom and help with the arrangements." Rose was Raphael's wife. They had met at a community college and Raph had gotten her pregnant. They were married now and living in a home in South Philadelphia. Surprisingly, Carmella took to Rose, and the two became close.

"By the way, I've been meaning to call you," Michael said. "I've been hearing that you're kicking butt with the sports betting." Raphael was overseeing a sports betting network in the city, and it was becoming a key part of the D'Angelo family's business. "I just want you to know I appreciate what you're doing. You're bringing in a lot of money."

"Thanks, Dad. Even I'm surprised at how well it's going. By the way, Gabe's been a big help. I couldn't have gotten where we are without him. He's got one of the Phillies' trainers channeling bets from the players, and I mean some big bets."

"Just be careful. When you've got high-profile clients, you got high risk of having the operation blow up in your face. They're not betting on their own games, are they?"

"No, no," Raph said, as if annoyed by the question. "They're mostly betting on basketball and football. And don't worry, we're being careful. But there is something I should mention. We caught some guys taking bets on the street who aren't part of our organization. We took them aside and told them they were on our turf and they needed to clear out."

"Who were they?"

"We're pretty sure they came over from New Jersey, the Carbone family."

"Did they leave?" Michael asked.

"Yeah, I went out and spoke to them myself. I brought some serious muscle along and they didn't want to fight. I let them know that if we catch them again, we'd break some bones."

"I'm glad you didn't get in a fight. The question is, will they come back and work our area without us finding out," Michael said.

"All of our guys are on the lookout, and I've even brought in some help to patrol our territory. I don't understand why they're doing this. They got Atlantic City and all of New Jersey."

"They've been having problems, Raph. We're doing well and expanding on our side of the river, but they're hurting in Atlantic City because we've opened new casinos over here. People here aren't driving over there to the casinos. I think the Carbone guys are coming over here to test us, to see if we notice."

"We're noticing all right. Where do you think this will end?"

"I dunno. Just keep your eyes open and keep me posted," Michael said with a sigh. "And try to avoid a fight. I don't want to start a war between the families if I can help it. The Carbones can be ruthless."

"One more thing, Dad. Will Maria be able to come to the party?"

"I don't see why not."

"I wasn't sure what the rules are."

"I'm sure she can come to a family gathering, especially on a Friday night. Besides, I know some important people in the church. They can bend the rules if I ask them. I'll have your mother call Maria with the details."

"Great. I haven't seen her in a while, and I know Rose would love to see her as well."

"Just a reminder—we don't talk business around Maria."

"Got it. Thanks for helping with the party, Dad."

CHAPTER 8

A week later on Friday evening, cars began pulling into the D'Angelo driveway in Chestnut Hill. A man in a security guard uniform directed the cars to park on a flat section of lawn to keep the driveway open for traffic. Maria pulled up and turned into the parking area. After sliding into her spot, she sat in her car and quickly searched through her brown leather designer handbag to find her makeup. The bag had been a Christmas gift from her parents before she entered the convent. She carried it on special occasions and kept it hidden in her apartment, as it would surely raise some eyebrows. Maria found her compact, quickly touched up her face with foundation, and applied some lipstick. She took a deep breath and reached into her bag for a tiny dispenser of Mon Paris, her favorite perfume. After applying the scent to her neck and wrists, she checked her face and hair again in the visor mirror. Of course, nuns and novices were not supposed to wear makeup or perfume, even when visiting family, but Maria knew she was about to enter a different world. Her mother and sister-in-law would be dressed to kill, and she wanted to fit in—or at least not look too out of place. She was pretty sure her whole family would have heard about her plans to enter the novice program. Maria looked forward to seeing her family but dreaded the questions that were likely to come.

Finally, she took a deep breath and got out of the car, carrying a small gift bag. As she approached the front steps, there were some tough-looking men in dark suits standing by the door each with their hands clasped together in front of them. The men parted when Maria approached, and the front door opened before she could knock or ring the bell. Maria had seen the likes of these men before, and she figured they were part of her father's security team. *But why are they needed at a birthday party for a three year old?* she wondered.

Carmella stepped through the door and gave Maria a hug.

"Maria, I'm so glad you could come!"

"Hi, Mom!" Maria said as she leaned in for a hug.

As they hugged, Carmella whispered in Maria's ear, "How are they treating you at the convent?"

"I'm doing fine," Maria replied, hoping there would be no more questions. She had come to the party for a short break from life at the convent. She didn't want to spend the evening talking about it.

"You look stunning, as always." Carmella's gaze traveled over Maria's white silk blouse, designer jeans, and light charcoal cardigan. "But aren't you required to wear a nun's habit?"

"Actually, at this stage of my training, we have some flexibility when we visit our families." Maria knew she was bending the rules with her fashionable outfit, not to mention the makeup and perfume. She had slipped out of her dormitory during the dinner hour when nobody would see.

"Father Pierce will probably be stopping by later, so you need to be on your best behavior," Carmella said, and Maria rolled her eyes at her mother's attempt at humor.

Maria was anxious to avoid further interrogation related to her life at the convent. "So, where's the birthday girl? I've got a little something for her."

The ladies walked arm in arm to the back terrace where the party had been set up. Clusters of people stood around talking and holding drinks from an open bar that looked well supplied and was manned by a bartender. Off to one side, a DJ played vinyl hits, trying to get some dancing started. So far, no one was taking the bait.

Carmella led her daughter to the family table, where Michael immediately stood up to welcome Maria.

"Hi, Dad," she said, pressing forward to hug him.

"I'm so glad you came, and congratulations—I hear you're doing well at the convent and at your new school!"

"Thanks, but I don't think I can call it a new school since I was there for six years. And thank you so much for helping my friend Julie. She likes Uncle Joey a lot, and she's very happy with her job and apartment."

"I'm always glad to help," he said. "And I hear you're going to be there a few more years before making any final decision?"

"I need to spend a few years as a novice before I can make final vows."

Michael gently placed his hands on Maria's shoulders and looked straight into her eyes. "Maria, I'm proud of what you've accomplished, but I also want you to be sure you really want to do this. You know you don't need to be a nun to teach, even at Catholic schools." It was the same thing her mother had said, and Maria realized the two had discussed the matter.

Rose stood a few feet away with little Tessa, greeting folks as they came in, each depositing gifts on a table already laden with presents for the three-year-old. Maria approached, and Rose exclaimed, "Tessa, it's your Aunt Maria!"

Rose immediately stepped forward and hugged Maria. "I'm so glad you came," Rose said. "By the way, you look beautiful. Is this the way nuns dress now?" They both laughed in a good-natured way.

"Thank you, you look beautiful as well," Maria said. She couldn't help but admire Rose's black party dress and her necklace, which almost certainly contained real diamonds and probably cost as much as Maria's car.

Raphael stood at the gift table with Tessa, who was preoccupied with her birthday presents. Rose shouted, "Raph, come and say hello to your sister!" When Tessa finally looked up from the pile of gifts, she bolted toward Maria and hugged her legs. Raph followed close behind.

"So, how is my favorite little niece?" Maria asked.

"Do you want to see my presents, Auntie Maria?" Tessa grabbed Maria's hand to lead her back to the gift table, but not before Raph approached and gave her a hug.

"Maria, thanks for coming. I don't get to see you enough these days!" Raph said.

"Come on, Auntie," Tessa said, tugging on Maria's arm. Maria handed her gift bag to Tessa. "Awesome!" Tessa shouted. "Can I open it?"

Raph stepped forward. "No, Tessa, we're going to open the presents later. Right now, we've got to go and sit with your grandma and grandpa."

Maria soon found herself at a table with her parents, Raphael, Rose, and Tessa. Maria sat back and smiled, quietly taking in the beautiful evening and the family's small talk—mostly about Tessa, her sleeping habits, and plans to send her to preschool next year.

After the small talk ended, Carmella looked at Maria. "Maria, tell us about this process you are going through."

"Sure, Mom. Just let me refill my drink." She thought if she could get away for a few minutes, her mother might forget she had asked the question.

Maria got up to walk to the drinks table as the DJ started playing "Just the Way You Are" by Billy Joel. The song was one of Maria's favorites—she tended to like older, romantic numbers. Maria ladled some punch into her cup and backed up to scoop some ice into her drink from a large bowl. As she turned, she bumped into someone and spilled a little of her punch. A man turned and stared at her for a moment.

"Whoops, I'm sorry!" Maria said as she grabbed some napkins to wipe her blouse.

"Maria? Do you remember me?" The man she'd bumped into touched her elbow.

Maria looked up at a tall man with chiseled good looks and an athletic build. Her eyes widened and she couldn't help but stare at him. She became aware of her heart beating. "Gabriel?"

"Yes, that's me."

"Sorry, I didn't recognize you at first," she said.

"You look great!" He smiled and stared at her a moment with a look of astonishment on his face. "You can call me Gabe, by the way."

"Thanks! It's been a few years, hasn't it?"

"Yeah, I think it was Christmas three or four years ago. And, oh yeah, I know that you played lacrosse at Villanova."

"How did you know?"

"I was there one day with the tennis team from Temple. I saw you playing on the lacrosse field."

Maria laughed. "So you were spying on me?"

"I suppose I was," Gabe said.

"Do you live in the city?"

"Yes. I have a townhouse in Queens Village." Maria recognized the neighborhood as an up-and-coming area in South Philadelphia settled largely by young professionals. Gabe continued. "Join me for a moment and we'll catch up," he said, pointing to a teakwood bench under a tree several feet away. Maria followed him and took a seat.

"Well, you probably know that I live at St. Helen's Convent. It's not too far from here."

"Yes, I had heard that."

Maria liked Gabe immediately. His posture displayed confidence, and it was clear Gabe spent time at the gym. He was friendly and had an unpretentious nature. So often, Maria noticed men she encountered constantly checked her out physically. Gabe simply gazed into her eyes, as if looking into her soul, and it thrilled her in an unexpected way. The two sat and talked, comparing notes about different family members they hadn't seen in a while. Gabe regaled her with funny stories about several times he had visited the D'Angelo residence when they were both children.

Out of the corner of her eye, Maria saw Rose lean over and whisper something to Carmella, pointing toward the bench where she and Gabe sat. Carmella placed her finger over her lips, as if signaling Rose to keep quiet. Maria glanced at her watch and saw that she had been sitting with Gabe for almost twenty minutes. It had seemed like no time at all.

"Could I talk you into dancing?" Gabe asked, as several other couples had started in an open space in front of the DJ.

"It's been nice seeing you again, Gabe, but I'd better get back to my table. I think they're about to cut the cake."

"It's great to see you again too. We'll have to continue this and catch up with one another." He took her hand, leaned in, and kissed her on the cheek in a way that was appropriate in an Italian family. Even so, Maria blushed. She could feel her heart beating again as she smiled and turned to walk away.

"I see you ran into Gabe. How is he doing?" her mother asked as Maria sat.

Maria felt uneasy about the whole interaction. "He's fine."

"You know he works for your father and is very successful."

Maria grimaced. She wondered why her mother went out of her way to point out what she already knew. Carmella had never kept her desire for Maria to find a husband and produce grandchildren a secret. Even though she had expressed pride, on occasion, that her daughter had chosen a religious vocation, Maria was now pretty sure her mother was having second thoughts about her becoming a nun. She remained quiet the rest of the evening and couldn't stop thinking about her encounter with Gabe. At one point, she glanced over at his table, and he was looking in her direction. He smiled as they made eye contact. A few minutes later, Father Pierce, the priest at

Carmella's parish, arrived and stopped by their table. After exchanging pleasantries, he offered a special greeting to Maria.

"Maria, it's so good to see you."

"Thank you, Father." Maria tried to be polite to her mother's priest, although she had never liked him. She felt he always fawned over her parents, treating them like royalty.

"We have a number of parishioners with kids going to school at St. Mark's, and I hear good things about your work there."

Maria wondered whether this conversation was for her benefit or for the benefit of her parents, as she suspected Father Pierce was involved in getting her a job so close to home. She was relieved when he stepped away—she felt she was being closely scrutinized when he was around.

Maria enjoyed seeing her parents together in a good mood and enjoying their time with the family, as she had not seen the whole family together very often in the past few years. She even enjoyed Rose's jokes about the convent. Maria admired how Rose had taken to motherhood and wondered what it would be like to have her own children.

As the evening ended, groups of guests were funneled out the front door, where Carmella was thanking them for coming. Maria somehow found herself a few steps ahead of Gabe in the line. After goodbyes and a hug to her mother, Maria paused briefly in the driveway, trying to find her car.

After Gabe walked down the front steps, he stopped and said, "Here we are again! I'm glad I got to see you tonight."

Maria smiled and her eyes brightened at the sight of him. She could hardly believe what she said next, but the words just seemed to tumble out of her mouth. "Gabe, we have a lake at the convent. We sometimes invite kids from the school out for an afternoon of fishing. It's part of a program at the school to introduce the kids to the outdoors. Would you be interested in helping sometime?"

"I'd love that! Just let me know when, and I'll do my best to clear my schedule for a few hours. You can reach me on the cell phone number on this card." Gabe reached into his pocket and produced a business card that read, "G. Rossi Enterprises." Gabe looked into Maria's eyes and flashed a smile before turning and striding to his car.

After Gabe left, Maria stood for a second in a daze. She was training to be a nun but had spoken to a man she was obviously attracted to, had invited him to meet her at the convent, and had even gotten his phone number. What was she thinking?

As Maria drove back to the convent, her head spun. She enjoyed being with her family and thoroughly enjoyed seeing Gabe. Other than Christmas, she had rarely been with her family during the past few years. Why couldn't she have had more experiences like this growing up? Now, it was almost as if she could imagine a different future opening before her. She could have her own family and wouldn't need to live alone in an apartment. Maria loved being with the sisters at the convent, and she loved teaching and interacting with the other teachers, but there seemed to be something missing. She wanted more of what she had experienced tonight. Maria drove into the parking lot but didn't go to her apartment. Instead, she entered the front door of the convent and walked straight to the chapel. Fortunately, there was no one present to see her fashionable clothes and makeup. It was dark, and there were dim lights illuminating the altar, creating an ambience that was quiet and peaceful. She lit a votive candle and dipped her finger in holy water from a font by the entrance, making the sign of the cross on her forehead. She knelt and prayed, trying hard to focus on the reasons she had chosen to come here.

◆　◆　◆

As Gabe drove away, he thought about how beautiful Maria had become. He couldn't get her image out of his mind, especially the dimples in her cheeks when she smiled. Gabe compared Maria's poise and glowing smile to other women he had met. Many of them would have suffered a meltdown after spilling a drink on a blouse as nice as the one Maria wore, but she had remained calm and taken the accident in stride. Gabe's mother had passed away, but he imagined taking Maria home to meet her and was sad he could no longer do that.

Not only had Gabe felt an immediate connection with Maria, he caught her looking over at him during the party. To top it off, she had invited him to an outing at the convent. *How could someone preparing to be a nun give such clear signals that she was interested?* Maria had mentioned she was working toward final vows in a few years. He had a flutter in his stomach as he thought of getting together with Maria again, but he decided he needed to keep his feelings in check.

CHAPTER 9

Special Agent Leon Dempsey was fifty-six years old and scheduled to retire from the FBI in less than a year. He was a veteran of numerous investigations and prosecutions of the Philadelphia Mafia going back decades, when names like Bruno, Testa, and Scarfo were frequently in the headlines. Dempsey had led the task force responsible for many successful prosecutions that had virtually cut the head off the Philadelphia mob and depleted its ranks. His task force had been so successful it had been inactive for the past two years. Now there were some signs the Mafia was coming back to life, so Dempsey convened a meeting in a conference room on the third floor of the William J. Green Federal Building on Arch Street in Philadelphia. It was time to revive the task force.

As Agent Dempsey entered the room, a handpicked team of junior agents ceased their banter and sat upright. Dempsey's administrative assistant followed with a cart containing stacks of inch-thick briefing folders that she began passing out, along with pads to take notes. While the papers were being shuffled, Special Agent Johnson Reed entered the room and sat in a seat next to Dempsey. Reed had been with the task force for ten years and was likely to succeed Dempsey as the new leader.

Dempsey began. "I want to thank you all for coming. Agent Reed and I have been working on this task force for a number of years, and we need to prepare you guys to pick up and carry the ball. As you know, we successfully prosecuted some major Mafia leaders, and most of them will be in prison for a long time. The last leader of the Philadelphia mob, Victor Molinari, has been released from prison but is serving his parole in Miami. We're watching him very carefully even though he is eighty-one years old. He's got four more years of parole, and he's not allowed to leave the state of Florida during that period. Our sources tell us he tried for some time to run Philadelphia from a distance, but that didn't work out."

Dempsey took a sip of coffee and pulled a page of notes from a file before continuing. "The current acting head of the mob here is Michael D'Angelo. He has supposedly repudiated the violence and infighting that plagued the old Mafia and has embraced a new type of organization.

"D'Angelo wants to reinvent the image of Mafia leaders as responsible businessmen focusing on legitimate business, such as legal gambling, night clubs, and construction projects. Let me underscore the word 'image.' D'Angelo has taken most Mafia activities 'under the radar' more than ever before. If you do your research, you'll find there have been no headlines or major news articles in the local papers about the Mafia for several years."

As Dempsey paused, Agent Reed spoke up. "The Mafia has done such a good job that most folks in our region don't even know who the leader of the mob is anymore."

Dempsey cleared his throat as a subtle reminder that he still had the floor. "But there's one way that D'Angelo is *not* staying under the radar: He's made a major effort to support charity and fundraising causes in the region. You'll find his name associated with homeless shelters, an upgraded wing at the children's hospital, and even the humane society. He has very cleverly repositioned himself as a wealthy benefactor of good causes rather than as the head of a crime family, and his strategy seems to be working, at least in the eyes of the public. On top of that, he has gotten very tight with the archdiocese of Philadelphia and carries a lot of influence with the Catholic church. There's even a report that D'Angelo's daughter has entered a convent."

Agent Natalie Perez, one of the younger agents, raised her hand, and Dempsey nodded. "If the Mafia leaders are now such model citizens, why are we so interested in them?" she asked.

"I was coming to that. First, I need to point out that most of what I've described represents some very clever public relations efforts by the D'Angelo family. Mixing legitimate business with illegitimate business has always been their tactic. It still is. We understand that they continue to have several illegal gambling operations in eastern Pennsylvania. We know some but not all of the locations. In addition, they have gone into high-stakes sports betting in a big way. These are not legal operations. They now run a sophisticated operation with computer access to all the latest lines on professional games, boxing matches, and horse races. In one of our investigations, we are even investigating a report that one of the Phillies' trainers is channeling bets from the players into D'Angelo's book-making operations, with individual bets in the one-thousand-plus range. In other words, we are interested because they are still in business and growing stronger."

Dennis McIntyre, another younger agent, spoke up. "You said they were moving toward legitimate business, including gambling. How are they doing that?"

Dempsey crossed his arms and frowned as if the question had interrupted his train of thought. "There is a section in your materials on their legitimate operations, but to summarize, we know they're taking ownership in legal gambling enterprises in places like the Pocono Mountains. Of course, to do this, they put forward an investor with a clean record, then find ways to control things behind the scenes."

"So," Agent Perez said, "are the investments in legitimate casinos the reason you said that the Mafia is coming back to life in our area?"

Agent Dempsey smiled. "The new casinos are part of it, but one of the main reasons we've decided to reactivate the task force is that some confidential sources are talking about a new development. Some of you may know the Philadelphia mob used to control southern New Jersey as well as the Philadelphia region. This continued through the reign of Victor Molinari as the mob boss of Philadelphia up until the time he was sentenced to prison. With Molinari sidelined, some high-level mob bosses in New Jersey wanted to cash in on the activities surrounding Atlantic City and control that region for themselves. The New Jersey faction was led by the Carbone family, the head of which was Bruno Carbone. When Molinari was sent to prison and his influence weakened, the New Jersey forces saw their opportunity and declared their independence. After Bruno Senior's death—supposedly of natural causes—his son, Bruno Carbone Junior, has now taken over leadership in South Jersey."

Dempsey paused, opened a bottle of water, took a sip, then continued. "We're getting reports of some tension between the D'Angelo and Carbone families. We don't have much solid information to go on, but as I mentioned, South Jersey is having trouble prospering in the face of all the new competition in Pennsylvania. So now the tables are turned, and the Carbones are looking across the river with envious eyes. Bruno Carbone Junior has a reputation for being ruthless and aggressive—he's the opposite of Michael D'Angelo. The informants say Bruno wants a piece of the business on our side of the river." Agent Dempsey looked up at the agents gathered. "And we don't want this tension to get out of control and repeat the bloodshed that occurred in the eighties and nineties."

Agent Perez spoke again. "Is the D'Angelo family using church connections for any unlawful purposes?"

"As far as we know, they're just using the church as part of their public relations efforts in a way that's unprecedented. After all, who would suspect a faithful supporter of the church to be involved in illegal gambling or money laundering?" Agent Dempsey's eyebrows rose. "But your question is a good one, and we need to keep our eyes open. I would challenge all of you to think further if there are ways the D'Angelos could use the church, not just for publicity, but to carry out their program."

Dempsey closed some files spread out in front of him. "I'm appointing Special Agent Perez as the lead agent on the ground. You'll all report to her in the field." He began handing out additional envelopes with specific assignments. "Remember, despite all the positive publicity and movement into legit organizations, this is still the Mafia. Don't get lax. I know these people and they *will* use violence, despite the claim that they are a kinder, gentler Mafia."

CHAPTER 10

Carmella and her daughter-in-law sat on the back terrace of the D'Angelo residence in Chestnut Hill in the warm afternoon sun, watching Tessa play on the swings.

"How are you doing, Rose?" Carmella asked.

"I'm good. Tessa keeps me busy. My biggest problem is I hardly see Raph. He comes home late, gets up early, and is off to work. Most nights, I'm already in bed when he gets home. When I ask him why he's late all the time, he just says it's business. I'm afraid that, someday, Tessa is going to be all grown up and she'll hardly know her father."

"Well, that's something we all experience in this business. It's what we married into. We have lots of benefits along with the struggles. Over time, it evens out. If you like, I can talk to Michael, and maybe he can encourage Raph to pay more attention at home."

"That sounds fine—just don't make it sound like I'm trying to interfere with Raph's work."

"Michael will understand." Carmella reached out and patted Rose's hand. "Just remember, we're family. We're here for one another."

During a moment of silence, Rose gazed out at the tulips that were starting to bloom before speaking. "Sometimes, I worry about Raph's safety."

Carmella sat back on the bench and folded her hands in front of her. "We all worry about our husbands. That's why I go to mass every day. I try to remind God of all the good things Michael does and ask God to look the other way sometimes when he does things that aren't so good."

"Say, there's something else I'm concerned about. Raph was talking about rumors that the family in South Jersey isn't happy. I don't understand it all, but I got the impression the boss over there thinks Philadelphia is hurting their business."

Carmella shrugged again. "Yeah, that's the Carbone family. South Jersey used to be under our control, but they broke away right about the time Michael became boss. He decided to let them go because they were more trouble than they were worth. Now they're making noise that we're too successful on this side of the river, and nobody comes to New Jersey anymore since they have lots of places to gamble here."

"Why don't we just say, 'Screw you! You guys left us, and now you don't like what you got. It's your own fault.'"

"Yeah, we could say that, and I bet some of our people have already said that, but that's usually not how problems are solved in this business. There must be some negotiation, and hopefully, both sides will agree on a peaceful solution. Sometimes we need to make compromises."

"You mean we might get a solution that's not peaceful?" The sun suddenly went behind a cloud, and Rose crossed her arms from the chill.

"I'm not going to sugarcoat it. The business we're in has lots of benefits, and our husbands make tons of money, but there are risks. My sister lost her husband. He was friends with a guy who was considered a rival to the boss, and they killed him for it. They were young, and she had a baby on the way." Carmella shook her head. "Heartbreaking. That's why Michael is trying so hard to get rid of the fighting and the violence. He'll do everything he can to avoid a war with another family."

"How can he do that if they start a fight?" Rose asked.

"Michael will work very hard for a peaceful solution. The last thing in the world he wants is a return to the old days when factions were fighting and killing one another. At the same time, he won't let the other guys walk all over us."

"That doesn't make me feel much better," Rose said with a wrinkling of her brows.

"Maybe you should start coming to mass with me to pray."

CHAPTER 11

A week later, Maria appeared at Sister Margaret's office for the monthly meeting the sister held with each of the young women who were novices, or soon-to-be novices. It was a time when the sister would discuss Maria's spiritual growth, as well as her progress in the program. Sometimes Sister Margaret would assign new projects or encourage a new direction in the woman's prayers and devotions. Maria approached this meeting with optimism, hoping Sister Margaret would announce the committee's decision to accept her into the novice program.

"Maria, please close the door and sit down," the sister said. The smile disappeared from Maria's face when she heard the sister's stern and formal tone.

After Maria did as she asked, Sister Margaret spoke again. "Part of my job as your spiritual director is to observe you, to interact with you, and to coach you as an individual along the way to the goal. Of course, the goal is to prepare you for your final vows. Is that still your goal?"

"Of course. I'm very grateful for all your help or any coaching you can give me along the way," Maria said, shifting nervously in her chair.

"Previously, you told us about your plans for an outing at the lake with some of the children, as well as a visitor from outside the convent who agreed to help. As you know, we approved the visit, and we're not saying you disobeyed us, but when a very handsome young man came in a fancy car and spent two hours with you, that caused a little bit of a stir among some of the sisters and the novices."

Maria's mouth fell open, and she gazed at the sister with a dazed look. Maria tried hard not to get defensive, but she felt she needed to explain the situation. "Sister Margaret, that was a relative, and I didn't know what kind of car he had before he arrived."

"Well, it's not just his car. It's the whole situation. Some of the sisters noticed you were wearing makeup, and you spent a lot of time very close to him."

Maria sat silently, not knowing what to say.

"We didn't know this at the time, but we understand you also attended a party at your parents' home a few days earlier, wearing makeup and some provocative clothing. We heard you spent time alone with a young man there as well. Was that the same man who visited the convent?"

"Yes, it was," Maria said with a sigh. She wondered how Sister Margaret knew about the party and her makeup and clothing. *And how did she know I was with Gabe at the party?* It must have been Father Pierce.

Maria's initial shock at the subject of the sister's questions began to turn to anger. She started to wonder why a double standard seemed to apply. After all, women come to visit priests all the time. Sometimes, they meet behind closed doors. No one ever seemed to care about that. Maybe this conversation was something like a test. She thought back to when she was in college just a little more than a year ago. She could speak to anyone she wanted, and no one looked over her shoulder, ready to call her in for "coaching."

Sister Margaret's next words revealed she was not merely testing Maria with this conversation. "Maria, when we met several weeks ago,

I told you we had some concerns about your breakup with a young man at the end of your time in college. Now the situation seems even more complicated. I'm going to recommend that the committee postpone its decision on your admission into the novice program for at least sixty days. In the meantime, we are going to assign you to a counselor who specializes in helping young women work through issues like this. You're going to need to do some soul searching and work hard to make sure your thoughts and actions are fitting for a young woman whose life is dedicated to God. In the meantime, you need to continue here, joining in with the life of the community. And you need to keep focused on your work at the school. Am I clear on all of this?"

Maria gasped and her mouth fell open. "Yes, Sister Margaret," she said with a weak and halting voice.

"Maria, you've done well in your training otherwise, and I'm not trying to turn this event into a big dark spot on your record. The point is we not only need to avoid things that break our vows, but we also need to be extra careful to avoid any appearance of breaking our vows—I'm referring to the vows of poverty, chastity, and obedience. We need to keep in mind what effect our actions may have on the religious community here. At times, that calls for sacrifice on your part. Do you understand?"

Maria tried to maintain her composure, but the sister's attempt to end on a positive note fell flat. The damage had been done. Maria nodded. "I will do my best to do better."

As Maria left Sister Margaret's office, she lowered her chin and walked away quietly, not even acknowledging several sisters who passed her in the hallway. Her eyes became moist as she thought about all the hard work she had expended to prepare for the novice program and now it seemed as though her acceptance was in doubt. Maria had never once failed when she set a goal. She also wondered who Sister Margaret was referring to when she said her actions had "caused a bit of a stir." Maybe the real cause of the stir was people not minding their own business. And how did her conduct violate, or even appear to violate, any vows? Was it unchaste to speak to someone like Gabe? Maria found herself harboring thoughts of resentment and even anger. When she realized this, she left for the chapel to pray for forgiveness.

CHAPTER 12

"Did I hear you right?" Michael asked. "Benny's moving between fifty and a hundred kilos a month right under our nose? I knew it was a lot, but I didn't know it was that much."

"Yeah," said Gus, "he's got a lock on the market here, and he's trying to expand his business. He spends half his time in Miami working with his suppliers."

Gus was Michael's closest advisor, his consigliere. Michael and Gus were in the Clubhouse, a meeting place in a remodeled warehouse the family maintained in South Philadelphia near the Navy Yard. Several of Michael's underbosses were present, along with Gabe Rossi, who was present by special invitation. Gabe's presence was a signal that he was on track to becoming a "made man," a full member of the family for life.

"Look," Michael said, shaking his head, "at thirty thousand a kilo, that's way too much product for Benny to bring in on our turf. We need to do something."

Gus and the other bosses nodded.

"So are we going to get back in the drug business?" Vinnie Fontana, one of the underbosses, asked.

"No, we're not. But if Benny Geller is moving up to three million dollars worth of cocaine a month, we need to get a piece of that. He can't be making that much money in our territory without showing some gratitude. Of course, we can provide protection in return. We can even help launder his money."

"Let me go back over how I found out about this," Gus said. "I've known Benny since he was selling drugs on the street. When he became a mid-level supplier, he used to supply some of our guys when Victor was in charge of the family. I saw him a couple days ago in a bar, and he invited us to get back in the business with him. Of course, I told him it was too risky for us and we weren't interested. When he told me how much product he was movin' I nearly fell off my barstool. I looked him straight in the eyes and told him he needed to start kicking up to us."

"So what did he say?" Michael asked.

"He said no. Part of his volume goes to the Carbones in New Jersey who *are* in the drug business. I told him he really needed to show some respect to the D'Angelo family, but he just said, 'I'll run my business as I see fit.'" Gus paused, then added, "He also said he had some powerful people on his side too."

"The bosses before me would have whacked this guy for the lack of respect he showed our people," Michael said, "but as you all know, I'm trying to get away from that kind of operation. If we can be a little patient and convince this guy to pay, we'll be a lot better off."

Gus said, "Yeah, I hear you. But what about his big suppliers? They might not like it if we put too much pressure on their golden goose in Philadelphia."

Vinnie jumped back into the discussion. "The cartels may not be happy, but I don't think they have any assets here that could do anything to us. They're not gonna risk sending guys up here to fight us on our turf. Besides, if Benny is gone, they can find somebody else and be up and running in a hurry. I bet Benny has some guys working for him right now that're just waiting for something to happen to him so they can step in. I'm more concerned about the Carbones across the river. They're already upset with us. If they find out we're squeezing their drug supplier, they'll go through the roof."

"I hear you, Vinnie," Michael said. "I kind of figured this is the way our discussion would go. As I said, I'm not in favor of whacking Benny, but I think we should hit him where it hurts. You're right about the Carbones, but I'm not going to let that stop us from doing what we need to do. If we have to deal with them, we'll deal with them later. I asked Gabe to sit in on this meeting and I'm asking him to work on a plan. We have sources who say Benny is leaving next week for Florida, and he'll be away two weeks. Word on the street is Benny has so much cash coming in he doesn't know what to do with it and he keeps a lot in his condo, along with diamonds and even some kilos of cocaine." Michael took a drink from the glass of scotch he had been sipping. "I want Gabe to lead a team to break into Benny's condo while he's gone and get some of the money we've demanded. Maybe we'll even find some merchandise. Gabe, are you ready to go with this?"

"I'll get right on it," Gabe said with a devilish grin.

CHAPTER 13

A week later, a white van with "Tri-State Tile and Flooring" on the sides pulled up to the front of the Barclay, a high-rise luxury condo that was one of the prime addresses in the city.

Gabe got out of the driver's seat and went into the lobby to the doorman's desk wearing a baseball cap and sunglasses. Another man sat in the passenger seat, and a third waited in the rear of the van. Gabe handed a letter to the man behind the desk—the letter had been printed on the letterhead of Benjamin Geller. He also handed the man a business card for Tri-State Tile and Flooring.

"As you can see, Mr. Geller has authorized us to enter his apartment to do a tile job," Gabe said.

"How come nobody told me about this?" the man behind the desk asked.

"I believe Mr. Geller is out of the country for a few days and he can't call. He said you'd need a signed letter so here it is."

The doorman paused as if deliberating whether to let them in.

Gabe continued, "This is going to be a big job, more than a hundred grand. Mr. Geller promised a big bonus if we get it done before he gets back. If you help us do that, we'll share some of that with you." He handed the doorman a sealed envelope. When the man opened it, he found ten crisp hundred-dollar bills inside. "That's just a down payment. If we can get in and out quickly, there's another similar envelope like that waiting for you." Gabe drummed his fingers on the desk nervously. If the doorman got suspicious and wouldn't let them in, the whole plan would be blown.

"Okay, whaddaya need?" the doorman asked.

"We need to get into the service elevator with our dolly and some boxes. Then, if you could meet us at Mr. Geller's unit, you can let us in and disable the alarm system. We understand you have a key and the codes in case you need to get in while he's away."

Gabe had done a lot of background work on the doorman and had discovered that he was a cocaine user. Gabe felt sure the guy wouldn't be able to resist a chance for some easy money that would feed his habit. That fact alone made an otherwise risky job feasible.

"Okay, take your van around the back to the loading dock. The sliding door should be open. There's a service elevator right inside, and I'll see you outside Mr. Geller's condo in about ten minutes."

"Great," Gabe said. "And by the way, please don't tell anyone about this job. It's supposed to be a surprise for Mr. Geller's girlfriend. She's with him on the trip and she knows people in the building. Mr. Geller doesn't want word to get back to her."

After the doorman let Gabe and his two companions into the condo, they went to work quickly, searching for valuables. Right off the bat, they found a kilo bag of cocaine in the bedroom—worth as much as $50,000 on the street—but they had expected more. After checking every drawer, cupboard, bookshelf, and even the refrigerator, Gabe shook his head.

"Benny's not going to be happy his cocaine is missing, but there's gotta be more here," Gabe called out to the others.

Just then, Gabe heard a shout. "I got sumpin' in the kitchen." It was Frankie Lombardo, one of Gabe's helpers. His nickname was Frankie Fingers, since he was a master safe cracker. When Gabe entered the kitchen, Frankie and Ange, the other helper, were swinging out a wall panel that was on a hinge. Behind the faux panel was a beautiful black safe, the old-fashioned kind with a mechanical dial and a large lever to engage or disengage the locking mechanism.

"This won't be too hard," Frankie said. "The electronic ones are harder, but I've opened them too."

"Let's just get to work, Frankie," Gabe said. "We've already been in here almost an hour."

Frankie opened a tool bag and pulled out a doctor's stethoscope and some tools. "I'm on it, boss." Ten minutes or so later, Frankie called to Gabe, who was enjoying the view of the city from a large picture window in the living room. "Got it, boss. Why don't you come and do the honors."

Gabe swung the door open and reached inside, grabbing several stacks of hundred-dollar bills, each about fifty bills wrapped with a paper sleeve. *Geller is going to be sorry he didn't play ball with us*, Gabe thought.

"Looks like about fifty stacks," Gabe said with a smile as he began piling them on the table. However, when he was done, he had counted seventy stacks, totaling nearly $350,000. "I think there's more," Gabe said as he felt a small compartment in the back of the safe. He reached in and pulled out a sack made of silklike cloth. He loosened the strings and dumped the contents. There were about fifty large, high-quality, uncut diamonds. Gabe began packing everything into a duffel bag.

"You guys did a great job. Michael will be very happy," Gabe said as they heard the unmistakable sound of a police siren. "Looks like we better get outta here," he said, and the three hurried back to the service elevator. As Gabe and the guys got in the van and drove away, he thought about Maria. He pictured her beautiful smile and he could imagine the smell of her hair. If only he could take her out and celebrate his success today.

CHAPTER 14

Each week a local priest came to the convent to hear confessions. This week, it was Father O'Malley from St. David's parish in Maple Grove. Maria liked Father O'Malley and felt she could trust him with whatever she had to confess. As Maria entered the booth and knelt, the priest slid open the small door in the partition. Through the screen, the priest looked like a dark, shadowy figure in the dimly lit compartment, but Maria always felt reassured by his warm and friendly voice.

"Bless me, Father, for I have sinned." Maria made the sign of the cross as she spoke.

"The Lord bless you, my child, and show grace and mercy to you in your time of need. How long has it been since your last confession?" The priest asked this question as a matter of habit, although Maria and the priest knew that women like her in the convent came for confession at least once a week.

"It has been one week since my last confession."

"Go ahead and confess your sins to the Lord. His mercy is everlasting."

"I felt anger at Sister Margaret this week."

"We often have feelings of anger," the priest said, "but it depends on why and what we do with those feelings."

"I feel angry and bitter, and I've been thinking about it all week. Last Saturday, I invited a relative to help me with the children during an outing at the lake. I asked for permission, and the sisters, including Sister Margaret, gave it."

"So why are you angry?" the priest asked.

"Sister Margaret called me in afterward and told me that my actions had the appearance of violating the vow of chastity I'm required to take. Then she postponed my acceptance into the novice program. I'm not only angry, I also feel hurt."

"It seems odd that she would postpone your vows over a simple meeting the way you described. Tell me a little more about the relative. I assume it is a man?"

"Yes," Maria answered softly. "He's really a distant relative, like a second cousin or something like that."

"I'm still thinking there must be more to the story for Sister Margaret to postpone your vows."

Maria did not recall Father O'Malley asking probing questions like this in the past. She grimaced and looked down before she spoke. "I guess there's more to the story," she said. "Sister Margaret also brought up that I had attended a birthday party at my parents' home, and she pointed out that I was wearing clothing that may have been inappropriate. She also mentioned I was wearing makeup and perfume. The man who visited me to help with the kids was there, and we sat talking on a bench for a time at the party."

"I see," said the priest.

"But honestly, Father, are those things sinful?"

"They aren't sinful in themselves, but they may not be appropriate for a young woman who is dedicating her life to God," the priest said. "By the way, how did Sister Margaret know about what happened at the party?"

"That's another sore point with me. Father Pierce from Chestnut Hill is the priest of my parents' church. He came to the party and must have been watching me. I can't figure any other way she could have found out. I wasn't hiding anything. What I did was out in the open among my family and some of their friends."

"You know you are in a period of instruction, my child, and that the sisters are working to help you develop a godly character. Sometimes that can be uncomfortable."

"Yes, I know that, but I feel it wasn't fair to accuse me of something wrong here. It was totally innocent. I can't stop having strong feelings of resentment about this." Maria didn't mention the fact that she felt attracted to Gabe. She tried to suppress that thought.

"Are you sorry for your feelings of anger?"

"Yes, Father. For these and all the sins I have committed during my life, I am deeply sorry."

"I absolve you in the name of the Father, the Son, and the Holy Spirit."

"Amen," Maria responded.

"Anger and many other undesirable emotions are not unusual for women training to become a nun when elements of the old life start to creep in. In this case, I perceive there may be deeper issues we don't have time to explore here. I'm not going to assign any penance, but I strongly suggest you seek a wise counselor who can help you work through this issue and any underlying issues."

"Sister Margaret has already told me I'm required to get counseling."

"There are some very skillful counselors available. I hope you work hard to take full advantage of their services," Father O'Malley said.

◆　◆　◆

Later that day, as Maria walked to dinner, she passed Sister Margaret in the hallway. The sister did not make eye contact with Maria or acknowledge her in any way, making Maria wonder if somehow Sister Margaret had gotten wind of her confession to Father O'Malley. Deep down, Maria knew the priest would never tell anyone what Maria had confessed. Still, Maria shuddered when she recalled Sister Theresa's admonition to keep on Sister Margaret's good side. Maria was clearly not on her good side right now. During dinner, Maria sat quietly and barely picked at her food. When dinner ended, the women stood and walked to the chapel for vespers, a service of evening prayer. The women were supposed to walk in silence, but one of Maria's friends, Emily, sidled up beside her.

"Are you okay?" Emily whispered.

"Not really. I think I'm in trouble," Maria whispered back.

"Everyone looks up to you, Maria. I don't see how you could possibly be in trouble. Do you want to talk about it?"

As they approached the doorway to the chapel, one of the nuns, Sister Laura, gave the two young women a stern look as she handed them copies of the scripture lessons that would be read or sung during vespers.

"Maybe later tonight," Maria whispered as they walked to their seats. Maria spent more time with Emily than the other women, but really didn't want to discuss with her what was bothering her.

Maria loved the vespers service, but after getting the cold shoulder from Sister Margaret, she found it difficult to pay attention. All she wanted to do was return to her apartment and work on preparations for tomorrow's classes at St. Mark's School. Maria loved her teaching job, and it was one of the few things right now that brought her joy and contentment. Some days she would be up until nearly midnight preparing for the next day's class.

Later that evening, Maria's cell phone rang.

"Maria, it's Gabe," the caller said after she picked up.

Almost automatically, Maria's face beamed with a smile, and she felt a flutter in her stomach. "Hello," she said. "I didn't know you had my phone number."

"Your father gave it to me. I'm sorry if this isn't the right number to use."

"No, it's fine," Maria said, but she began to feel nervous about the call. After all, her contact with Gabe had already gotten her in hot water at the convent. But she was feeling down right now, and Gabe's friendly voice seemed to be just what she needed.

"How was your day?" Gabe asked.

"Oh, it was fine," Maria said, knowing she was not being truthful. She definitely did not want to unload her problems on Gabe. "I think I mentioned at the party that I'm teaching sixth grade at St. Mark's School. I'm really enjoying it." That much was true. "How was your day?"

"Great. One of my projects turned out really good. I was in such a good mood I decided to give you a call." Gabe continued, "I wanted to tell you that I had a lot of fun the other day at the lake. If you ever need help again on something like that, please give me a call."

"Yes, that was fun. I hope we can do it again sometime," Maria said, realizing she was encouraging the type of contact that got her into trouble.

"I'm glad we had a chance to get reacquainted at the party. I was busy that week and almost had to turn down the invitation. I'm so happy I went."

Maria was at a loss for words. "Ah, yes. It was lots of fun. As you can imagine, I don't get to go to a lot of parties."

"Look, Maria. I will probably be up in your neighborhood next week. If you like, I'll treat you to a latte at Starbucks if you're free. We could meet after you're done at school."

Every fiber of Maria's being wanted to accept the invitation, and the sisters would probably never know, but she felt it was too risky to meet with Gabe again. If word somehow got back to the convent, she'd be asked to leave for sure. At the same time, Maria didn't want to scare Gabe off with the story of how her vows were being postponed because of her contact with him.

"That sounds lovely, but right now is not the best time. Next week is pretty busy here. Maybe some other time."

"Okay, I'll look forward to it," Gabe said.

Maria thought she detected a hint of disappointment in his voice. "Thanks again, Gabe. I guess I'd better go. I still have a lot of work to do on my lesson plan for tomorrow." After they said goodbye, Maria had a mixture of feelings. She was very happy Gabe had decided to call, but she felt she was nervous during their conversation. She hoped Gabe hadn't noticed.

Chapter 15

Agent Dempsey called another meeting of the task force at the Philadelphia field office. This time Agent Perez took the lead, using slides projected onto a screen in the conference room.

"I'd like to report on a new development based on a report we received from the Drug Enforcement Administration," she said. "The DEA has been keeping surveillance on Benjamin Geller, who is reputed to be one of the largest distributors of illegal drugs in the region." Agent Perez flashed a picture of Geller on the screen. "Geller lives at the Barclay, and while the DEA was watching him they noticed the doorman at the condo was acting suspiciously. His name is Charles Evans." The next slide showed a mug shot of Evans. "The details are not important, but the bottom line is that they picked Evans up for possession with intent to distribute cocaine. After questioning him, they were able to turn him to be a witness against Geller."

"So how does this relate to our task force?" Agent McIntyre asked.

"I'm coming to that. Not only was Evans getting his supply from Geller, but he believes he was tricked into letting some workers enter Geller's condo. The DEA allowed me to question him, and he positively identified one of the men from photos I showed him." Perez next displayed a slide of a police mug shot. "This is who Evans identified. His name is Frank Lombardo, and he's a member of the

D'Angelo crime family. The important thing about Lombardo is that he's a master locksmith who can crack just about any safe or locked vault. In case you're wondering, Evans couldn't identify the other two members of the break-in crew."

Agent Dempsey spoke up. "So, we can assume Lombardo wouldn't be there unless the crew was planning to open a safe in the condo."

"That's right," Perez said. "And given the amount of cash Geller was bringing in, the crew probably walked off with a lot of money, maybe some drugs as well."

"Were the police involved after the break-in?" Agent McIntyre asked.

"No. Geller didn't report anything," Perez answered. "This fits with what our confidential informants have been telling us, namely that the D'Angelos are pressing Geller to kick up money to their organization from his drug sales. We heard Geller has been refusing to play ball, so this break-in was probably payback."

"Where does this stand with the DEA?" Agent Reed asked.

"They have an active investigation, and they're getting close to bringing a case against Geller. They're at a crucial stage and they've asked us to stand down from taking any action related to Geller that might impact their investigation."

"Of course, we won't take action related to Geller since that's their area of responsibility," Agent Dempsey interjected. "But at the same time, we can't let it interfere with our investigation of the D'Angelo family."

"Is there any security camera footage?" Agent Reed asked.

"Yes, but we don't have a clear image of anyone's face. These guys obviously knew what they were doing," Agent Perez answered.

"Let's send the footage to Langley," Dempsey said. "Sometimes they can identify images that everyone else has given up on."

"It's already on the way," Agent Perez responded.

"Isn't it unusual to turn a small-time dealer like Evans so quickly?" Agent McIntyre asked.

"Evans knew he was already in big trouble for letting the D'Angelo crew into the condo and he feared for his life. My understanding is the DEA offered him witness protection and he accepted," Perez said.

"We need to remember this is not just some interesting evidence about a break-in," Agent Dempsey said. "We know Geller is a major supplier to the Carbone family across the river, and that the Carbones are relying on the drug trade to keep afloat. They are probably going to view the break-in as an attack by the D'Angelos on one of their core business operations. I think we've got a powder keg here ready to detonate."

CHAPTER 16

St. Peter's House was about a twenty-minute drive from the convent. When Maria arrived, it looked like a relatively plain one-story multi-purpose building that could have been a school, or perhaps administrative offices for a school, at one time. The receptionist directed Maria to the office of Sister Anna, the counselor Maria had been required to see. The door to the sister's office was open, and Maria walked in. It was small, but cozy and comfortable. Sister Anna greeted Maria with a smile and urged her to sit in the chair across from her desk.

Maria noticed Sister Anna's pleasant appearance. She'd pulled her silver hair back under her habit, and her smile and cheerful demeanor quickly put Maria at ease. She was the opposite of Sister Margaret in every way.

"Welcome to St. Peter's House. I'm so glad you were able to come," Sister Anna said, reaching across the table to take Maria's hand.

"Thank you. It's nice to be here. I had no idea there was something like this in the area."

"Yes, a lot of good things are happening here. This is a Catholic social service agency that handles counseling for pregnant women and mothers. We also work on adoptions and various types of out-patient counseling, everything from marital problems to substance abuse. I don't get involved in the substance abuse part, but one of my specialties is counseling young women preparing for a religious vocation, mostly in the novice stage. I love this part of the job, and I'm always thrilled to meet sisters-in-training like yourself."

Sister Anna offered Maria some coffee or tea, but Maria declined. After Sister Anna poured herself some coffee, she returned to her chair and said, "I'm guessing that you are probably viewing these sessions as a punishment. Am I right about that?"

Maria crossed her arms. "I'm not sure . . ." She struggled to speak. "I mean, Sister Margaret called me in and told me they were going to delay my vows because of something I did, and she told me I was required to get counseling."

"I wouldn't blame you if you thought this was some sort of punishment or discipline," the sister said. "But I'm going to ask you to try not to think of it that way. My goal is to help you understand your own goals and needs and to help you discern God's calling on your life, whether that ultimately means taking your final vows or serving God in some other way. Of course, if I can help you deal with any fears, frustrations, or anything robbing you of your joy, I'm here to help with that as well. Are you with me so far?"

"Yes," Maria said with the beginning of a smile. She was feeling even more at ease with the discussion.

"The second thing you need to know is our discussions will be totally confidential. I won't report back anything you tell me to the convent or to anyone else in the church. We'll probably need several more sessions together, and at the end, I will make a recommendation *to you* about your commitment to the religious life, and it will be up to you to follow or not follow it. I've been doing this a long time, Maria, and when we're done, almost without exception, the young women I counsel will see the reasons for my recommendation, and they will usually follow it."

"Okay, I guess that sounds good."

"So, let's start at the beginning, Maria. Why do you think the sisters at the convent required you to come for counseling?"

"Sister Margaret told me, or at least she strongly implied, that I was violating the vow of chastity I'm supposed to take. Well, I mean, she said it gave the appearance of violating the vow of chastity," Maria said.

"At least from her point of view, why do you think she came to that conclusion?" Sister Anna asked.

Maria repeated the story of how she met Gabe at her niece's party and rekindled their friendship, including the details about her wearing makeup and perfume that Sister Margaret had pointed out. She went on to describe the outing at the lake and the discussion she had with Sister Margaret afterward.

"So did you know Gabe before your niece's party?" the sister asked.

"I had known Gabe growing up but didn't see him that much. I was told he was a distant relative, like a second cousin or something."

"How would you describe your relationship with Gabe right now?" the sister asked.

"I'd consider him a friend. I enjoy talking to him," Maria answered.

"Tell me a little more about him."

"Well, he seems to be a very warm and friendly person. He's kind and considerate, as far as I can tell. When we talk, it seems like he is really listening to me. Yes, I know he's a good-looking, single man, but is it wrong to be friends with someone like that?"

Sister Anna looked down and made some notes in her book. "I'm not here to judge you. I'm just trying to understand your relationship with Gabe. But let's shift gears now and come back to Gabe later. Tell me a little bit about your family, especially your parents."

"My father is a successful businessman, but I have to confess I don't know much about what he does. He's involved in construction, and I think he's also an owner of some resorts and hotels. I wish I could tell you more."

"Do you talk to him very often?"

"Not as much as I'd like to. He's very involved in his work, and I don't get to see him much. That's been true as long as I can remember." Maria paused as the sister continued to write in her notebook. "I might as well get this out in the open—I've heard rumors that he's involved in some things that aren't legal."

"Do you think there's any truth to the rumors?" the sister asked.

Maria looked straight at Sister Anna. "My father is a good man. He's honest and fair and he supports a lot of charities. He's also a big supporter of the church."

"Is your father available if you just want to talk to him?"

Maria grimaced and thought for a moment. "Sometimes he's hard to approach. So maybe I'd have to say he's not always as available as I'd like," Maria answered.

"How about your mother?" the sister asked.

"She has always been busy too. Sometimes it seems like the main time I spent with her was when she was driving me to school, or to sports or other activities. Other than that, we didn't do much together, at least after I became a teenager. I think she spent most of her time at church or church activities. She also did work for charities."

"Did you have dinner as a family?"

"Usually my dad didn't make it home in time. We had a housekeeper who did lots of the cooking, and she would put dinner out for me and sometimes my brother, Raph," Maria said. "Then when we were together for dinner as a family, usually on a Sunday, we'd have company and didn't have a lot of talk about our immediate family in the conversations. I should say that even though it didn't happen a lot, my father was very kind and loving when he *was* with me. I guess we did talk more when I was younger, but since around the time I finished high school, I haven't been able to talk to him as much."

"How do your parents feel about you pursuing a religious vocation?" the sister asked.

"At first, they seemed happy. I think they even bragged about me. But lately, I'm getting the impression they're not as enthusiastic."

"What makes you say that?"

"Well, for one thing, they've started asking me if this is what I really want to do. They've also told me I can be a teacher in a Catholic school without being a nun."

"That's true, isn't it?"

"Yes. I'm filling in now for a woman who teaches sixth grade and is out on maternity leave."

"So why do you think they changed their tune?"

"My impression is they thought I was just going through a phase and that I'd grow out of it."

"Is it just a phase?" the sister asked. "You don't need to answer that now. In fact, I think this is a good place to end. You can think about the question and come back to it later."

CHAPTER 17

While Maria was having her first visit with Sister Anna, Gabe was less than a mile away, looking at some property that might be suitable for a gambling joint. While he was driving, his phone lit up with a text message from an unknown sender, but it was clear from the tone of the message that it was Michael.

My house. Now.

The boss wanted him to come to his home in Chestnut Hill right away. Michael's terse message made Gabe nervous. Given his successful heist, he had no reason to think he was in any trouble. Or did he? Bosses in the underworld could be unpredictable. More than a few soldiers had been summoned to see the boss at a nonpublic location, never to be heard from again. The worst scenario would be if Michael was waiting for him in a car to go for a drive. That usually spelled trouble. He couldn't help but think of Salvatore Tessio in *The Godfather* and how the family took him for a ride to get rid of him. The movie scene was troubling because things like that really did happen in the Mafia world. Gabe couldn't think of anything he might have done to offend the boss. Did Michael think he skimmed some money out of Benny's safe or his condo? Michael had given no hint of such an accusation. In fact, he had been highly complimentary of Gabe's plan and the way he had executed it.

Was there something about Gabe's contact with Maria that had upset Michael? Young men in the Mafia had been badly beaten or even killed for the way they treated the boss's daughter. But it was Michael himself who had urged Gabe to come to the birthday party and make an effort to get reacquainted with her. Michael had said she needed a friend. Bumping into her was fortuitous, but it led to a long and pleasant conversation and an outing at the convent. It seemed like he had done exactly what Michael asked him to do and more.

A few days ago, Maria had sounded happy to hear from Gabe when he called her in the evening. Gabe couldn't imagine she had complained to her father about it.

When Gabe pulled into the driveway, he breathed a sigh of relief that there was no car parked out front and no one beckoning him to get in. As he walked up to the house, he prayed Michael had not sent Carmella away for a few hours. He was relieved again when Carmella came to the door and greeted him. He doubted very much that any harm would come to him inside the boss's home, especially with Carmella around.

"Hello, Gabe. Nice to see you. Michael is in his study."

Gabe's confidence grew. When he entered the study, Michael stood up and gestured for him to sit in the seat in front of his desk.

"You've had quite a week."

Gabe nervously stumbled for words. "It's been a really interesting time," Gabe said as he stared at a framed photo on the wall of Maria playing lacrosse.

"Nice photo, isn't it?" Michael said, and Gabe turned to Michael with his face flushed with embarrassment. "That was taken when Maria was in high school. It was a district championship game, and Maria scored the winning goal. By the way, thanks for making the effort to get to know her."

"Oh, that's okay. It's been a pleasure."

"I should also thank you for spending that afternoon at the lake with her. She told us how good you were with the kids."

"Again, it was my pleasure. I'm happy to be a friend to her."

"In fact, believe it or not, we heard some of the other nuns were a little put out when they saw you with her and they've postponed her vows to become a novice."

Gabe's face turned ashen, and he felt a tremor run through his body. *Is this why Michael called me to his home?* Maybe Michael was angry that Gabe went too far and got Maria expelled from her program. No doubt Carmella was furious about this as well, so her presence in the home did not provide any safety for Gabe.

Gabe looked at Michael and tried to say something but words failed him. His mouth just dropped open. Finally he said, "I'm sorry. I had no idea . . ."

Michael smiled. "Gabe, get a hold of yourself. It's all good. Maria's mother and I think it's a mistake for Maria to take final vows to become a nun for life. Maybe you can help her to see that. Keep up what you're doing, and if the convent doesn't like her having you as a friend, it's all the better."

"Well, I . . ." Gabe grimaced and continued to stumble with his words.

"I said it's okay. I have confidence you'll be a good friend to Maria and you'd never do anything to hurt her. All I ask is that you don't mention this to Carmella. She doesn't know I asked you to do this."

"All right," Gabe said with a sigh.

"But I didn't call you over here to talk about Maria. We got word that Geller is back from his trip and is obviously not happy. We think it's time to pay him a visit and offer him the opportunity to start doing business under our protection, at least on this side of the Delaware River. He'll have to start paying his dues, of course."

"So how will that play out? Are you going to send Gus? Doesn't he know Geller?"

"Actually, we'd like you to make the contact. The break-in was your operation, and we'd like you to do the honors. You can talk to Gus about when and where to find Benny."

Gabe nodded. "I'll get right on it."

Gabe left Michael's home taking satisfaction that his boss had assigned him another important job. He had not been officially inducted into the family as a made man, but he sat for a moment in his car and ran his fingers through his hair, wondering what he was supposed to do about Maria. How could he be a real friend to her when her father was trying to use him as a tool to get her away from the convent? Gabe wondered if he'd be able to look her in the eyes if he saw her. He needed to be more honest with the woman he was falling in love with.

CHAPTER 18

Gabe hadn't slept well the last few nights. He not only thought about the difficult position he was in with Maria, he was also nervous about the present assignment. But now he needed to be totally focused as he spotted Benny Geller sitting alone at a table in the bar at the Rittenhouse Hotel. Geller was sitting next to a large picture window facing an outdoor garden terrace. As far as Gabe could tell, Benny had no security people close by. It was now or never, he thought.

Geller faced Gabe as he approached, but sat expressionless, staring at his drink.

"Mr. Geller?" Gabe spoke softly.

"I'm sorry. Do I know you?" Geller asked.

"I'm not sure we've had the pleasure of meeting. I'm Gabriel Rossi, and I work for Michael D'Angelo."

"So what has that got to do with me?" Geller frowned.

"The family sends its condolences for your recent misfortune."

"What do you know about any misfortunes?"

"Word on the street travels quickly."

Geller slammed his hand on the table, and several patrons turned to look. "You bastards! You're the ones that did it? Get out of my sight!"

Gabe couldn't tell if Geller really knew or was just bluffing. This was not going the way he had expected. He stepped forward, knowing his window to speak was shrinking fast. "Here's the bottom line. You were given an opportunity to do business under our protection and you turned it down, and now you've seen some consequences. I assure you, if you don't step up and pay your dues, the D'Angelo family is coming after you. So, shall I report back that you're willing to cooperate?"

Geller calmly took a sip from his drink and gave Gabe an icy cold glare. "What do you think I'm gonna do? The people in charge are afraid to talk to me, so they send a punk that nobody knows."

"I don't think you want me to report back those words."

Geller stood and pointed to the door. "Just get out! Leave before I call security! Tell your boss he's gonna regret what you're doin'!" Once again, several people at the bar, as well as the bartender, turned and looked.

"Is everything all right, Mr. Geller?" the bartender asked.

Gabe answered, "Yes, we're finished here."

Gabe stormed out of the hotel bar to the curb. He raised his arm for the driver, who was waiting for him, stepped in the rear door, and slammed it closed.

◆　◆　◆

After the meeting with Geller, Gabe's driver dropped him off at the Clubhouse. When Gabe entered, he found Michael and Gus seated in the main meeting room, nursing glasses of scotch. There was a bar off to the side, and Michael signaled to the bartender to bring one for Gabe. He was nervous about how the meeting with Geller went and felt bad he had lost his cool. He had been thinking how to put his actions in the best light.

Gabe sat down. After he took a good sip from his drink, he didn't wait for the obvious question. "I gave Geller the message loud and clear, but he's refusing to play ball."

"Did he know it was us who got into his condo?" Gus asked.

"He pretended to act surprised, but I'm sure he knew," Gabe said, taking another swig from his drink.

Gus waved a hand at him. "Don't worry about it, kid. I didn't think he was going to just cave in and tell you right then that the money was coming. But now he knows we're watching him closely and that we can get to him. I wouldn't be surprised if he leaves town again for a while. He'll probably beef up security at his warehouses."

Gabe knew better than to ask any questions at this point. In his present situation, it was better to keep his mouth shut and wait for the bosses to speak.

Michael said, "You did all right, Gabe. We'll take it from here." Michael looked toward the door, and Gabe took the cue to leave.

CHAPTER 19

Geller's condo was only a block from the hotel. As soon as he got home, he placed a call to his contact in the South Jersey mob, Frank Pasquale, a captain who oversaw distribution of Geller's products.

"What the hell's going on, Frank? I've got the D'Angelos all over me. They're threatening to shut me down if I don't kick up to them," Geller said.

Unlike the Philadelphia family, South Jersey was deeply involved in the distribution of illegal drugs and marijuana. Geller made major shipments to mob-owned sub-distributors in Camden, Atlantic City, and other locations.

"So, what gives? Are you going to keep the product coming to our locations?" Frank asked.

"Of course," Geller answered.

"Okay. Sit tight. I'll look into it from this end."

The call ended.

A few minutes later, Geller's phone buzzed—it was Bruno Carbone Jr. After inheriting the leadership role when his father had died a year ago, he'd quickly eliminated several of his rivals, and their bodies had been found in the salt marshes outside of Atlantic City.

"Benny, so tell me what's going on in the City of Brotherly Love," Junior said.

"The D'Angelos are gonna shut me down if I don't kick up money to them."

"Oh yeah? Maybe they're just bluffing."

"I don't think so. They broke into my apartment and stole half a million dollars from my safe," Geller quickly replied, exaggerating the number. "You know, Michael D'Angelo pretends to be such a nice guy, supporting the church and all that. They even say his daughter is in a convent. But he's just as bad as any of the crooks who were in charge over here in the past."

"Don't they have security at that place where you live?" Junior asked.

"They got past it. So, you see my dilemma? It's not just the money. Almost half of the product I move goes over to your side of the river. If I pay them, they'll be getting a cut of our New Jersey business."

"Benny, that's not gonna happen. In fact, I've been wanting to talk to you about expanding your shipments to new locations in South Jersey, if you can handle it."

"Yeah, I can handle it if you help me get the D'Angelos off my back."

"We're having other problems with the D'Angelos, so keep the products coming, and we'll deal with them."

"Yeah, you better do something before it's too late," Benny said and hung up the call.

CHAPTER 20

In the days following her meeting with Sister Anna, Maria immersed herself in her work—she was trying her best not to think too much about Gabe and the gnawing questions about her future. Fortunately, her students consumed most of her attention, and she enjoyed working with them. At the convent, the young women at various stages of becoming a nun were required to sign up for service projects off-site. Something in Maria's mind led her to sign up for a solitary project away from prying eyes. She settled on working at a soup kitchen at St. Paul's parish in the Germantown section of the city.

She arrived home tired after her first evening at the soup kitchen, still needing to spend time preparing for tomorrow's classes. As she entered her apartment, her private cell phone rang. It was Gabe.

"Hi," she said, feeling a flutter in her stomach. After the events of the past week, Gabe's voice was a welcome diversion.

"Just wanted to see how you're doing."

"I'm fine," she said. "Between school and other activities, I'm pretty busy and I haven't even started to prepare for my classes tomorrow."

"I've got my hands full too," Gabe said, "so I'll try not to keep you too long. I've been thinking more about our outing at the lake the other week. I really felt we were doing something worthwhile. Maybe I should do more stuff like that."

"I just got back from helping at a soup kitchen. Maybe you should try it out. Many of the people who come don't have any other options for food. When you see the people come in, you feel like you're really doing something to help them."

"Could I come and help you sometime?" he asked.

"Well, I work at the soup kitchen at St. Paul's in Germantown Thursday evenings and Saturday mornings. Why don't you come Saturday morning and I can introduce you to the people who run it. Could you be there by eight?" When she said this, she could hardly believe that she'd planned again to see Gabe. This time it was away from the convent, where no one would know. She hoped Sister Anna wouldn't ask her about seeing Gabe again, but she still felt a little angry at Sister Margaret and wanted to prove to herself that she could be friends with Gabe without doing anything wrong.

"Sure, that'd be great. Maybe we can get a cappuccino at Starbucks afterward."

"We'll see," Maria said. She knew going to another public place with Gabe would be pressing her luck.

"Could I ask a favor?" Maria asked.

"Of course."

"Let's not tell them we know each other. I don't want people to think I have friends or family show up to help me every time I go on a service project."

"No problem at all. It's not like I can't talk to you when I'm there."

"That's fine. We'll just pretend we didn't know each other before you came to check out the soup kitchen."

"I'm looking forward to it," Gabe said.

Maria smiled as she ended the call.

◆　◆　◆

On Saturday morning, Maria looked up from the serving table and saw Gabe entering the church basement where the soup kitchen was

90

set up. Gabe's grin when he saw Maria was contagious, and she greet-ed him with a cheerful smile. When he approached her, he leaned in for a hug. Maria obliged, notwithstanding her request that Gabe act like he didn't know her.

"You look great, as usual," Gabe said.

Maria blushed and smiled again, having a perception that Gabe held the hug just a moment longer than normal. "Glad you could make it. Let me introduce you to someone who can help you get start-ed," she said, and she took Gabe by the arm and led him to an older helper who was setting the tables.

After the soup kitchen got under way, Maria stood behind a metal table dishing out a simple meal of scrambled eggs and sausage while Gabe had been assigned to police the dining area, picking up empty paper plates and cups and wiping the tables clean. Maria and Gabe had hardly been able to exchange a word during the meal as a steady stream of hungry patrons had shown up for the free breakfast. After the meal ended and the two had finished helping with the cleanup, Maria met Gabe outside the church where his car was parked.

Maria looked into Gabe's eyes and smiled. "Thanks for coming. I could see for myself that you enjoyed helping the people who came here this morning."

"Yeah. There's something about helping people who need it. It feels good, but I guess you already know that. Call me again if I can help," Gabe replied.

"Sure. Maybe you'd like to try helping on a Thursday evening?"

"Actually, that would be great. I won't have to get up so early!" The two laughed. "Are you still up for Starbucks?" Gabe asked.

"Actually, I'd better get back to my apartment. I have a lot of work to do to prepare for classes next week." Working at the soup kitchen was one thing, but going out afterward really seemed too much like a date. Still, she was sorry she couldn't spend more time with him.

"That's fine. Maybe some other time," Gabe said.

Maria glanced over Gabe's shoulder and recognized his car parked in front of the church. She hadn't seen it up close when he came to the outing at the lake. It was a BMW, and not one of the smaller, entry-level models. Maria stared at the car and in an instant imagined getting in the passenger side and driving off with Gabe. It didn't matter where they went, as long as she could be with Gabe and they could share some time just talking and enjoying each other's company.

"Are you okay?" Gabe asked, interrupting Maria's silent gaze at the car.

"Oh, sure, I'm fine. I was just thinking about something I need to do. I have a busy day tomorrow and I should go. Thanks again for coming," Maria said as she reached out and squeezed Gabe's upper arm.

"You're welcome. See you Thursday," Gabe said. He smiled and turned toward his car.

Maria smiled and turned to walk back into the church to pick up her bag. When she turned, she saw the priest standing on the sidewalk about fifty feet away in front of the main entrance. He was talking to someone. She drew closer and as she turned to enter the door to the fellowship hall, the man speaking to the priest looked in her direction. It was Father Pierce. Maria hurried into the building, hoping he didn't see her.

CHAPTER 21

A few days later, Michael and Gus sat in the meeting room of the Clubhouse. Michael had told Carmella he had a late-night meeting and not to wait up for him. It was after midnight, and no one else was around.

"You sure you wanna do this?" Gus asked. "It's not too late to call it off or scale it back some."

"We've already talked about this. I'm not gonna let Geller move all that product under our noses and then snub us. He's lucky we didn't whack him. Victor certainly woulda done that. Besides, Rudy is gonna call us in a few minutes. We got a bunch of moving parts in place, and it would really screw things up to change the mission at the last minute," Michael said.

"I hear you about the need to take action, but my source says the truck might stop in New Jersey. If we mess with a delivery to the Carbones, there'll be hell to pay. And what if the truck has armed security? Somebody could get hurt."

"Have faith in Maestro," Michael said. "He'll have the situation under control."

When the call came in, Michael put his phone on speaker. "Maestro, where are you?"

Rudy was a trusted solider in the D'Angelo family; he'd earned his nickname "Maestro" by being resourceful and effective at projects assigned to him.

"I'm parked just a few blocks from South City Bakery," Rudy said. South City was a commercial bakery Geller owned. In addition to the bakery business, he used it to warehouse and ship drugs out to his distributors. The business was a perfect cover because trucks with the company name were constantly coming and going, with flour and supplies coming in, and baked goods, mostly freshly baked loaves of bread, being shipped out to grocery stores.

"Is anything going on?" Gus asked.

"No, it's quiet. Nobody is around," the Maestro said. All of a sudden Michael and Gus heard loud static and a scratchy voice.

"Copy that, ready to roll. Did you guys hear that?" Rudy asked. "The target truck is pulling through the factory gate and heading in our direction. It'll be here in a couple of minutes. Hold on, I've got to pull down my ski mask. Let me know if you have trouble hearing me."

"We can hear okay," Michael said. Despite his intent to promote a more peaceful Mafia involved in legitimate businesses, moments like this thrilled Michael. It reminded him of his younger days when he was working for the old boss, Victor Molinari. "What happens next?"

"When Geller's truck gets close, my truck and another van will pull into the street to block it. I've got earbuds so we can still talk when I get out," Maestro said. Michael knew Rudy and his men would be heavily armed as they approached the bakery truck.

Michael muted his phone. "We don't know who's in the truck. I told them to get the driver and any passengers out and disarm them. I promise we won't hurt anyone, and Rudy won't let any of our guys get hurt," Michael said, looking straight at Gus. "By the way, are we sure about our inside information?"

"Yeah," Gus answered. "My guy inside the factory is reliable. He says this truck has a big shipment of Geller's stuff that's going to be dropped off with his distributors in the area. As I said, there might be a stop in New Jersey," Gus added, reinforcing his misgivings over the mission.

After Michael unmuted his phone, he heard Rudy. "Geller's truck is stopped. I'm getting out now." A moment later Rudy and his men were screaming at the driver to get out. "He's alone in the cab," Rudy said.

"Hands up where I can see them . . . I said 'hands up!'" Rudy shouted.

By now, Michael knew Rudy's men were putting zip ties on the driver and shoving him to the side of the street. They would tie his feet with cord to keep him from running away and they'd search him for weapons. "Danny, take Sal and Leo and open the back of the truck. Be careful, somebody might be inside," they heard Rudy say.

"Maestro, can you hear me?" Michael said loudly. Michael and Gus heard only some indistinct voices and some banging noises. Michael called out for Rudy again, sighed, and began tapping his fingers on the table as another minute went by.

"Sorry, I couldn't answer a minute ago," Rudy said. "We got the back door open and all we see are stacks of bread and some heavy cardboard boxes. Danny is opening the boxes. Danny, whaddaya got?" Rudy shouted.

Michael and Gus heard some indistinct voices. Then, "Looks like we hit the mother lode. S'got to be about thirty kilos of white stuff—and it's not flour."

Michael did a quick calculation and figured there was about a million dollars' worth of Geller's product. "Okay, grab a few bags and bring 'em here for us to check out. Then torch the rest," Michael said as he turned to Gus with a big grin on his face.

"Danny is pouring some gasoline on the cargo to start the fireworks. We'll be outta here in two minutes," Rudy said.

Michael could picture the truck and its cargo going up in flames. "Good job, Maestro. We'll see you back here. Just make sure no one is following you."

"Sure thing, boss," Rudy said and he disconnected the call.

Michael turned to Gus. "I figure one of two things is going to happen. Either Geller will call you and try to negotiate a deal, or he'll go right to Carbone. Either way, we've sent a strong message."

"I'm worried about a response from the Carbones. We need to be ready."

"We'll be ready," Michael said with a look of determination on his face.

CHAPTER 22

Maria approached her second session with Sister Anna with trepidation. She'd been thinking about the question Sister Anna had asked in the first session, whether living at the convent was just a phase she was going through. Of course, she loved her life teaching and living at the convent. She knew she didn't want to leave the convent and her friends, but she wasn't exactly sure how to answer the question other than that she was seeking to discern God's will, which seemed like a cop-out. Also, Maria did not want to tell the sister she'd been with Gabe at the soup kitchen a few days ago, since the sister had promised they'd return to a discussion on Gabe. Maria bit her lip as she waited for the sister to return with cups of coffee. Sister Anna seemed good at digging out details, and that's what worried Maria.

"Last time," Sister Anna began, "you told me about your father being busy and the fact that it's hard to find time when he's available to talk. You told me a little about your mother, so let's talk more about her."

"Okay," Maria said. It wasn't a question she was expecting, and it put her a little off balance.

"You mentioned she's always been busy with her church and charities. How would you describe your relationship with her today?" the sister asked.

"She's still busy. I wish I had a closer relationship with her," Maria said. "And now, she seems to spend more time with my sister-in-law, Rose. Maybe that's because my mother likes to be with Tessa, her granddaughter. I guess in the present stage of my vocation, it's not possible to spend more time with her. Don't get me wrong. My mother didn't neglect me when I was growing up. She was constantly on my case, but not in a bad way. She drove me to school, took me to sports practices and other activities, made sure I studied and did my homework, and made sure I went to church. In high school, she was very strict and monitored my friends and my activities."

Sister Anna made a few notes in her journal and then said, "She was being more of a mother than a friend to you, which is good. It's one of the reasons you were successful at college and at your teaching job. But it seems now that you are grown up, you'd like to be in a position where you and your mother could enjoy each other's company more."

"Yes, I think that's true."

"You said she was strict and monitored your activities. Would it be a fair statement that she made most of your choices for you?"

"Yes, definitely."

"This included what schools you attended, what activities you pursued, and even what you did at home?"

"Yes."

"How about your choice for college?"

"I was accepted at several colleges, but my parents—especially my mother—made it clear that they wanted me to go to Villanova, I guess because it's close to home."

"When you entered the convent, was that your decision or theirs?" the sister asked.

"That was definitely my decision," Maria answered.

"Was that the first major decision you made about your life?"

Maria sat in silence and looked toward the ceiling for a moment before she spoke. "I think it probably was," Maria said.

"Did your parents support it?"

"I could tell they were lukewarm about it at best. My mother started talking about how she had hoped I would have grandchildren for her. But they didn't stand in the way either."

"Well, you were in your twenties and finished college. I guess they couldn't really stop you," the sister said. Maria didn't say anything. "I guess you were glad to make your own decision about the direction of your life for a change."

"I think I was." The sister made some notes. "Are you suggesting I joined the convent because it was a decision I could make without my parents' approval?" Maria asked after another pause.

"It's interesting that you would ask that question," the sister said. "Do you think it was the reason?"

Maria felt troubled at the thought that her choice of a religious vocation may have really been just an attempt to get out from under her parents' control. Yes, she could have gotten married and pursued teaching without going to the convent, but that's exactly what her parents wanted her to do. Maria crossed her arms over her chest. "But I was seeking God's will! Maybe deep down that thought was there, but I was praying every day about it. And Sister Theresa invited me to a retreat, and I enjoyed it."

"I'm not arguing with you or judging you. I'm sure you *were* seeking God's will. I just want you to probe your own heart and examine the things that motivated your decision," the sister said. "Sometimes when we gain an understanding of how we got where we are, we can make better decisions now and in the future," the sister said softly with a smile.

Maria marveled about the way the sister had approached the question of Maria's motivations. Of course, neither she nor the sister could prove or disprove Maria's real motivations. However, the sister had planted a thought that was entirely plausible, maybe even probable. Maria wouldn't be able to forget it as she thought about pursuing a religious vocation.

"Let's shift gears," Sister Anna said. "Tell me about your friends."

"Do you mean my friends at the convent, or friends I've known from before?" Maria asked.

"Start with the convent."

"Well, I'm friendly with a lot of the women in my program. There's a group of about five of us who sit at the same dinner table every night. We're not supposed to talk, but we do share a few whispers."

"Who's your best friend in the group?" the sister asked.

"I guess it would be Emily. We don't get much chance to talk one-on-one, but I talk to her the most. I've known her since I first came to the convent for a retreat. She's also a teacher at a school in Glenside, St. Mary's School. We compare notes sometimes."

"Have you told her about your friendship with the young man we discussed last time? I think his name was Gabe."

"No," Maria said. "I've kept that under wraps at the convent after I got called out on it."

"Have you socialized with Emily outside of the convent?"

"Not really. I drove her to the store a few times since she doesn't have a car. And oh, I forgot to mention, I've become friends with one of the teachers at the school where I teach. Her name is Joanne. We usually have lunch together. She's promised to invite me for dinner sometime, but it hasn't happened yet."

"Would it be a fair statement that most of your interaction and talking with Emily and Joanne is about your teaching or your life at the convent?" the sister asked.

"I suppose so. Joanne is married, and she talks about her little boy, but I haven't met him yet."

"So, other than hearing about Joanne's child, you and the friends you've mentioned have never told each other about your families? And you've never gone anywhere together other than an errand to the store?"

"That's right."

"What about friends from college?" the sister asked.

"I had some friends at college, mostly on the lacrosse team, but I've lost touch with them."

"Let me ask you this, Maria. Imagine a different life where you are not in a convent training to be a novice. Suppose you got married. Who would you pick to be your bridesmaids?"

"Wow, that's a good question. I suppose I'd have my sister-in-law, Rose, as a bridesmaid. I like her a lot, but we really don't have much in common. And maybe my cousin Diane. She works for my Uncle Joey, who owns a bunch of restaurants in the city. I like her a lot, and she's close to our family, but I have to admit I don't know her all that well," Maria said.

"What about Emily or Joanne, the young women you mentioned as friends?"

"I don't know. Maybe after I get to know them better."

"Earlier, you mentioned the young man you met at the party, Gabe. Where does he fit in?" the sister asked.

"I've known him for many years but only recently gotten to know him better. I enjoy talking to him," Maria said.

"Other than at the party and the outing at the lake, have you seen him any other time recently?"

Maria paused and dropped her chin. "Ah, I saw him at the soup kitchen where I worked last week. He volunteered to help."

"I think you mentioned earlier that you enjoy talking to him and have shared lots of stories about your relatives. Do you talk to him on the phone as well?"

Maria could sense where this was going. "Yes, I've seen him a few times, and I've talked to him on the phone, but I've only known him, at least on a closer level, for a short time. Less than a month. I consider him a good friend. Since he's a distant relative, we seem to have some things in common," Maria said. Maria was pleasantly surprised that Sister Anna did not call her out for having continuous contact with Gabe.

"What do you like about your friendship with Gabe?" the sister asked.

"He's warm. He's friendly, and he seems genuinely interested in what I have to say. I can't give you specific examples, but I just get that feeling when I talk to him," Maria said.

"How do you feel when he calls you? I assume he's called you on the phone. For instance, what feelings do you get that are different from when, say, Emily calls you or talks to you?"

Maria thought for a moment. She knew she had to be careful. "I guess Gabe is a special friend. I'm always happy to hear from him."

"Do you have plans to see him again? Would you be willing to see him again?" the sister asked.

"No, I don't have plans. He might help again at the soup kitchen, I guess. He seems to like doing that kind of work."

"We've got to stop now, but I want to mention two things. First, you've told me you are fond of your friends at the convent, but I think it's important for you to cultivate some female friendships that go deeper than the friendships you've described with Emily and Joanne. God made us to be social creatures, and we are never truly happy until we can share our lives with others. People like me, and maybe you someday, develop friendships in religious vocations in a different way. But they are real friendships. There's a nun where I live, Sister Renee, whom I've known since I was a novice. We get together on a regular basis, and I can talk to her about anything. We've even gone on vacations together. I think what started our friendship is that we both love to go walking outside, and we went out on walks and hikes together. I suggest you start by finding someone—maybe Emily or Joanne—and see if there's something you have in common. It might be as simple as going on walks or baking cakes. Then, do it together."

"Thank you. I will try to do what you say," Maria said, thinking Joanne would probably love to go for a walk in one of the local parks.

"And last, just be careful about Gabe. I'm not going to tell you what to do. God may be using this relationship to help you discern his will for your life. It's possible God may have different plans for you than being a nun. If that is the case, it's better for you to leave based on your own prayerful decision and not because the convent asked you to. We'll talk more about this in the future."

CHAPTER 23

Michael had arrived early at Francesca's in South Philadelphia. He had invited Gabe to meet him for lunch. Michael had always loved Francesca's and decided early on he wanted it to be part of his organization. Although it was quiet and unassuming, it had come to be known for its excellent Italian cuisine. The owner, affectionately known as "Uncle Joey," was not really a relative but a close friend of the D'Angelo family organization. With the help of the D'Angelos, a large banquet room in the back of the restaurant had been remodeled, expanded, and turned into a private casino with blackjack tables, roulette, dice, and slot machines. Joey and the family both prospered from the joint venture. Michael was a regular at the restaurant, and the waitress brought him a glass of his favorite wine without his asking for it. As he took a sip, Joey approached the table with Gabe.

"Your guest has arrived, my friend," Joey said with his hand on Gabe's shoulder in a friendly way. "Can I get you anything?"

"The veal parmesan special for both of us, and bring Gabe a glass of the house wine," Michael said. "Have a seat, Gabe. I think you'll like the special. Joey's chef is one of the best."

"Thank you," Gabe said.

"After lunch, I want to show you the renovations we've made to the back room. As you know, our little enterprise here is doing quite well."

Gabe oversaw several gambling operations for the family, including the sports betting, but he hadn't had much to do with this casino. Michael decided not to tell Gabe why he was getting a tour until afterward.

"How are things with Geller?" Gabe asked, displaying a growing confidence in talking to the boss.

"We're working to bring him around. We hijacked one of his trucks the other night and found a large load of cocaine on the way to his distributors. Now his distributors are gonna be short of product for a few days," Michael said with a smirk as he munched on a fresh dinner roll. Michael didn't mention the fact that his consigliere had some misgivings about the operation. "By the way, have you spoken to Maria lately?"

"She asked me to help at a soup kitchen in Germantown. I'm invited to come back again and I think I might go," Gabe said.

"You should do it. I'm pleased that you're being a good friend to her," Michael said. "How is she doing otherwise?"

"Great, as far as I can tell," Gabe said after taking a good sip of the wine. "She is really busy between teaching and her activities at the convent, but she always seems happy when I call."

"Has she mentioned anything about her progress on the vows that were postponed?" Michael asked.

"No. Not at all. I don't think she knows I'm aware of that situation."

"I'm sure you cheer her up," Michael said. "Just keep me posted on how she's doing and remember, the fact that I'm encouraging you to be a friend to her is our little secret, okay?"

"Of course," Gabe said. Gabe gave Michael some reports on the various operations that were under his supervision as they finished up their lunches.

Just then, Joey approached the table, bringing a strikingly attractive woman with a low-cut dress and luxuriant black locks. "Are you ready for Diane?" Joey asked.

"We're always ready for Diane," Michael said as he leaned in to kiss her on the cheek.

"She does a fantastic job handling the books for Francesca's and my other restaurants," Joey said with a smile before withdrawing to the kitchen.

"I think you've met my niece, Diane D'Angelo," Michael said, looking to Gabe.

Gabe's eyes lit up at the sight of Diane as she leaned in and shook his hand.

"Long time, no see, Mr. Rossi," Diane said.

"What was it, three or four years ago at the New Year's Eve party?" Gabe asked.

"That sounds about right," she said.

"Diane's going to show us around the back rooms," Michael said, and she led them to the rear of the restaurant where she unlocked a large wooden door leading to a hallway. After they passed through the hallway they entered a large, well-appointed hall with beautiful oak-accented blackjack tables, tables for roulette and dice, as well as several rows of slot machines.

"This is beautiful," Gabe said, admiring the room and its marble pillars and attractive artwork.

"Diane works for the restaurant part-time, but her real job is managing our casino here. Most importantly, she sets up our high-stakes poker games a coupla nights a week. Why don't you show us the game room, Diane?"

"Right. I should point out that all our equipment in the main hall is top-of-the-line, and we have state-of-the-art security cameras to keep an eye on things," Diane said as she led them into a side room with a large round table, fancy leather chairs, and a faint smell of cigar smoke. There was a bar off to the side with a refrigerator and countertop for food service. "This is where our VIP poker games take place. Many of our clients are well-known in the community, some are even on the city council."

"How do you maintain security here?" Gabe asked.

"We have some security guys on-site, and sometimes they patrol the neighborhood to make sure we're not attracting anyone's attention and warn us if there's any law enforcement approaching. We've also got security cameras in all the rooms," she said.

"Sometimes I drop by to greet the poker players, especially someone new," Michael said. "As charming as I am, no one wants their picture taken with me, but they're all photographed with me by the security cameras. It's an insurance policy to keep the VIPs quiet about this place."

Next, Diane led Michael and Gabe through a small door in the hallway into an office where there was a desk and a bank of monitors. Diane flipped a switch, and the monitors came to life, showing multiple views of the main casino room and direct overhead views of the gaming tables and the poker table in the room they had just left.

"We use these monitors to keep an eye on things, and I've got some helpers to watch these during the night. We're careful who we invite, but occasionally we spot cheaters and show them to the door," she said. "Needless to say, they're not invited back."

For a moment, Gabe stared at the futon in Diane's office. "Yes, it can become a bed," Diane said as though she knew what Gabe was thinking. "The poker games go all night, so sometimes I can sneak out and take a short nap. Other times, if I'm working late, I can do the same thing."

Diane ended the tour by showing them the heavy, steel-reinforced door leading to the alley behind the restaurant. "If the restaurant is full, we steer casino patrons to come and go through this door. There's a camera so we can see anyone who rings the doorbell."

"Thank you, Diane, for the tour," Michael said. "Gabe and I will go out the back and walk around the block to the front." While walking,

Michael put his hand on Gabe's shoulder. "The reason we had this tour is because I'm putting you in charge here. It's our biggest cash cow and one of our most important operations."

Gabe stopped and his mouth dropped open. "I don't know what to say, Michael. Thanks for having confidence in me."

"It's a lot of responsibility, but it won't require a lot of extra effort. Diane has things under control here. In case you were wondering, Diane is single. Diane's fiancé, Eddy DiNunzio, was killed about ten years ago. There were factions, and we had a lot more of that going on back then. Diane never married, although she's had many suitors. She was pretty shattered after her fiancé died, so I offered her a job helping to get this operation started. I knew she was bright, but she exceeded everyone's expectations. The poker games alone bring in millions. She's able to attract the kind of poker players we need, and the house takes a big rake every game. I'm sure you'll work well with her."

"I look forward to it," Gabe said with a smile on his face.

CHAPTER 24

A few days after her second meeting with Sister Anna, Maria had worked late at school. When she got back to her apartment, it was almost time for dinner and vespers. She was exhausted and didn't feel well. Following protocol, she phoned the convent office and spoke to the sister on duty.

"I'm not feeling well, and I think I'll just stay in my apartment this evening."

The voice at the other end said, "I'm sorry to hear that. Is there anything we can do for you? We can send your dinner over if you like."

"No, thanks. I'm not very hungry."

In fact, a headache had started at the base of her skull. She took two Tylenol and stretched out on her bed. She didn't feel like sleeping but couldn't rouse herself to work on lesson plans either. She would have to do that later.

Soon, she dozed off until the phone rang. As she went to pick it up, she felt a moment of hopeful anticipation.

Maybe it's Gabe! But she was soon disappointed.

"Hello, Maria?" the voice said.

"Yes," she answered, half awake.

"This is Father Pierce."

Maria quietly sighed and shook her head. The last time she had spoken to him had been at her niece's birthday party.

"I happened to be over at St. Paul's the other night at a meeting with Father Nathan. I assume you were doing volunteer work at the soup kitchen?"

"Yes," Maria said, having an idea where this conversation was headed and dreading the thought.

"I couldn't help but notice you were with the same young man who was with you at the party at your parents' home. And wasn't this also the man who visited you at the convent a few weeks ago?" the father asked.

"I wasn't with him at my parents' house," Maria answered with a sharp tone as her headache began to throb. "My parents invited him, and he's family. He's a cousin, and he wasn't with me at the party. And he was a volunteer at the soup kitchen." Maria knew she was bending the facts about Gabe being a relative, but she wanted to make a strong point.

"Of course. I just wanted to caution you that when a young woman who is preparing to be a nun spends time with an eligible bachelor, it can raise some eyebrows," the priest said.

Anger began to rise in Maria, but she tried to remain civil. "Thank you for your concern, but I'm disappointed that a member of the clergy feels the need to make critical comments about something I do that's totally innocent."

"Believe me, Maria, I have no intent to criticize you or to speak to anyone else about this." Maria started to see this conversation as a veiled threat. "I'm just looking out for your interests and don't want to see this cause any trouble for you."

"Thank you, Father Pierce, but I'm sure your parish has bigger fish to fry than a soon-to-be novice speaking to her cousin at a soup kitchen." She was aware Father Pierce's assistant priest had been disciplined for inappropriate touching of young boys in the choir. She drove the point home. "None of us is perfect, and no one who works with us is perfect. Sometimes we need to look straight ahead and just move forward."

The priest didn't answer.

"Also, you should be aware that the gentleman you saw is Gabriel Rossi, and he works for my father. He is a very successful and highly regarded employee, and my father is fully aware that Mr. Rossi and I are friends. If that is a problem, I suggest we take it up with him."

Maria could hardly believe what she had said. She knew her father had influence, but had no idea how powerful it was.

Maria's last statement hit its mark. Father Pierce did not want to tangle with Michael D'Angelo or a soldier named Rossi. Nor did the priest want to create any complications with a large benefactor to his parish.

"Yes, of course," he said. "I'm sorry for the misunderstanding. I'm so glad to see you working at the soup kitchen. It's a wonderful ministry."

"All right," said Maria, "I've got to be going now. Good night, Father Pierce."

"Good night, Maria. Keep up the good work."

Maria tried to settle back into bed to get rid of her headache when her phone rang again. *It couldn't be worse than the last call,* she thought. But when she saw where the call was coming from, her face turned ashen and she realized it *was* going to be worse.

CHAPTER 25

Four men sat on the second-floor veranda of an expansive house overlooking the bay in Margate, New Jersey, on an unseasonably warm spring evening. A golden sunset glittered over the ripples of the bay and the green marshland in the distance. Two older men, Hank Maranzano and Sal Rizzo, sat on cushioned lounge chairs. In the center, facing the bay, a younger man sat with bulging biceps hanging out of a tropical-style Tommy Bahamas camp shirt. The younger man, Bruno Carbone Jr., had succeeded his father as head of the Mafia in southern New Jersey a year ago. The other younger man—Tony Bianchi, the newly appointed consigliere—was dressed in a simple navy-blue polo shirt and faded jeans and wore a pair of retro-style Ray-Ban sunglasses. Bianchi had replaced the consigliere Bruno's father had appointed and relied on for many years. The four men represented Junior's inner circle.

"I called you here due to the situation in Philadelphia. You guys know my father split New Jersey off to be our own territory. The D'Angelos really didn't give a damn because they really didn't need us. So, what happens? They expand on their side of the river and get new casinos approved all over the place. They also open their own private casinos that operate without approval of the Gaming Commission. They push the casino business so much that nobody needs to travel over to Atlantic City anymore, and we're dyin'. Well, not exactly dyin', but we got problems. My father reached out to Michael D'Angelo and said, 'Maybe you got enough now, and you're starting to hurt us.' Did the D'Angelos pull back at all? Hell no."

"So, how can we expect them to pull back over there on their own territory when they're makin' lots of money?" Sal asked.

Bruno lit a cigarette and took a few puffs. "There's other ways of handling this," he said. "The D'Angelos are opening casinos in the Poconos, where the New York families have some investment. My father approached D'Angelo himself and said maybe we can invest with you in the Poconos, or maybe we can open a new operation together up the river from Philadelphia. We were tryin' to be fair and resolve this peaceably. My father reminded him the D'Angelo family was doin' stuff like that with New York families, but it fell on deaf ears. My father believed families aren't supposed to compete with one another, but that's what we have here."

"They're probably pissed off that we broke away from them," Hank said.

"Yeah, yeah, but families split off in a lot of cases and they get over it," Bruno said. "Besides, they didn't suffer at all when we broke off."

"I still know people over there," Hank said. "And maybe we should give it some time. I think we can work with them."

Bruno gave each of his bosses an icy stare. "You know the answer to that, Hank. Our casino business has been going down, and we were forced to get into the drug business to save our asses. So, what does D'Angelo do next? They threaten our main supplier in Philadelphia. They tell him he's gotta kick up twenty percent of his take, even though half of what he sells goes to New Jersey. They break into his condo and rob him," Bruno said. "And in case you all didn't know it, they hijacked one of his trucks the other night and burned it up."

Hank leaned forward. "Yeah, we got some problems for sure. So whadda we do about it?"

Bruno had known Hank for most of his life, since the older man was a carry-over from Bruno's father's regime. Hank threw his lot in with Junior when the old man died, and his decision saved his life—others who didn't follow Junior weren't so lucky.

"We need to hit the D'Angelos where it hurts and let them know we aren't gonna sit back and let them walk all over us," Bruno said, holding up an empty glass to signal another round of drinks to an attractive woman standing just inside the house.

"So, are we willing to risk war between the families?" Hank raised his eyebrows. "You know what that means. None of us will be safe. You won't be safe. Plus, we'll have the cops and the FBI all over us. Is that a risk worth taking?"

Bruno stood up, walked to the railing, and stared out over the bay.

"The time for talking is over. My father tried to talk to the D'Angelos. They wouldn't listen. Michael D'Angelo won't even take my calls. What kind of respect is that?"

"I hear you loud and clear. But let me just say this, and then I'll shut up." Hank sat up in his chair. "I used to work with them. There's back channels we can use. Maybe there's a way we can get what we want without going to war."

Bruno didn't answer Hank directly. "What I need from you, from all of you, is complete loyalty. I'm not going to let these people walk all over me. If we go back and try to negotiate, they'll see it as weakness, and we'll lose. You guys know when my father broke off New Jersey, they screamed about it at first, but they didn't do anything. They backed down. Michael D'Angelo doesn't have the stomach for a war between the families. He's too busy trying to suck up to the church and convince everyone over there what a nice, regular guy he is, donating to the Boy Scouts and the SPCA."

"So, what's the plan?" Sal asked.

"We hit 'em hard where it hurts," Junior answered. "If we do nothing but talk, they'll never respect us. I'm not talking about whacking anybody, but they hijacked a truck delivering product to our distributors. They beat the driver up and burned up the truck. I think that demands a strong response, and it needs to happen quick. Geller is not going to pay 'em anything, so it's clear they aren't going to leave him alone. If we let things slide, our drug business is going down the shit hole, and we need the money to prop up the casinos until business gets better. If we don't stand by our biggest supplier, how will we ever keep the goods flowing in our direction?"

"Do we have a target and a plan to hit it?" asked Hank.

"Yeah. Their most successful gambling joint is in the back of a restaurant in South Philadelphia. Tony here has worked up a plan, so I'll turn it over to him now to explain how it's gonna go down."

<h1 style="text-align:center">CHAPTER 26</h1>

Maria answered the call that came in right after she spoke to Father Pierce. The moment she hung up, she grabbed her car keys and her phone and headed to the parking lot. Maria didn't call the convent office even though she was breaking curfew by leaving at this hour. She had even missed vespers after telling the nun on duty that she wasn't feeling well. None of that mattered to her now. She was normally a good driver, but tonight she paid little attention to the speed limits. In a little more than ten minutes, she pulled into St. Jude's Home. No one was at the reception, so Maria took the elevator to Sister Theresa's floor. When she arrived at the room, the sister was lying face-up on the bed with her eyes closed and her mouth slightly open. Her breathing was labored. A nurse was in the room making notes at a computer stand that could be wheeled around.

"You must be Maria," the nurse said, looking up from the keyboard. "I was the one who phoned you."

"How is she? I mean, what's her condition?" Maria asked.

"She hasn't been responsive since this morning. The doctor was just here and he said she might not make it through the night."

Maria teared up and could barely speak. "Why didn't someone call me sooner?"

"I'm sorry, hon. I just came on shift and the nurse from earlier left me a note to call you. I don't know why she didn't call you herself. I'm also supposed to tell you Sister Theresa didn't name any next of kin. She named you in her living will. You're the one who decides when we can remove the oxygen." There was a tube looped around the sister's head, with outlets supplying oxygen into her nose. "The doctor said if we remove it, she won't suffer any longer and she'll pass more quickly."

Maria sat in the chair by the bed, put her head in her hands, and began to weep. "Please don't leave me, Sister." She took the sister's hand into both of hers, lifted it up, and kissed it. After a few moments, Maria gently laid the sister's hand down, grabbed a tissue from the nightstand, and wiped her teary eyes. Maria sat with Sister Theresa for another hour, praying, occasionally taking her hand, hoping she could get some response, if only a squeeze. There was none. A local priest came by and said the last rites over the sister, then he left. The nurse told Maria last rites was a common occurrence at the home, and there were local priests who were on duty at various times.

As she sat with the sister, she noticed she would breathe three or four times, then pause before her breaths began again. Maria couldn't bring herself to disconnect the oxygen. Even so, a little after midnight, she noticed Sister Theresa breathed several times and paused, but didn't start breathing again.

Maria stood by the door and shouted. "Help! Could somebody please come!"

The nurse came in and knew instinctively what the problem was. She took her stethoscope and listened for a heartbeat. "I'm sorry, dear. She's passed. I'm sure she's in a better place. I'll just leave you with her for a little while," she said before walking out.

Around two in the morning, the nurse came into the room. "You look tired," she said. When Maria looked up, she continued. "You should go home and get some rest. We can take it from here. We'll take good care of Sister Theresa. St. Jude's will make all the arrangements, and I'll have the funeral home contact you about the service. I'm sure they'll want your input on planning the funeral."

Maria thought back to one of her last visits with Sister Theresa and what she said. *You were one of my best students and you've become one of my best friends. I can see that God has great plans to use you in his kingdom.* Then she thought of how excited the sister had been when she entered the convent to begin her training. Maria would visit from time to time, and Theresa always asked about her day-to-day experiences at the convent. She'd often give helpful advice on how to grow and learn during her training. As Maria left and walked toward the parking lot, she felt a sense of determination to make Sister Theresa proud. She decided to rededicate herself to serving God without any entanglements that might hinder her. Deep down, she knew one of the entanglements was her growing connection to Gabe.

Chapter 27

The following Saturday, Maria stood by Sister Theresa's casket at the Catholic cemetery in Flourtown. She had just come from a mass that had been held in the sister's honor. Now she was among a modest crowd of nuns and a few priests who had known the sister. Tom Jenkins and a few older teachers from the school were in attendance for their fellow teacher's funeral. Maria stared at the casket in a tearful daze, thinking about times she had spent with Sister Theresa. She remembered one time when she was considering entering the convent.

"Sometimes, it's helpful to imagine yourself at the end of your life," the sister had said, "and try to think how you will feel about the choices you are faced with right now."

Surely, Maria thought, if she lived a life like Sister Theresa—a life that blessed so many people, especially her students—she would never have any regrets about dedicating her life to God. Up to this point, the sister's death had given her a renewed sense of dedication to the religious life where she could pursue things of eternal value. Yes, her parents had a good point that she could serve God without becoming a nun. She knew that was true. But if she got married and had a family, there would be many interruptions and distractions from the spiritual life. Wouldn't it be better to end life like Sister Theresa?

Maria was shocked out of her daze when she realized the priest in charge was saying the final prayer of committal.

Eternal rest grant unto her, O Lord,
And let perpetual light shine upon her.
May she rest with the souls of the faithful departed…
Through the mercy of God…
Amen.

As the small crowd began to disperse, Maria looked up and could hardly believe what she saw. There was Gabe standing on the other side of the casket wearing a handsome pinstripe suit and tie, with his arms locked respectfully in front of him. He must have been standing behind some of the other mourners. Maria wondered how he had found out about Sister Theresa's passing and her funeral. She had never seen Gabe dressed in such a becoming manner. When she looked at him, she couldn't help but smile, and he smiled calmly and nodded. As the visitors began to walk to their cars, Maria took a quick look around to see who was present. When she determined that neither Father Pierce nor anyone from her convent was around, she walked toward Gabe and he waited for her.

Maria placed her hand on his arm. "Thank you so much for coming, Gabe! How did you find out about the funeral?"

"Your father mentioned it to me, and I made some calls to find out the details," Gabe said.

"I'm sorry I didn't tell you, but I had no idea you might want to come."

"When I heard about Sister Theresa and how close you were to her, I wanted to come and offer my support to you."

"That's so thoughtful of you," she said. "By the way, there's a little reception for Sister Theresa at St. Jude's Home where she lived. It's not far from here. Are you interested in coming?"

"Sorry, but I need to get going. And I'm very sorry for your loss. I know Sister Theresa meant a lot to you," Gabe said.

"I've known her since I was in eighth grade, and she became a mentor to me."

"I know how important mentors are," Gabe said. "Look, maybe we could meet up again like we did at the soup kitchen. Are you still working there?"

"Same as before, Thursdays and Saturdays."

"I'll give you a call sometime about it, okay?"

"Sure," she said. "Thanks again for coming. It was good to see you."

As Maria continued toward her car, she began to wonder how her father knew about the funeral and why he would tell Gabe.

CHAPTER 28

Diane readied the casino for the Tuesday night poker game in the back of Francesca's Restaurant. There were scheduled to be at least five players, maybe six. The guest of honor tonight was Henry Townshend, a member of the city council. Henry was an at-large member and the only Republican on the council. Even though in the minority, he was a powerful mover and shaker in the city, with a network of close contacts in the mayor's office, the city council, local businesses, universities, and even some major labor unions. Townshend came from a wealthy family in the Main Line and could easily afford the high-stakes game at Francesca's or, more accurately, the game held in a back room at Francesca's. Townshend had not previously played at the casino, and Diane had been told to front $25,000 of Townshend's stake in the game. This was to make sure Townshend would, in a sense, be in debt to the casino and the D'Angelo family.

Shortly before the players were scheduled to arrive, Gabe poked his head in the door to Diane's office. "Hey, beautiful cousin, ready for the game tonight?" Gabe asked.

"Of course. Congratulations on your promotion. I guess I should call you 'boss' now," Diane said. "So what brings you around to hang out with us peons?"

"The big boss asked me to stay around here tonight, but don't worry, I'll stay out of your way. I'm meeting Gus for dinner and I expect I'll be in and around the casino afterward."

"You'd better stay out of the poker room. I don't want the guests to get nervous. By the way, what's with all the security tonight? Michael asked me to bring in some extra guys to watch the street and the back alley."

"You didn't hear this from me, but the Carbones in New Jersey are making some noise and Michael wants us to beef up security at our gambling locations."

"I'd heard some rumors about that. Are we expecting trouble tonight?"

"No, it's just a precaution. If we were expecting anything, we'd cancel the poker game and probably close the casino tonight."

"Speaking of security," Diane said, "I was just about to check the camera system. Do you want to have a look?"

"Sure," he said.

Diane led the way to the bank of screens she had shown Michael and Gabe a few weeks ago. The feed looked good, showing various views in the poker room and the main casino floor, as well as the front and rear entrances to the property. "Go and stand in the poker room by the table near the side of the bar," she said.

No sooner had Gabe gotten to that location than she walked back into the room with three photos of Gabe from different angles. "Wow, that was quick," Gabe said.

"We've got a big shot from City Hall coming tonight. Henry Townshend. Ever heard of him?"

"Yeah, I didn't know he was a poker player."

"They say he's quite a player and he likes big games. I'm sure you know Michael will be dropping in to greet him, and we'll have a bunch of quality stills of Townshend shaking hands with the leader of the D'Angelo family."

"So you'll be here all night?" Gabe asked.

"Oh yeah, and then some. After the game, I've got to reconcile the accounts and cash the players out. Some will walk away with some nice stacks of cash and others will need to pay up. We give credit to the regulars so they can pay later. We'll have coffee and some pastries for those waiting to settle up. After the guests leave, I'll probably go home and crash for a few hours and then come back tomorrow afternoon to finish up the accounting for the game and the casino receipts."

"I haven't had a chance to look at any financial reports," Gabe said. "How do we do on the poker game?"

"That's because we don't publish reports. I have figures on my laptop that I share with Michael and the bosses, and someone from the Clubhouse will come over in the morning to pick up our proceeds. On a good night, the house could take in six figures on the poker game alone," Diane said with a smile. "We can do just as well in the casino on a good night."

"I think you told us before that there can be up to one hundred poker games in a year?" Gabe asked.

"Theoretically, that's true. It's probably closer to seventy or eighty games."

"Amazing," Gabe said as he marveled at the thought that Michael had put him in charge of such an operation.

"You should probably have one of these," Diane said, handing Gabe a small earbud device. "This will enable you to hear the feed from the security guys on the inside and on the street." She handed him a small metal device about the size of a pack of matches. "If you press this button, you can transmit your voice to all the security guys."

◆　◆　◆

At eight, the poker guests started to arrive.

"Sid! Great to see you," Diane said with a huge smile. Sid Greene owned several meat-processing plants that supplied grocery stores and butcher shops throughout the region. Diane suspected he had more than that going for him based on the amount of money he could spend on the games.

"Diane, it's a pleasure as always." He leaned forward and kissed her on the cheek.

"We've got a great game planned tonight. Can I get you something to drink?"

"The usual, thanks."

Diane proceeded to pour him one of the fine Kentucky bourbons from the shelf. Most poker players seemed to favor whiskey or scotch. Soon, Diane turned to welcome another regular guest.

At last, around 8:20, Henry Townshend entered the room—a tall, slim man with a full, thick head of wavy gray hair that was almost certainly held in place by spray or pomade.

"Council Member Townshend! Welcome to our game," Diane said, shaking his hand. One of the cocktail waitresses immediately offered to take his trench coat, revealing an elegant, navy-blue pin-striped suit. No doubt he would shed the jacket once the game started.

"Please, you can call me Henry."

Diane smiled and squeezed a button on a second transmitter in her pocket. In less than a minute, Michael D'Angelo appeared and began shaking hands with the guests. After a few perfunctory welcomes, he came to the councilman.

"Councilman, I'm Michael D'Angelo. Welcome to our little gaming room." Michael extended his right hand and shook Townshend's while gently putting his left hand on the other man's upper arm, giving the appearance of two old friends. "If there is anything we can do for your comfort or enjoyment, we are here to serve you."

Townshend greeted Michael with a forced smile. He squinted at Michael but said nothing. Michael's role as the Philadelphia mob leader was one of the best-kept secrets in the city, but Townshend appeared to be in the know.

"I won't be staying, but I hope you have an enjoyable time. I'll leave you in Diane's capable hands." He glanced at Diane, who smiled in response. The house now had some very embarrassing, if not incriminating, photos of Townshend.

Diane stepped forward and introduced the dealers and the cocktail waitresses. After mingling for a few minutes, the players grew anxious to do what they had come to do, and they sat at the table and began their game.

CHAPTER 29

Later that evening, after his dinner with Gus, Gabe took a walk on the streets surrounding the restaurant. He did not acknowledge the security personnel in parked cars at various locations but simply nodded slightly as he walked by. Suddenly, when he was about a block south of the restaurant on Tenth Street, his transceiver came to life.

"A white windowless van heading south on Ninth Street and slowing down in front of the restaurant entrance. It's proceeding south," said one of the men watching the neighborhood. Suddenly, the voice on the transmitter shouted, "The van is turning in the alleyway to go behind the casino!"

Gabe hit the button on his transmitter. "Code black. Looks like bad guys in a white van by the rear entrance! The guys in the casino need to get to the back door to guard it. Also, anyone out front needs to watch the front door!" Gabe ran toward where the alleyway came out on Tenth Street.

Gabe's transmitter sounded again, and one of the men on security spoke. "The van slowed down by the back door but then continued down the alley."

When the van exited the alley and drove by, Gabe looked toward the street. The vehicle traveled at a normal speed, but the windows were dark, and he couldn't see the driver or any passengers. "Did you get pictures?" Gabe shouted into the transmitter.

"Yeah."

"Okay, let me know if you can find out anything about the van."

A few moments later, the voice on the transmitter spoke again. "The plate is registered to a Michael McNamara at an address in North Philadelphia. It's not a commercial plate, so it may have been stolen."

"Okay. Everybody stay on high alert," Gabe said before he called the Clubhouse for extra backup to keep an eye on the streets, including two armed men to be stationed near the front of the restaurant. There was already an armed guard watching the rear door leading to the casino.

Gabe continued his patrol, walking around the block. After nothing happened for the next hour, he began to think the vehicle might have been totally innocent and of no consequence.

Several hours later, around 1:00 a.m., the security team had not reported any more activity. Gabe got tired of walking, so he returned to the casino. There were no customers in the main casino area, so the attendants had started to close up. Gabe entered the kitchen, which had also closed, but some warm coffee had been left in the coffeepot. Gabe took a cup, returned to the video room, and tried to watch the poker game, but it was hard to follow without the sound feed. Gabe would love to have called Maria, but it was the middle of the night on a school night. He decided he would call her tomorrow evening. Wednesday evening would be quiet. The casino would be closed, and even the restaurant would be closed early.

Gabe dismissed the extra security force around 6:00 a.m., after the poker players had cleared out and the normal hustle and bustle was beginning on the neighborhood streets. Diane had handed off the cash proceeds of the night to D'Angelo family couriers and had left for home to get some sleep after an exhausting night. She thanked Gabe and the security team for preventing any interruptions in the game. Diane would be back later in the day to finish up the accounts for the restaurant and casino. As Gabe walked toward his car a few blocks away, his phone rang.

"Gabe, it's Michael. I heard you guys had a little excitement last night," Michael said.

"Yeah. A van passed in front of the restaurant and then entered the alley, but we were on it. We swarmed the front and back entrances and the van passed and that was it. It might have been innocent and unrelated to us."

"Or, it could have been the Carbones checking out our security."

"Right," Gabe said, tired from being up all night and not wanting to get into an extended conversation.

"Well, you guys handled it well. Keep up the good work," Michael said.

CHAPTER 30

The next day, Wednesday, when Maria got back to her apartment, she had barely shed her coat when the phone rang.

"Hi, Maria. Is this a bad time?"

Maria knew Gabe's voice, he didn't need to identify himself. "Hi, Gabe. No, not bad at all. I just walked in the door." Maria felt butterflies in her stomach. She hadn't spoken to Gabe since Sister Theresa's funeral, and she couldn't help but smile when she heard his voice.

"Are you putting in overtime?" Gabe asked.

"No, I was visiting a friend who invited me to her house for dinner. She teaches at the school." Maria was careful to emphasize that her friend was a woman.

"I hadn't heard from you since last week, so I wanted to see how you're doing."

"Thanks for calling. I keep thinking how nice it was to see you at the funeral." Maria wondered whether that had been a wise thing to say. "How are you doing?" she asked.

"I just woke up a few hours ago. I was working on an event at one of our restaurants, and we had to have some security people there. I ended up staying all night to keep an eye on things."

"Do you usually keep such late hours?" Maria asked, wondering to herself why her father's events always seemed to need security people.

"No. It was a special occasion and things just went late," he said. "By the way, I saw our cousin Diane. She's a manager at the restaurant."

"Oh, are you talking about Francesca's?" Maria asked. "I didn't know my father owned that place."

"You're right. We don't own the restaurant, but we use space there for events."

"That must have been quite an event if it went all night," Maria said.

"So, how was your day?" he asked, as if trying to change the subject.

"School was fine. The days go so quickly for me. After school today, I went to Joanne's home for dinner. She's married and has two young children. I enjoyed being with them and their kids. Don't tell anyone I said this . . ." Maria paused, wondering if she should confide in Gabe, but then decided it would do no harm. "It's really nice to get away from the convent once in a while. And it's nice to be with a young family. Joanne has a lot to do, teaching at school and then coming home and spending time with her kids. Actually, she can check on them during the day since they are at the preschool on our campus."

"I'm like you. I like being around a family," Gabe said. "My father died when I was young, and my mother passed away a few years ago. I have a brother in New York, but I don't see him much, so I don't have much of a family life."

"That's too bad," Maria said. "My family is close by, and I still don't see them that much. It was fun being with them at the party a few weeks ago."

"Your parents are great," Gabe said. "Your father is almost like a father to me. He's my mentor." He paused a few seconds. "Maybe it's out of place for me to ask you this, but in your line of work, I mean your career in the church, in a way, you're giving up family life, aren't you? So how do you deal with that?"

"Well, the usual answer to that question is the church becomes our family, and that's kind of true. We get close to the people we live and work with at the convent, and they are my 'sisters,' not just in a religious way, but they're like sisters in real life."

"I can see that, but not having children of your own is a pretty big sacrifice, isn't it?"

"I won't deny that."

"Does that bother you?" Gabe asked.

"In fact, I have a counselor right now who is helping me work through questions like that. You probably know I'm at a stage where I haven't taken final vows, and my counselor is helping me figure out if this is really my calling," Maria said.

"So you're not locked in at this point?" Gabe asked.

"No, if I decide this is not right for me, I can go to my superiors and explain my decision. If they agree, they'll release me with their blessing."

"So if they don't release you, are you still free to leave?" Gabe asked.

"No, it doesn't work like that. It's just a question of whether they think I've prayerfully worked through my decision. If they think I'm making a hasty decision, they'll encourage me to spend some more time thinking about it. But they won't force me to stay."

"I think I understand," Gabe said. "Again, you don't have to answer this if I'm out of place, but can't you serve God or the church without being a nun? Sort of like your friend Joanne?"

"Now you're starting to sound like my parents," Maria said with a laugh. "Your question is fine, and yes, you can serve God even if you're not a nun. For me, I've spent more than a year at the convent and I've loved being here. So for now, working toward my vows is my path forward. But as I said, that decision is not finalized yet." Maria said, wondering if she should be speaking to Gabe this way.

"I'm glad I've gotten to know you a little better after we met up at Tessa's party," Gabe said, "and I'm glad you have time to consider your choices. It's a big decision."

CHAPTER 31

Diane woke on Wednesday, the day after the poker game, at two in the afternoon. She'd not returned home until nine that morning and had managed to get a few hours of sleep before heading back to the restaurant. After taking a quick shower, she grabbed a folder with handwritten receipts from the night before to enter on a computer she kept at home not connected to the internet. Before entering the numbers, she re-checked the receipts, chip purchases, the revenue from the casinos, and worksheets she had made at her office, as well as the costs of liquor, refreshments, and supplies. The combined revenues of the casino and poker game after expenses were a little more than $149,000—not bad for a weeknight. The restaurant's cut was more than $5,000. No wonder Joey Romano was happy with the arrangement. The deal he had at Francesca's almost seemed too good to be true.

Diane arrived at Francesca's around four. Wednesdays generally were quiet, and she meant to make the most of the lull to catch up on the restaurant's bookkeeping. Sometimes she worked on the books for Joey's other two restaurants. There were also some housekeeping items from the previous night's poker game, including arrangements to clean the poker room and casino facilities, restocking the liquor, cigars, and other supplies, and reviewing the credit accounts several of the regular players enjoyed. Most importantly, Diane had to begin preparing for the Friday night game, which would start her whole work cycle all over again. Fortunately, the casino was closed today, and the restaurant would likely close before ten.

At nine, Diane entered the kitchen and ran into the chef, Tony Bonetti. Tony was a short, stocky man with a handsome face and a full head of black hair that he tried to comb back, but it tended to spill back over his forehead. He was recently divorced and had a "thing" for Diane. She genuinely liked Tony, although not in the way he would have liked.

"Hi, Tony!"

"Well, hello, Diane. Didn't realize you were still here." He looked at her with a gleam in his eye. "Can I get you something?"

"As a matter of fact, I was wondering if you had any of your killer veal parmesan left." The dish was one of Tony's specialties and one of the most popular entrées in the house.

"For you, I'd make anything!"

A few minutes later, he brought a plate as requested, along with a small side salad, some fresh-baked rolls, and a glass of the house merlot. The wine was excellent, and she finished it. Almost immediately, Tony came by with the bottle to refill her glass.

"Oh, don't give me too much, maybe half a glass. I have some work to finish tonight."

"Sure thing, Diane," he said, filling her large glass about three-quarters full.

As Diane sat in the kitchen, she took several deep breaths through her nose. Something wasn't right. "I think I smell gas. Do you smell it?" she said.

Tony paused and sniffed. "Yeah, I think I do. I turned the ovens off an hour ago. They were still hot enough to heat your food, though," he said. All the ovens and cooking surfaces ran on propane gas. There were also several gas-powered refrigerators. "I can't turn the refrigerators off, but I checked over there and didn't smell anything in that area. The smell isn't strong. I'll call the gas company first thing in the morning. They respond quickly if there's a possibility of a leak."

"Good. It's probably nothing. Although, there is a definite smell. It's best to be safe."

Diane took her plate and salad dish to the dishwashing area. When Tony wasn't looking, she scraped the remains of her oversize helping of veal into the garbage. It was far too much for her to finish. Diane carried her glass of wine back to her office and sat at her desk to put the finishing touches on the restaurant books and records for today.

Diane went to work on the restaurant receipts before going over the work schedules for the casino for Thursday night and Friday night. She heard Tony close up the kitchen, leaving her alone in the building. She closed the doors to her office and locked them from the inside. She could see the views of outside from the four security cameras to make sure no one was trying to access the premises.

At around ten, she found herself nodding off, so she decided to stretch out on the couch in her office for a little nap. Usually, she could nap for a half hour, wake up, then finish her work before midnight. But last night's all-night vigil, the veal parmesan, and the generous servings of wine she'd drunk all combined to put Diane in a deep sleep.

CHAPTER 32

At 2:00 a.m., as Diane slept soundly in her office, a white windowless van pulled into the alley behind Francesca's with its headlights off. Six blocks away, Bruno Carbone Jr. and Tony Bianchi stood on the roof of a parking garage looking through binoculars with a direct line of sight to Francesca's. A third man sat waiting in the driver's seat of the sedan in which they had arrived. They could see the front of the restaurant but not into the alleyway.

In the alley, about fifty feet from the rear door, just out of the view of the restaurant's security cameras, the van paused, and a man stepped out of the passenger side. He wore a hooded runner's parka pulled tightly over his head. He also wore a clear plastic mask that distorted the features of his face to prevent identification through security camera footage.

The hooded man reached into the car and grabbed a Gamo air rifle with a scope. He raised the gun and aimed at the only streetlight in this part of the alley. There was a quiet pop, and the streetlight went dark as pieces of glass dropped to the ground. Another light over the door of the restaurant had not turned on—possibly motion-activated.

The intruders had decided there was no need to disable the security cameras. In the dark, the cameras would not pick up much detail and would be harder to take out. If someone was watching the cameras, they would dispatch someone to check it out either way. Regardless, the men in the white van didn't plan to be there long.

In front of the restaurant, two additional cars patrolled the surrounding streets. They had confirmed no guards or security personnel were in sight. The cars could act as blocking vehicles to get in the way of any police or other cars that showed up in pursuit of the van.

The van pulled up and stopped in front of the door. The light did not switch on. Within seconds, the two men in the van were outside, setting up an extendable three-piece ladder to the roof.

As Bruno Carbone and his consigliere stood on the rooftop of the parking garage, he zeroed in on Francesca's through his binoculars.

"I can't see anything. What's taking so long?" Bruno asked. It was unusual for a boss to be this close to an operation of this type, but Bruno had insisted.

"Don't worry. Our guys are working in the shadows behind the building. They'll call if there's any problem."

"Wait. I think I see something on the roof."

"That's one of our guys," Tony answered.

One man had climbed to the top of the building holding two paracords and began pulling one cord hand over hand as a five-gallon gasoline can rose at the other end. He did the same with the other cord. Just as the men had observed in drone footage, there were two vents near the rear section of the roof. The climber quickly poured one can of gasoline into a vent leading to the kitchen and a second in the vent leading to the casino area. He then dropped a device, slightly larger than a pack of cigarettes, into the kitchen vent. The device was similar to the "improvised explosive devices" encountered by American soldiers in recent wars.

The arsonists decided a second IED was not needed—the fire in the kitchen would spread quickly to the casino area, where the rest of the gasoline had been poured. The man on the roof scrambled down the ladder and loaded the ladder and cans into the van. In a moment, the van was moving toward the street. They had completed their mission in less than three minutes, except for one final detail. About half a block from the front of the restaurant, one of the men dialed a number on a cell phone to detonate the IED. They heard a faint thump as the device exploded inside the building.

Just then, Bruno Carbone's phone buzzed. The caller said, "The candles on the birthday cake have been lit."

"It should be a good party. Nice work, fellas."

Carbone looked toward the restaurant with pleasure as he saw thick black smoke pouring out the vents. As the first fire truck siren could be heard in the distance, Bruno and his consigliere turned to their car. They would be home in New Jersey in their untraceable vehicle before the D'Angelos even knew what hit them.

The fire would cause extensive damage inside the building, closing the casino for many months. No one would be injured, and there would be no damage to the surrounding buildings. As Bruno opened his car door, he saw a bright flash out of the corner of his eye. He had just enough time to turn back before the sound of the blast hit him. A huge fireball had shredded the roof of the restaurant, tossing wood and debris high into the sky.

As the roar died down, Bruno asked, "What the hell was that?"

"That was definitely not supposed to happen," answered Bianchi.

"What do we do now?" asked Bruno.

"Damned if I know."

The two stood, mesmerized by the sight unfolding before them. What was supposed to be a small fire, easily brought under control, had quickly turned into a raging conflagration that had already spread to the surrounding buildings. Fire truck sirens grew louder and several police cars were approaching. Bruno began to realize this would be a front-page news story. The police and FBI would be all over this. He was sure that the D'Angelos would figure out who was behind the fire, and they would be out for revenge, big-time.

CHAPTER 33

Michael D'Angelo, Gus, and several of his top bosses sat in front of the large screen television at the Clubhouse for a rare morning meeting. The group sat in front of the bar, which was closed other than for a pot of coffee brewing. The group rarely used the television other than for sports events when the bosses were gathered late at night. This morning was different. Michael turned the set on and flipped through channels until he found the news.

"This is Jim Garner with the Channel Five Action News Team. A major fire has struck South Philadelphia. Shortly after two this morning, a six-alarm fire started at an Italian restaurant known as Francesca's on Ninth Street near its intersection with Christian Street. The fire apparently started from a gas leak at the restaurant and quickly spread to surrounding buildings. Action News Reporter Vince Horden is live at the scene. Vince, what's it like where you stand?"

"Jim, the scene here can be summarized by one word: devastation. Witnesses spoke of hearing a boom and seeing a large fireball last night that literally blew the roof off what used to be an upscale Italian restaurant here on the quiet streets of South Philadelphia. The two commercial buildings on either side also appear to be severely damaged if not a total loss. There's also severe damage to buildings immediately behind the restaurant. Normally, the streets here are busy with people visiting commercial establishments with local bars and restaurants open late into the evening…"

Michael and the group sat watching the scenes of the smoldering ruins of what used to be Francesca's Restaurant, as well as their successful casino. Suddenly, Michael stood up, shaking his head as he hit the off button on the TV controller and threw it against the wall, where it burst into pieces and scattered around the room. He turned to Gus and his underbosses just as his phone buzzed.

"What?" he said.

"Michael, it's Gabe."

"Where are you?"

"I'm down by the restaurant with Joey."

"Is he there right now?"

"No, he's in his car making some phone calls."

"Is everybody okay?"

"The restaurant closed at ten, and everybody is accounted for . . . except Joey says Diane was working in her office when he left. I've tried her cell phone, but she's not picking up."

"Get over to her apartment and make sure she's okay. She's probably still asleep."

"I'll call you back from there," Gabe said as Michael disconnected the call.

He turned back to his team. "What's on the security camera footage?"

Gus sighed. "We got the feed here and we've looked at it. Right at two in the morning, the lights in the alley went out, and a van pulled up to the door. It's very dim and hard to see any details. They must have shot out the streetlight. It looks like two guys carried a ladder to the roof, and one climbed up. We can't see anything on the roof, but the guy came down a couple of minutes later. He must have dropped something in one of the vents."

"Did we have someone here watching the live feed?" asked Michael.

"No, we don't usually do that at night when the casino and restaurant are closed." Gus shuffled on his feet. "It wouldn't have mattered. The guys drove off in the van in less than three minutes. They would have been gone before we could get anyone over there. I think the pricks who did this assumed they'd be picked up on camera even in the dim lighting."

"What about the gas leak? Was that part of the attack?" asked Michael.

"It looks like a coincidence. Joey says Tony told him there was a faint smell of gas before closing that evening. They were going to get it checked in the morning. There's nothing unusual there."

"So, I don't think there's any doubt that this is payback from the Carbones for hijacking Geller's truck and the other stuff we've been doing to get their drug seller to pay up." Michael slapped the table.

After a brief pause, Gus spoke up. "I doubt they intended the fire to be so big. Bruno Carbone is an asshole, but he's not totally stupid. Now the cops and maybe the FBI are going to be asking questions, and this will backfire on New Jersey. But he's also forced us to act, and he can't expect us to sit back and do nothing."

"They wanted to hurt us, but they hurt an innocent family who owned the restaurant. That's not the way any of the families in this part of the country operate," Michael added. "We can recover, but how is the Romano family going to come back from this? We need to hit the Carbones back hard, but be smarter about it." Just then, Michael's phone rang again, and he immediately hit the speaker button.

"Michael, I just left Diane's apartment and she's not there." There was a tremor in Gabe's voice. "I found her car parked a block from the restaurant."

"Is there anywhere else she could be?"

"I spoke to Joey and Tony, the chef. She was in her office when they left at ten." There was a pause. "They said sometimes she'd sleep on the couch in her office if she worked late. They also said she would never walk home that late at night."

Michael's gut roiled. "Okay, Gabe. Come down to the Clubhouse if you can." He disconnected the phone and looked at his advisors. "This changes everything," he said.

CHAPTER 34

At the FBI field office Thursday afternoon, Special Agents Dempsey and Perez sat in a small conference room, joined by Agent Reed, who was still Dempsey's second on the task force.

Agent Dempsey pointed to Perez. "Tell me what you've found."

"You know the basic details from the news. At two, a major fire broke out at Francesca's Restaurant, destroying several of the surrounding buildings. At the beginning of the fire, or soon after, there was an explosion, suggesting a gas leak. I spoke to the fire marshal this morning, and he confirms there was a leak in the building, but they haven't pinned down where it started. The big news is the fire marshal says there was a significant amount of accelerant inside the building in at least two locations. They are running tests to confirm, but the accelerant is presumably gasoline."

"You said there was a significant amount of accelerant. How much would that be?"

"The fire marshal can only guess, but he thinks there could have been five to ten gallons or more dumped in the building."

"Why would somebody use that much accelerant in a building with a gas leak?" asked Agent Reed. "All you would need is a small spark or fire near the leak, like a burning cigarette."

"Great question. I don't think you would use much accelerant, if any, if you knew there was a gas leak," Perez answered.

"Which means whoever dumped the accelerant probably didn't know about the leak," said Dempsey. "What about the restaurant owner? Has he been interviewed?"

"Yes, the Philadelphia PD talked to him this morning before the fire marshal discovered the evidence of arson. His name is Joseph Romano, and the restaurant was opened by his father about fifty years ago. He said he had a call about the gas leak at about ten from his chef. The chef reported a smell of gas and said he had left a message for the gas company to come and check it out in the morning. We've confirmed the existence of that voicemail. At the time, he said all but one employee has been accounted for. Later this afternoon, we learned that the bookkeeper, Diane D'Angelo, was working late and was still at the restaurant when the other restaurant employees left. That would have been around ten. Unfortunately, her car was parked near the restaurant, and she's not been found, so she's presumably a casualty of the fire."

"That makes the arson a homicide. Is the owner a suspect?"

"The homicide division of the PD is interviewing Romano right now," said Agent Perez. "They've had him there for a few hours. Just before the meeting, I got an update from one of the detectives, and both Romano and the chef seem to have solid alibis, but the Philadelphia police are checking them out. We've put together a financial team to check out how the restaurant was doing, and everything so far suggests it was very successful and making lots of money. Romano says neither he nor the restaurant had any debts to speak of. The Romano family owned the building. But I should add that we are basing this on what the Philadelphia PD got out of him in the interrogation and from last year's tax returns. The owner says all books and records were on the premises with no outside backups. The same is true of security footage. The cameras and the system were all burned up in the fire."

"Let me back up a bit," said Dempsey. "You mentioned the missing woman is Diane D'Angelo? Any relation to Michael D'Angelo or the D'Angelo crime family?"

"There may be a connection there. We're running that down right now."

"The PPD has already asked Romano about Ms. D'Angelo. He says she was a very loyal and hardworking employee. One of the best he's ever had. The fact that she was working late supports his statement. He said she sometimes worked so late she slept on the couch in her office rather than making the trip home in the middle of the night. The chef also confirmed she was an outstanding employee and that she was good friends with all the other employees. I don't see anything that would suggest she was involved," Perez explained.

Agent Reed spoke up again. "So, if the lady was still at the restaurant, someone must have broken in and poured gasoline all over the place without setting off any alarms, and either she didn't hear it or slept through it. Let me ask you this. Is there a way to get accelerant inside the building from the roof?"

"I suppose someone could get up there with a thirty- or forty-foot ladder. There are ladders that long that can collapse into a shorter length so it would fit in a truck or a van," Agent Perez said. "I've saved the best for last in my report, and this highlights your question about Ms. D'Angelo's family connections."

Perez had already given Dempsey a preview of this part of the presentation. It was one of the reasons this meeting had been called.

"Francesca's Restaurant has been patronized by leaders of the Philadelphia mob in recent years. It's not one of the more prominent locations that we've associated with the mob, but this goes along with their recent efforts to keep a low profile. Joseph Romano has a clean record. Assuming he wasn't behind this arson, we don't have any solid evidence of any crimes. That could change when our financial team digs deeper. But my final point is we have a confidential informant who says there was a backroom gambling operation at the restaurant.

Of course, any hard evidence of that has gone up in smoke, unless we can find some good witnesses. Due to the fire, we've just begun looking into this location, but we will continue to do so."

"If there was a gambling operation at this location, I find it hard to believe we didn't know about it," said Agent Reed.

Agent Perez shrugged. "There may be lots of smaller operations in the region where we have typically deferred to the state and city law enforcement authorities. It's possible some of these could have grown into something significant without our awareness."

"So, Francesca's may have had a gambling operation hiding in plain sight, so to speak. Does the Philadelphia PD have any information on it?" asked Dempsey.

"If they do, they haven't shared it. We've certainly asked," Perez answered.

"If Mr. Romano was hosting the gambling operations at his restaurant, I doubt if he was doing it for free. If we can get some evidence of that, we can charge him and try to get him to turn on the parties that were in charge of the gambling," said Dempsey. When the others didn't speak, he continued. "If this is a gambling operation tied to the D'Angelo family, then that puts the arson investigation in a different light. I don't think the restaurant or the D'Angelos would blow up their own cash cow. I think we need to expand our investigation across the river in light of the information we received concerning tension between the two families." He looked at his partners. "Thank you, Agent Perez, for great work in a short time. I know you will be continuing to work this case. I'd like some review of satellite images to study the roof of the restaurant to see how accelerant could have been dropped in from the outside. Also, I'd like a review of all the security footage on bridge traffic to and from New Jersey on the night of the fire. Let's see if we recognize anybody. Let's also canvass the neighborhood for any security footage that might show the vehicles involved in the arson. Agent Reed, let's talk to the FBI field office in Newark to let them know where this may be heading and see if they have any insight on the activities of the Carbone family. Last, if this looks like the beginning of a war between the Philadelphia and New Jersey crime families, we're going to have to take the lead, and we'll need to make this clear to the Philadelphia PD. Let's meet again tomorrow for an update."

CHAPTER 35

Gabe decided to stop home for a quick change of clothes before heading to the Clubhouse. As he was grabbing his keys and heading to his car, his phone buzzed again. Michael's voice sounded hoarse and tired.

"Gabe, are you on your way over here?"

"Yeah. Should be there in about twenty minutes."

"I need you to go back to Diane's apartment right away and get her laptop and any other computer equipment. Make sure there are no financial books or records relating to the casino or the restaurant. Joey is being questioned, and we don't want any trails leading to us. You know what to do."

"Got it." Gabe knew Diane was missing, and it was a prudent step to get her computer. But a wave of sadness overtook him as it was clear that by sending him on this errand, Michael was assuming the worst. He drove to the apartment, found a spot on her block, and parked. For the second time, he began randomly ringing buzzers for the twelve apartments in the building at the entry to the small lobby. This was an old trick that usually worked to gain entrance into a locked front door to a lobby. Finally, someone buzzed him in, probably assuming it was a delivery. Gabe pulled his baseball cap down and kept his head low. Avoiding the elevator, he walked to the stairwell and quickly ran up to the third floor. He expected the police might check the security cameras if they searched Diane's apartment.

Gabe put on a pair of latex gloves. He didn't have a key but was able to pick Diane's lock in about thirty seconds. His heart sank when he entered and caught a faint smell of Diane's perfume. There was even a photo on the wall in which he saw himself and Diane at a birthday party when they had been kids.

A desk sat by the window with a laptop and some neatly stacked files. There were also some notebooks and bound journals with her writing in them—a pre-electronic form of spreadsheets. He went to the kitchen and found a large canvas bag, the type someone would carry into the grocery store. Gabe quickly unplugged Diane's laptop, put it in the bag, and began stacking the files and journals in the bag as well. There was nothing in the drawers except some USB thumb drives. These were most likely where she stored files for the casino and restaurant. Gabe pocketed them, then quickly checked behind hanging pictures and looked at the books on her bookshelf to make sure there were no hidden compartments. Similarly, he rifled through the drawers in her bedroom. It felt like a violation to look in the drawers containing Diane's undergarments, but he found a revolver and a box of ammo, which he put in his bag, so it was not a wasted search. A small drawer on her vanity contained a felt-lined shelf for jewelry. He left it there.

Gabe looked in all the usual hiding places in the bathroom, including the toilet tank and under the sink. Last, he strode to the kitchen. A rolodex lay on the kitchen counter, which he took. There was no landline. Gabe knew Diane had a personal cell phone for "ordinary" calls and a burner phone for family business that she kept with her at all times. Both had undoubtedly burned up in the fire.

He checked the cupboards and found only plates, bowls, silverware, and similar items, as well as a pantry stocked with cans of soup, crackers, spaghetti sauce, and the like. There were several large, plastic containers of sugar and flour, which Gabe probed with a long fork, then looked in the freezer. He noticed a frozen pizza box that looked like it had been opened. He pulled it out and opened the flap on the side. There was no pizza inside, but several thick stacks of cash—hundreds and twenties. It looked like about $20,000. Gabe did not suspect Diane was skimming money, but she often received large tips from the players and cash bonuses from the casino, creating too much cash to take to a bank without raising suspicion. Gabe stuffed the cash in his bag and threw the pizza box in the trash.

Gabe happened to glance out the window to the street. Just then, two police squad cars pulled up and parked in a "no parking" zone in front of the door. Two cops got out of each car. Gabe decided he needed to get going, so he grabbed the canvas bag, which was now heavy, and left the apartment. As he pulled the door shut, he encountered an elderly man in the hallway with a small white poodle on a leash. The man stood in front of a door down the hallway and appeared to be groping in his pockets for a key.

"May I help you?" the man said, looking over at Gabe.

"Oh no. I was just checking on Diane."

"Is she okay?"

"She wasn't home." Gabe noticed the man staring at the canvas grocery bag. "I was just dropping off some stuff for her."

"You can leave it with me if you like."

"Thanks, but I need to see her. I'll try back later."

With that, the man continued to open the door to his apartment. Gabe hoped the man hadn't gotten a good look at his face in the dim light of the hallway. He raced in the direction of an exit sign at the other end of the hallway. In the stairwell, he turned back toward the thin glass window over the doorknob.

He watched the four officers emerge from the elevator along with someone who looked like he may have been the building supervisor. They began to knock on Diane's door.

"Miss D'Angelo, are you there?" the one cop shouted. It appeared to be a wellness check.

Joey had probably told the police Diane was missing. After a few moments, the man without a uniform pulled out a set of keys and opened the door. Gabe wondered why four officers were needed for this. Then he figured they would use the wellness check to look around for any records of the restaurant or the alleged gambling joint. Gabe slipped down the stairs and out a back door to his car, where he dialed Michael's number.

When Michael answered, Gabe said, "I've found some stuff, which I now have with me—otherwise, the apartment is clean. The police came right after I finished, but they didn't see me."

"Good. Meet me at the Clubhouse, and we'll talk."

Despite the sadness he felt about Diane, when he heard Michael's voice, he thought of Maria. "Does Maria know Diane is missing?" he asked.

"I haven't spoken to her about it. Why don't you call her? She'll appreciate hearing from you. Tell her I'll talk to her soon."

Gabe hit Maria's number immediately after disconnecting. He knew her classes at the school were finished by now.

"Maria, it's Gabe."

"I'm so glad to hear from you. I was worried when I saw the fire on the news. You were at the restaurant the last time I spoke to you. Is everything okay?"

After a pause, Gabe took a deep breath and said, "Diane is missing."

"Oh my gosh, no!"

"She was working late last night." Gabe swallowed against the tremor in his voice. "I checked her apartment, and she's not there, but her car was parked near the restaurant."

"Did you look anywhere else? I mean, maybe she went out for breakfast."

There was silence for a moment.

"I don't think so. Her car was still parked by the restaurant, and she wouldn't walk home from there," Gabe said.

"Oh no!" Maria said as she began to weep. "Was anyone else hurt?"

"No, everybody else at Francesca's is safe and accounted for."

"Has anyone told Diane's family?" Maria asked with a tearful voice.

"I don't know. I'm on my way to see your father. I'll ask. I'm sorry about the news. I'll let you know if I find out anything more. He's got his hands full right now, but he said he'd call you soon."

CHAPTER 36

Gabe walked into the Clubhouse later that day and found Michael nursing a glass of bourbon in the club room by the bar. Gus was getting up to leave, but Michael beckoned him to stay when Gabe walked in. Gabe took a seat at the little table with them. The atmosphere was glum as there had still been no sign of Diane.

"I just had a long meeting with my captains. We had a lot to talk about. Tell me what you found in Diane's apartment," Michael said.

"I got her computer and some spreadsheets for the restaurant. There are some file folders I haven't gone through yet, and she also had a bunch of thumb drives in her desk." Gabe put them out on the table. "They contain computer files. I assume it's stuff related to the restaurant and casino."

"We'll get someone to go through everything if you don't have time."

"I can do it," Gabe said.

"Anything else?" Michael asked.

"I found a gun in her bedroom. It's in the bag with the other stuff. Also, there was some cash hidden in the kitchen freezer, about $20,000." Gabe pulled the stacks of money out of the bag and put them on the table. "There was some jewelry, but I left it in her bedroom. Otherwise, the police won't find anything if they search."

Michael took several stacks of cash and slid them across the table to Gabe. "That's for your good work."

Gabe started to reach for the stacks but stopped. "Did Diane have any family?" he asked.

"No, but thanks for asking. Her mother died of cancer a few months ago. She lived in Allentown," Michael said. "She's got a brother who's a worthless piece of shit, but I don't know where he is. No need to be concerned about him."

"I made a call to Maria," Gabe added. "She seemed pretty shaken about Diane. I think you should talk to her when the dust settles a little bit around here." Most people who worked for Michael would not have made such a bold suggestion, but Gabe had enough confidence to speak freely.

"Back to what I called you here for," Michael said. "The fire is the work of Bruno Carbone Jr. He's a punk who's out of control. His father would never have done anything like this. If Junior was here, I'd do to him what he did to Diane—burn him alive. But our contacts tell us that Bruno has gone into hiding for a while, supposedly until things calm down. He's probably out of the country."

"So, do we wait for him to come back?" asked Gabe.

"We've got another plan. Bruno has a cousin named Nickie Perrelli who runs a big service station just off the New Jersey Turnpike on Route seventy-three in Cherry Hill. It's a truck stop. He's also got a fleet of trucks, and he's in the transportation business. Perrelli isn't a member of the Carbone family, but he grew up with Bruno, and they are quite close. The Carbones rely on Perrelli for transportation needs. He moves slot machines and other equipment around the casinos, and he picks them up for servicing and repairs, for example. But the big thing we learned is Perrelli's truck stop is a drop-off for drugs from Geller. Perrelli moves them from there to locations all over South Jersey. So if we take Perrelli out of the picture, it's gonna hurt the Carbones big-time."

"I'd like to help pull it off." The look on Gabe's face made it seem like he was ready to carry out the hit himself.

"I thought you'd say that, and we need someone like you who's smart and who can think on their feet. Someone I can trust completely. But this is going to be a very risky job, and we need to bring in a specialist." Michael slugged back the rest of his bourbon. "We've got Jimmy Salerno on board. He's the best of the best. We're bringing him in from St. Louis, and he's on his way here to stake out the job. Since you want to help, you can be his driver and backup. You'll be the only one in our organization ever to see this guy face-to-face. He usually doesn't allow anyone else to be involved, but we made it worth his while."

"I'll do whatever you ask me to do." Gabe knew that, in the old days, a soldier had to handle a hit in order to be officially inducted into the family. Whether or not that rule still strictly applied, it was clear his job would satisfy the requirement and would clear the way for Gabe to become a made man in the organization. That would involve a ceremony where Gabe would take a blood oath, literally cutting his hand to drain blood onto a picture of a saint. In that oath, he would promise eternal loyalty to the family, placing the family above his own interests, his own family, and even his religious convictions, on pain of death. There was no walking away after taking that oath. In some ways, it was like taking final vows to become a nun.

CHAPTER 37

The next morning, Special Agent Dempsey reconvened the meeting at the FBI field office to discuss the fire on Ninth Street. Agents Reed and Perez were present, as well as Agent McIntyre. They called Agent McIntyre "Mac" around the office, and he was working with Agent Perez on the matter.

"Agent Perez, tell us what you've got. Why don't you start with the missing woman."

"I spoke to the Philadelphia PD's lead detective on the arson case. Unofficially, it's also a murder investigation. They paid a call to Ms. D'Angelo's apartment yesterday for a 'wellness check.' No one answered the door, and the supervisor let them in. When they confirmed the apartment was empty, they had a look around. There was no computer, no cell phone, no files—nothing with any relation to the restaurant or any gambling operation. There was a closet full of clothes and an unpacked suitcase."

"Any security footage?"

"I was just getting to that. The super provided footage from Wednesday evening through Thursday afternoon when the police visited the apartment. There was no sign of Diane. On Thursday morning, a man entered the lobby and took the stairs. The super didn't recognize the man as there wasn't a clear shot at his face. The footage didn't show the man leaving."

"Don't tell me. The guy was wearing a baseball cap and kept his head down, right?" asked Dempsey.

"Pretty much."

"Is there any other way out of the building?" Agent Reed asked.

"There's a fire exit on each floor, leading to a second stairwell in the rear. The door can only be opened from the inside."

"So it's possible the mystery man went out the back door?" Agent Reed asked. "And if he was carrying anything, we don't have any footage of it."

"It's possible. It's also possible he lived in the building and didn't go out the rest of the day. But we'd have to look at photos of all the male residents to rule that out."

Agent Dempsey raised his hand to interrupt. "My gut is that it's all too neat and clean. The woman was the bookkeeper for a restaurant we strongly suspect had illegal gambling. All the records were burned in the fire. Her apartment is clean, and she's missing. Suppose our working hypothesis is that she was killed in the fire and the people running the gambling—most likely the D'Angelo family—got to the apartment and cleaned it up before the police could get there. Maybe the mystery man was the one who got there first. Can anyone shoot that down?"

"Maybe," Agent Reed said. "But suppose Ms. D'Angelo was in on this. She made sure the people at the restaurant knew she was there when they left. She let the bad guys into the building to spread the accelerant. She cleaned out the cash and got out of there. Now everyone thinks she's dead, but she's sipping a margarita on a beach in the Caribbean. Maybe it wasn't just the money. She could have had her own reasons for wanting to check out."

"Mac and I have worked that scenario. Stay with me," Perez continued. "We think some additional evidence makes Leon's scenario more likely. In particular, the fire marshal's lab tests came back. There were two hot spots that tested positive for gasoline. Both were under ducts that vented to the roof. One of them tested positive for thermite, and some remnants of an electronic device were found close by. That suggests a remotely detonated explosive device."

"Or detonated by a timer," added Agent Reed.

"Yes. Either way, there would be no need for an explosive device if the arsonists got in the building," Agent Perez said. "They could spread their accelerant, light it, and leave. As we said yesterday, it's not likely they would have used that much accelerant if they were relying on the gas leak."

"So a second part of our hypothesis is that the arsonists quietly got on the roof and poured accelerant and maybe dropped an explosive device down a vent," Dempsey added.

"Why wouldn't the arsonist just break in the front door, throw gasoline around, and leave?" Agent Reed asked.

"Breaking in the front or rear doors would have set off alarms. We also believe the rear door was reinforced and would be difficult and noisy to break in. Either way, there's no telling how long it would take to get to the casino area once they were inside. We think they decided to eliminate that risk and approach quietly from the roof without setting off alarms," Agent Perez answered.

"Anything more on the fire?" Agent Dempsey asked.

"As a matter of fact, yes. We checked the bridge traffic, and there's nothing definitive showing that Carbone or any of his known associates crossed in either direction. But a crossing is not hard to conceal. What we do have is Bruno Carbone leaving on a privately chartered jet from Atlantic City to San Juan on Thursday morning."

"Bingo. He's expecting retaliation and wants to lie low for a while, out of the country. Do we have anything on his whereabouts in Puerto Rico?" asked Dempsey.

"No. We got the flight record several hours after he arrived, so we had no one looking for him. I've alerted the field office in San Juan to keep an eye out. They told me he probably got on a private plane to hop to one of the other islands in the Caribbean after arriving in San Juan. We don't have accurate passenger manifests for all the private flights out of Puerto Rico.

"I need to move on to some other important items," Agent Perez said. "We got some security footage from the other businesses close to the restaurant." Perez distributed copies of a grainy photo showing a man getting out of the rear door of a Lincoln Town Car. She passed out a second photo showing an enlargement of the man's face. "This is Henry Townshend, a member of city council. He's about seventy-five feet from the front entrance to the restaurant. There's also a rear entrance, where we suspect any players would enter for gambling or poker. He's alone and has a reputation as a high-stakes poker player. I'm guessing he didn't want his car to be seen pulling up to either entrance. He probably didn't realize he was on other security cameras."

"Did the Philadelphia detectives ask Romano if the council member dined at the restaurant that evening?" Reed asked.

"Not specifically. They did ask him if there were any noteworthy guests at the restaurant. He said there weren't. It was a slow night. I imagine they'll follow up and ask him specifically. Perez added, "We also have an unknown subject on our footage who appears to have walked by the same security camera that got Townshend. He walked by twice, like he was circling the block. The image of his face is very poor quality, and we can't do anything with it. I've sent it to Quantico, and if they can enhance it, they'll run it through the facial recognition database. It'll take a few days for them to get it all done."

"Have the Philadelphia detectives talked to Townshend yet?" Dempsey asked.

"No, they wanted to check with us. I think they realize they're getting in over their heads. Plus, Townshend is very influential in the city. He votes on their budget, yada yada yada. I think they'd rather have us be the bad guys on that one."

"Okay, folks," Dempsey said as he pushed back from the table. "We're hot on the trail, but somehow the major actors keep getting one step ahead of us. We need to find a way to get out front before the situation goes down the crapper. I think we're on the verge of a potential mob war between two families. Agent Perez, why don't you take the lead on talking to Townshend? If nothing else, we can nail down the fact that there was gambling at the joint, probably illegally. Let's watch the airports to see if the D'Angelos go looking for Carbone. That will be tough, but we've got to try. Let's get a warrant to search Ms. D'Angelo's apartment. We'll have a forensic team go over it inch by inch. We should also canvass her neighbors to see if they saw anyone enter her apartment. By the way, I assume no one found her remains. Let's double back and check on that. Maybe we need a team to go through the rubble. Let's do a daily briefing like this unless Agent Perez tells me there is nothing new to report."

◆　◆　◆

Later that day, Councilman Townshend's private line buzzed and he picked up.

"Councilman, I met you Tuesday night. Are you on a secure line?" the caller asked.

"Yes, it's a private phone registered to my wife." Townshend recognized Michael D'Angelo's voice and knew better than to greet the caller by name. You never know who might be listening in. He was nervous about taking the call but wanted to hear what this was about.

"We have sources that say there were security cameras on Ninth Street near the restaurant, and there is footage of you getting out of a car Tuesday night. We encourage you to be very discreet if anyone questions you about this."

"Of course. Thanks for the heads-up." Townshend was sharp enough to understand Michael's message. Being "very discreet" was another way of saying "keep quiet about the poker game." Townshend didn't need to be convinced that telling the police about his attending a poker game sponsored by the D'Angelo family was out of the question. It could be a career-ending scandal for him, not to mention the dangers of getting on the wrong side of the local Mafia family. Townshend would find a way to keep quiet if the police or FBI questioned him. He would even lawyer up if necessary.

CHAPTER 38

On Friday evening, Maria received a call from her father.

"Maria, how are you?"

"I could barely sleep last night thinking about Diane. Is there any more news about her?" she asked.

"I'm sorry, but no. I'm afraid we need to assume the worst."

Maria sniffled, barely holding the tears back. "Will you let me know about her funeral?"

"Of course," Michael said.

"How's Uncle Joey doing? Hasn't the restaurant been in his family forever?"

"He's doing well, under the circumstances. Yes, the restaurant was in his family for seventy years. It's going to be hard to bring it back."

"Wow. I heard they were investigating arson. They don't suspect Uncle Joey, do they?" Maria asked.

"No, it was a very good business. He would never do anything to hurt it," Michael said.

Suddenly, some troubling thoughts filled Maria's mind. "But why would anyone deliberately burn down a restaurant? The news even made it sound like someone planted a bomb, and isn't our family business involved with the restaurant?" As soon as she asked these questions, Maria wondered whether she had crossed the line.

"Yes, Joey has always been a close friend, and I'm sure he never did anything to deserve having his restaurant destroyed like that." After a pause, Michael continued. "I can tell you we would never do anything to cause harm to Joey or the restaurant."

"I know that," Maria said. "I just can't understand how anyone would want to hurt a restaurant like that."

"There are some bad characters out there, and I hope they pay for what they did."

Maria decided not to pursue the subject further even though she remained concerned about the fact that her family was involved with a restaurant that somehow experienced such violent destruction. She sniffled and took a deep breath to regain her composure. "It's all just so sad," she said. "Joey is in my prayers every day. Of course, Diane is as well. By the way, how's Mom doing?"

"She's upset about Diane. She requested a mass at her church to be said for her."

"Have her let me know when it is. I'd like to go with her if that's possible."

"I will. And, Maria, I'm sorry I couldn't call you sooner. I knew you were very sad about Diane and the fire. You might hear some things in the news about our family ties to the restaurant. Don't believe everything you hear. Joey's a close friend, and we've spent a lot of time at his restaurant related to our business. It was a wonderful place. But the media will try and twist things."

"I know, Dad. I know you've worked hard to build a successful business. Just hang in there."

"One more thing before you go. I know you've become good friends with Gabe. I want you to know that he's a good man. He's very loyal to our family, and you can trust him."

"I know he's a good man." Maria left it at that, wondering why her father had brought it up. She felt encouraged that her father approved her friendship with Gabe, but it didn't make the decision about her vocation any easier.

CHAPTER 39

That same evening, Gabe sat in a quiet bar on South Thirteenth Street, nursing his second pint of ale. A deluge of thoughts flowed through his mind as he pondered the past few weeks of his life. He was working for an organized crime family in Philadelphia, making more money than ninety-nine percent of those his age. He guessed this made him a "one-percenter." Although the family aspired to shift its focus to legal enterprises, Gabe had been promoted to oversee a substantial operation engaged in illegal gambling in the back of a restaurant in South Philadelphia. Not only that, the restaurant and gambling operation had been bombed and burned to the ground, probably by a rival crime family, killing a cousin he cared about.

Of course, no one blamed Gabe for this tragedy. All signs pointed to a job cleverly pulled off by the mob in South Jersey, and the families were on the verge of a violent blood feud. Now, although the family shied away from the violent ways of the past, Gabe was about to plunge into the center of a plot to kill an associate of the South Jersey mob in cold blood. Gabe had willingly volunteered for this job to avenge his beloved cousin, but as he got closer to the act, he was having some second thoughts. Not only that, the FBI would now actively become involved in the investigation, and Gabe's role in the plot—not to mention his other illegal activities—could lead to a long prison sentence.

On the other hand, Gabe's successes could lead to membership as a made man in the D'Angelo family at an exceptionally early age. His rewards would be many, but he'd be stuck in the family business for the next forty years or more, if he lived that long. To walk away from the family was a violation of a sacred oath taken at initiation, on pain of death. In addition, as a practical matter, anyone who walked away was deemed a loose end who might decide to talk to authorities.

The family did not like loose ends.

Gabe supposed he might already be a loose end if he tried to leave the organization before becoming a made man. In any case, if Gabe were arrested and faced charges, it would be hard to resist the temptation to cooperate with authorities to reduce or even elimi-nate a prison sentence. Seventy-year-old Mafia dons could spit in the face of the authorities. They weren't afraid of dying in prison. But what about a thirty-year-old like himself with his whole life before him? The way things were going these days, Gabe felt that the odds were probably about fifty-fifty he'd someday be faced with a choice of cooperating with authorities or violating his oath to the family. That day could be soon. If Gabe decided to cooperate, he'd have a target on his back. Like many others in this situation who decide to testify against the Mafia, his lifeless, mutilated body would probably be found with a dead canary placed on his head—the Mafia's way of pointing out those who agreed to sing. Gabe doubted even Michael's kinder, gentler version of the Mafia would tolerate someone who rat-ted out the organization or its leaders.

What if the government could protect him for his cooperation? The best he could hope for was relocation in an out-of-the-way place in the witness protection program, cut off from family, friends, and everything in his previous life, including the money he'd made in the Mafia. That was not the most cheerful prospect.

At the root of Gabe's anxiety was another fundamental problem, maybe the biggest problem of all in his mind. He now realized he was falling in love with a woman who was preparing to become a nun. Gabe had only recently gotten to know Maria, but his heart ached at the thought of losing her, even though he didn't really "have" her yet. If Gabe could somehow deepen his relationship with Maria, could he talk her into leaving her religious vocation? Maybe, but would a person like Maria agree to be with someone who worked for the Mafia? Sooner or later, he would have to tell her the whole story. He couldn't keep such a secret from a wife or lover for very long. And then there was the question of whether Michael would ever approve of Gabe becoming more than a friend to Maria. Things were fine as long as Gabe was following Michael's instructions to befriend Maria as part of a larger plot to get her away from the convent. Having a relationship with the boss's daughter could be a risky proposition.

With these thoughts swirling around in his mind, he kept coming back to the same conclusion. Leaving the Mafia right now was not really an option. He would stay on course, perform his assignment, and become a member of the organization if that door opened. He would work hard and save as much money as he could. Maybe someday he could talk Maria into leaving her vocation and running away with him. They would disappear together. After all, weren't there specialists in making people disappear and relocating them with a new identity? Gabe already had nearly a million dollars stashed away. All he would need would be a few more million to live comfortably. And it wouldn't take long to save that much as a member of the D'Angelo family.

Chapter 40

On Saturday morning, Maria had arranged to go on a walk in Fairmount Park with Joanne. Joanne asked if she could bring her three-year-old in a stroller, an accommodation that Maria was happy to make. Joanne's husband would watch her other child, still a baby, for a few hours. Maria picked up Joanne and her little boy, Teddy, and they drove to the park. Their plan was to walk south on a trail on the west side of Wissahickon Creek, stop at the Valley Green Inn for coffee, cross the bridge, and return on a trail that paralleled the other side the creek. It was a cool, sunny spring morning as they began walking, and Maria marveled at the rays of sunlight that penetrated the thick canopy of trees along the trail. Getting out in the fresh air and sunshine was wonderful after being in a classroom all week teaching. They walked along for about an hour and said little as they took in the scenery.

Arriving at the Valley Green Inn felt like stepping back to an earlier time, thanks to the white stucco walls and black shutters, along with the wood pillars on the porch and small white posts for tying up horses—a carry-over from the inn's early days. A stone terrace overlooked the creek where a flock of Canada geese frolicked in the water.

After watching the geese for a few minutes, the little group took a seat at a table on the porch. The women ordered coffee, and Joanne punched a straw through the little hole in a carton of fruit juice she carried for Teddy.

"I'm so glad we did this," Joanne said. "This is so nice. I live so close and never realized this was here."

"I'm glad too. I really needed this. A friend suggested this place. I think it's what got her hooked on hiking as a hobby," Maria said, referring to her recent conversation with Sister Anna. She was still feeling bad about Diane and was happy for something to occupy her attention.

"So how are you doing, Maria?" Joanne asked. "I know you're busy at the school. Plus, you have your duties at the convent. It must be taxing at times."

Teddy began to cry.

Maria reached toward the stroller. "May I?" Joanne nodded, and Maria picked up Teddy and gathered him into her arms. As she sat down, Teddy immediately calmed down.

"I prefer being busy," Maria said. "I love teaching, and I enjoy life at the convent. But sometimes, I do think about a different life, one like yours, having a husband and a family." Maria felt she knew Joanne well enough to open up to her. "They tell the women in our program it's okay to think about such things during the next few years before we make final vows. We need to work through this and be sure of our calling."

Joanne took a sip of her coffee and nodded. "I don't have to tell you that I love being a mom. It's not easy, but I wouldn't trade it for anything. I love teaching too," Joanne said. "I'm familiar with the novice process. We've had several women in the novice program teach at the school."

"I didn't know that," Maria replied. She hadn't mentioned to Joanne the fact that her vows to become a novice had been delayed.

"One of them stands out in my memory. Her name was Sister Veronica. We called her Ronnie. I think she lived where you're staying."

"I hadn't heard of her," Maria said.

"There used to be a program that allowed us to take our class to an environmental studies center operated by the public school, and we usually went a couple times a month. While she was there, she met a man who taught in the public school. Apparently, they started seeing each other on the sly. One day, Ronnie cleared her things out of the convent, and she just left. She married the guy, and they moved away," Joanne said.

"That's quite a story," Maria said. "I bet that didn't sit well with the convent."

"No, it didn't," Joanne said. "The way she handled it didn't sit well with the church either, for that matter." She looked at Maria and said, "I don't mean in any way to compare you to Ronnie, but you're an attractive woman, and I'm guessing you've probably had opportunities for relationships. I know you would never in a million years handle it like Ronnie did. The point is, if you have strong desires to be married and have a family, and I'm not saying that is necessarily your case, it's best to work that decision out with the help of your superiors at the convent. There's nothing wrong with wanting a family. If you ever want to talk about this, I'm here for you."

Maria had heard the pitch about the benefits of leaving her vocation on friendly terms but was touched by Joanne's expression of concern for her. "Thank you. I've been thinking a lot about this lately. Can I share something with you?"

"Of course, go ahead."

"I have a distant relative who works for my father. I met him years ago but met him again at my niece's birthday party. His name is Gabe, and he's about thirty years old. The best way I can describe it is that we have struck up a friendship. We haven't gone anywhere alone, but he came over once to help with an outing for the kids. It was all in the open, right on the grounds of the convent. Another time, he volunteered at a soup kitchen where I was working. I know we can't be more than friends, and he respects that. The thing is, if I were free, he's the kind of man I would want to be with."

"I think I understand." Joanne did not probe further. "I don't envy the position you're in, having to make such a big decision about your life, and I won't tell you what to do, but I can say one thing. I've seen the way you interact with kids, and even the way you interact with Teddy, and I think you'd be a great mom."

Maria still cradled Teddy, who was sleeping soundly. She handed him back to Joanne.

"Thank you. I supposedly have two or three years to make my decision. At the convent, they tell us not to rush it. I'm still working at becoming a nun, and I enjoy the program. But if I'm not supposed to be a nun, I'd sure like to know sooner and get on with my life. I wish God would just send me a sign," Maria said.

"I think he will, and I hope you can recognize it when it comes."

CHAPTER 41

On Monday morning at six thirty, Gabe found a gray Honda Civic parked on the street in front of his home, just as he had been told he would. He approached the car wearing sunglasses and a baseball cap, which made it hard to see his full face. Following the detailed instructions he had been given, he had no wallet or ID with him. His cell phone was left hidden in his own car, which was parked around the corner, several blocks away. Gabe got in the Honda and retrieved the key under the driver's side mat on the floor. Beside him on the other front seat was a small gym bag holding a wallet with a new ID and fifty dollars in cash. There was also a burner phone and a map outlining the way.

He quickly consulted the route—straightforward, driving north on Fifth Street to the Ben Franklin Bridge, crossing the bridge to Route 30, then on to Cherry Hill and his New Jersey destination. He had already checked the route at a public computer at the library and memorized it, along with several detours to use if necessary. Salerno had given strict instructions not to leave any route searches on his home computer.

Gabe cut over to Fifth Street on Pine and headed north. There was no more than the usual amount of traffic. The congestion increased when he passed Market Street, but he had only three more blocks to the bridge ramp. Fortunately, most of the bridge traffic was coming into the city at this hour, not leaving. It was smooth sailing across the bridge until he got off the ramp to Route 30, where traffic slowed. Gabe fidgeted in his seat and tapped his fingers on the steering wheel. He wished he had his cell phone to determine the cause of the delay on his map application. Gabe stayed focused on driving the route with the flow of traffic, which helped keep his mind off the job he was rehearsing.

Finally, he reached Route 30, which was clear except for the numerous stops at traffic lights. Gabe's heart began to pound as he saw blue lights flashing in his rearview mirror. Traffic slowed as the squad car got closer. Gabe began rehearsing the script he had been given in case he was stopped and he shivered with fear as he wondered what would happen if the police pulled him over and ran his license plate. However, the trooper approached in the passing lane and glided right past Gabe. He felt a surge of relief. He now realized he had been breathing rapidly as his panic abated.

The rest of the trip went by in a blur. Then, suddenly, the truck stop was upon him. It was a standard-looking truck stop with large lanes on one side where trucks could fill their tanks with diesel fuel. There were smaller, car-sized pumps under an awning in front of what appeared to be a sizeable convenience store that offered everything from food to showers. Gabe hit the brakes and turned in. When he scanned the lot and saw the spots he was supposed to park in, he realized they were both taken, and Gabe made a mental note to ask what to do if he found the spots taken during his trip on Friday. Of course, Gabe would be driving Salerno on Friday, and he would know what to do, but Gabe wanted to be prepared. For now, he pulled into the next available spot, which was several spots closer to the entrance to the convenience store and cashier for gas purchases. Gabe opened a map that partially covered his face from the view inside the store. His cap, the map, and the tinted car windows would have to be enough protection from any security cameras pointed in his direction. He looked at his watch and saw that it was seven fifteen. The trip had taken thirty-five minutes.

Gabe glanced to his right and saw a short, stocky man with dark, balding hair emerge from the store, carrying a clipboard. Gabe had received a parcel with several photos of the target and he recognized the man as the one he would help to kill in four days. A thin, younger man followed Perrelli outside. The younger man wore a shirt with a logo that appeared to say "Highway 30 Service." The young man said something, and Perrelli laughed with a cheerful smile on his face. Perrelli seemed like an ordinary guy, almost someone who Gabe would enjoy having a beer with.

Gabe started to have a sickening feeling as he thought that this guy with the cheerful demeanor would be dead in a couple of days and Gabe would be witness to the murder. He wondered if Perrelli had a wife and children who would grieve his death. There were twelve gas pumps, but Perrelli and the younger man looked at only the three closest to the store entrance. Perrelli handed the clipboard to the young man, nodding with a smile. He pointed to an entrance near several repair bays at the end of the building and returned to the inside of the store. The young man proceeded to look at the remaining pumps. The station wasn't crowded, but there was a steady stream of customers pulling up to the pumps and some entering the store.

Gabe noticed a woman who looked to be about thirty with long black hair pulled back in a ponytail walk into the store, holding hands with a little girl who was about four. Gabe sat still for a few minutes, as though he was studying routes on the map he still held in his hands. A few minutes later, the woman emerged holding a Styrofoam cup of coffee. The little girl trailed behind her, holding a small bottle of orange juice.

Gabe began to imagine the unspeakable act he would be helping to accomplish. What if there were children in the store on Friday when he brought the hitman to do the deed? Would any children be present to witness Perrelli's violent death? Would he be contributing to a traumatic experience that would haunt the children for the rest of their lives? He began to feel sick, and he hit the buttons to open both front windows. It wasn't enough. Gabe opened the door and leaned over, throwing up on the blacktop parking lot and barely avoiding splattering the car parked next to him. Fortunately, there was no one inside. When Gabe got back in his car, he sensed something on his left. He turned to see a man leaning over and looking in his window. The man's face was barely twelve inches away, and Gabe jolted back in horror like he had seen a ghost. It was Perrelli.

"Is everything okay, buddy?" Perrelli asked through the still-open window.

"Ah, yeah, I'm okay," Gabe said with a hoarse voice. "I'm sorry about the mess. I can clean it up." After the words came out, Gabe realized he should have just said he was okay and kept quiet.

"Don't worry about it. We'll take care of it. Just feel better, okay?" Perrelli said with a smile on his face. He tapped the roof of the car in a friendly way and walked off.

Gabe started the car and began to back out of his spot. When he got to the service station exit, he had to wait for an opening in traffic so he could drive out onto the highway. It seemed to take forever, but finally, Gabe drove to the planned rendezvous point where cars would be switched. He didn't switch cars like he would on Friday but continued to drive home. Gabe began thinking his trial run had been a disaster. Parking right in front of the convenience store entrance, getting sick, and having a face-to-face encounter with Perrelli were not in the script, and he wondered whether he had compromised the operation. But the more he thought about it, the more he felt that nothing that happened really mattered. Perrelli was going to die and wouldn't be able to identify Gabe after Friday. Gabe also knew he'd been careful about cameras, wearing a hat and keeping his head down.

Gabe had been told to park a few blocks from his home and leave the keys under the floor mat. He was to leave the wallet, ID, burner phone, and map in the car. When he arrived in his neighborhood, however, Gabe phoned a number on the burner phone to report in on his trial run.

Someone answered his call with a strange-sounding voice—as though it had been run through a device to distort it. Gabe assumed it was Jimmy Salerno.

"Well, how did your trip go?" the distorted voice asked.

"Fine," Gabe answered. He decided not to mention the parking problem, or the part about throwing up and encountering Perrelli.

"Did you see the target?"

"Yeah, he was actually standing outside talking to someone when I got there."

"Any trouble finding the place?"

"No, the directions were fine. There was some traffic along the way, and it took me thirty-five minutes to get there."

"Okay, let's meet fifteen minutes earlier than we had planned at the café on Friday. Anything else I should know about?" the voice asked.

"No, I think that covers it," Gabe said, hoping Salerno didn't have anyone staking out the service station who might have seen what really happened.

♦ ♦ ♦

Later that day, Gabe was due to visit an important client of the sports betting operation he oversaw—a trainer for the Philadelphia Phillies named Rudy McDowell, who collected bets from players to place with Gabe. The bets were large, generally more than $500. Of course, Gabe would not accept bets on Phillies games, and none were ever requested by the trainer. Most bets were on NBA games. Other times of the year, the bets were on NFL games and sometimes hockey or college football. Gabe visited Rudy a couple of times every week to collect funds and occasionally to distribute winnings. It was not unusual for Gabe to pick up four or five thousand dollars at a time from Rudy.

When Gabe pulled into the stadium parking lot, Rudy was standing by his car smoking a cigarette, as though his reason for being there was simply to take a smoke break.

"Rudy, my man. I assume you've got something for me?" Gabe asked.

"Hey, Gabe. Yeah, I sure do," Rudy said, handing a tan-colored envelope to Gabe. "Let me tell you what I got." Gabe stuck the envelope in the inside pocket of his windbreaker, and he took out a little notebook as Rudy began describing the bets that were listed on a piece of paper.

"Thanks, Rudy," Gabe said. "That's some nice action today. Tell the players I wish them the best of luck." Gabe reached into his pocket and pulled out five crisp hundred dollar bills. "That's a little something for your efforts," he said, winking with a smile.

"You want to count what was in the envelope?"

"No need. I trust you," Gabe said.

Rudy always paid in full what was due and paid on time. The arrangement worked for those placing bets as well. They didn't need to deal directly with Gabe or his organization, and it was easy money for Rudy. The betting continued throughout the year as Rudy worked at the stadium during the off-season up until spring training.

As Gabe raised his hand to wave goodbye, Rudy spoke up.

"Just a second. Today I got something for you to show how much I enjoy working with you," Rudy said, handing Gabe another envelope. "It's two deluxe box seats for the game against the Mets coming up Friday night." Gabe doubted he'd feel like going to a game Friday night—after the job he expected to do that morning. But he had another idea what to do with the tickets.

Gabe took his time going home. First, he dropped off the money from Rudy at the Clubhouse, where he had to enter the bets into a logbook. The sports betting operation took place in a large room in the rear of the Clubhouse, and Gabe spent another half hour there talking to several of the employees who worked the computers entering bets that were called in. Afterward, Gabe made stops at the grocery store and the state liquor store before arriving home. He put a frozen pizza in the oven for dinner. He shared the Mafia superstition about home deliveries of pizza. More than a few Mafia members had been whacked by someone pretending to be a pizza delivery man.

After dinner, Gabe poured himself a bourbon with ice in a large iced-tea-sized glass to calm his nerves, then settled in front of the television and tuned in to a Phillies game. By the time he had finished half the glass, the effects of the bourbon were coursing through his system and he felt relaxed for the first time in several days. Gabe refilled his glass at the end of the third inning, and by the fifth inning, Gabe was sound asleep on the couch. He dreamed about the service station in Cherry Hill. He saw Perrelli standing in front of the store, smiling and laughing just as he had when Gabe watched him from his car. Suddenly, there was a boom, and Perrelli's head blew apart in an explosion of blood and gore. Next to Perrelli's body, he saw the woman and her little girl screaming. Perrelli's blood had splattered all over them. Gabe awoke with a scream, jerking upward on the couch. The television gave off an eerie glow in the now-dark apartment. Gabe managed to hoist himself up and stagger into his bed, where he passed out.

Chapter 42

The same evening Gabe calmed his nerves with bourbon, Michael entered his bedroom, where Carmella was up late reading. Normally she was asleep, but tonight she was wide awake. As he began getting ready for bed, Carmella put her book down.

"Are you okay, Michael?"

"Yeah, I'm fine."

"You've been quiet lately. You're either off at your clubhouse or you're home and we hardly talk."

"I've had a lot on my mind lately."

"I'm sure you have. What I'd like to know is how we got ourselves in a situation where our most profitable operation gets burned down and our niece gets killed in the process," Carmella said as she sat up in bed. She was clearly not in the mood to sleep.

"That's not fair," Michael shouted. "We didn't cause the fire. The Carbones burned it down because we were so successful without South Jersey. They could have attacked any number of our locations."

"But they didn't, because they knew the casino was our cash cow. They wanted to hurt us, and they picked the best target," Carmella said. "And you've seemed more upset about the loss of your gambling operation than the death of your niece."

"Of course I'm upset about Diane, and believe me, we're taking some very strong action on that. But I'm also nervous about the fire, because the police and the FBI are now looking closely at it, and that's a major threat to our whole organization. There are too many loose ends. Joey and maybe others know we had unlicensed gambling going on, and Joey knows we pull a lot of cash out of the poker games and the casino."

Carmella shifted in the bed and grimaced. "I thought the plan was to get away from illegal businesses? Why did you even set up a casino at Francesca's?"

"Don't pretend you don't remember, Carmella. When I took over the organization, I needed some financial successes to prove my ability and solidify my control. Having a source that produces millions of dollars in cash every year was a big help. We wouldn't be where we are today without that success."

"And where are we? We were successful without the casino, but now it seems like half of the city government is in on this. Our dear friend's restaurant was burned down, and your niece was killed because of it. And what about the loose ends you mentioned?"

"Well, besides Joey and his staff, there are the card players. If the FBI has anything to charge any of them with, they'll push them hard to talk and tell all about the poker games." The two lay silent for a moment before Michael continued. "Actually, I think we're safe with most of them, especially the regulars. They won't talk. But I'm a little worried about Henry Townshend. I don't know him, but I do know he's a politician and will try to save his own skin. And he knows enough about the game to hurt us."

"You mean he knows enough from playing just one night?"

"He saw the amount of money in play, and if he has a brain, he saw the dealer taking a rake for the house from the large pots. We also staked him twenty-five thousand at the start of the game, which is something we do for VIP guests on their first visit. He's a public official with influence in city government. If his eyes were open, he saw

Diane getting thousand-dollar tips, and he may have given her one himself. He can't truthfully say it was just a friendly poker game with some associates."

"Wouldn't he have to incriminate himself to tell those details?" Carmella asked.

"Sure, but it depends on what else the police or the Feds have on him."

"So, what can you do about it? Don't you have photos of him shaking your hand or were they burned up in the fire?"

"Yeah, we got them and they're all backed up off-site. They're very powerful when a politician is trying to save his career. But if the Feds can bring charges against him, his career will be over anyway."

"So, what are you going to do, whack him?" Carmella asked in a sarcastic tone.

"No. I had a talk with him. I think he got the message that he doesn't want to get in trouble with our organization. Sometimes that fear is the most effective tool we have."

"What about Gabe? He knows the whole operation inside and out."

"Gabe is loyal. He understands the code of silence and the consequences of breaking it. Besides, I don't know what grounds they would have to question him."

"Hasn't he been seen at the casino?"

"He spends time there but never in the card games. Nobody would know him in the casino room. I doubt anyone other than Joey knows about Gabe."

"I'd hate to think what would happen if Gabe got picked up. He's young and has his whole life in front of him. If they got any leverage with him, he's not going to want to spend the next ten or twenty years or more in prison. And you're sure Joey can't hurt us?"

Michael shook his head. "Joey is as loyal as they come. He runs a clean operation and has no records related to the gambling. In fact, all his financial records were destroyed in the fire. Gabe got hold of the records Diane kept in her apartment, and they are either destroyed or safely stashed away. Joey can say he rented some rooms out for card games. That's all he knows, and no one can prove otherwise."

"Who picks up the money from the casino and card games?"

"One of our soldiers from the Clubhouse drops by every day, except after nights when the casino is closed. Diane is the only one who deals with him."

"Sooner or later, there's going to be some publicity about a gambling operation, even if they can't pin it on us," Carmella said. "And what about our public image, and what about our daughter in the convent?"

"We'll have to deal with it."

"Is that all you can say? 'We'll have to deal with it'?" Carmella said, raising her voice. "And what about the promises we made to each other about keeping Maria out of the business?"

"What does that have to do with any of this?" Michael asked.

"Don't think that I don't know about your little scheme with Gabe to try and lure Maria away from the convent," Carmella said with a sneer on her face.

"I don't know what you're talking about. There's no scheme."

"Don't worry, Gabe didn't tell me anything, but it doesn't take a genius to figure out what's going on. You get Maria attached to Gabe, and she'll want to quit the convent if they don't kick her out first. Admit it, Michael, you told Gabe to get close to her for just that purpose. You're either going to get our daughter hurt or you're going to get her involved with the business."

"I admit I asked Gabe to keep an eye on her. I thought she could use a friend. If that helps her decide not to take the vows, so much the better. I think we're on the same side of this, aren't we?" Michael asked. "How does that go against what we promised each other?"

"Well, hooking our daughter up to the brightest rising star in our organization isn't exactly keeping her away from the business."

"Don't be silly. She's not hooking up with Gabe."

"I saw the way they looked at each other at the party, and it was more than friendly," Carmella said.

"I think you've got a good imagination. Gabe is a solid guy. He won't step over the line."

"Well, they've already delayed her vows to become a novice. She'll never forgive us if the convent asks her to leave and she finds out we—I should say you—were behind it." Carmella abruptly reached over and switched off the light, then she turned away from Michael.

Michael felt there was no reason to argue further, so he simply turned his light off and lay back in the bed. A half hour later, he heard Carmella's rhythmic breathing, but he couldn't fall asleep. The conversation had brought to light a problem he had not adequately considered, namely, the risks of sending Gabe along on the mission to take out Bruno Carbone Jr.'s cousin. Carmella was not aware of the plan, but her mention of the risks of Gabe testifying about the gambling operation if he were arrested had gotten Michael's attention. If Gabe were arrested and charged with murder after the Carbone hit, the police and FBI would have huge leverage to pressure Gabe to mitigate his sentence by testifying against the family.

Gabe knew just about everything. Would someone thirty years old choose a life in prison or a much shorter sentence for cooperating? Who could blame him for avoiding a life sentence? Michael quietly slipped out of bed, opened the medicine cabinet, and took an Ambien. He was sure he would make some changes in the plan after a good night's sleep.

CHAPTER 43

Michael's words to Carmella about Henry Townshend turned out to be prophetic. At eight thirty Tuesday morning, Agents Natalie Perez and Dennis McIntyre entered the chambers of Councilman Townshend in City Hall. They had seen him enter the office fifteen minutes earlier, and city council was not in session today.

They were greeted by a handsome Black woman who sat behind a desk in the reception area in front of a bank of file cabinets. A large nameplate on her desk said "Stella McCann, Assistant to Councilman Henry Townshend."

She greeted them cheerfully. "May I help you?"

The agents identified themselves and flashed their badges for the receptionist to see.

"We'd like a word with Councilman Townshend," Agent Perez said.

"I'm sorry. Do you have an appointment?" the receptionist replied.

"We need to speak to him right now." The agents moved toward Townshend's door.

"Okay. Please give me just a moment." She picked up a phone, hit a button, and spoke. "Councilman, Agents Perez and McIntyre from the FBI are here and they need to speak to you." After a pause, she turned to the agents. "He'll be right out. Just have a seat. Can I get you some coffee?"

"Thank you, but no. We'll just wait here." The two agents continued to stand over the receptionist's desk, glaring at her.

A few moments later, Townshend appeared in the doorway to his office.

"Well, Agents Perez and McIntyre, what can I do for you on this fine day?" Townshend said with a slightly nervous-looking smile. He appeared to be straightening a suit jacket he had just put on. Bright red suspenders were visible underneath.

Townshend backed up a step and extended his arm to beckon the agents into his office. The stately office held a wall of old books on wooden shelves and another wall of photographs of the councilman with well-known politicians, including a large portrait with President Reagan. A masculine tobacco smell, the kind that came from cigars and pipes, permeated the office. Townshend pointed at two large leather chairs in front of a magnificent antique oak desk, then he took a seat on the opposite side. He noticed Agent McIntyre staring at the desk.

"Do you like the desk?" he asked. "It belonged to Philander Chase Knox when he was attorney general under Theodore Roosevelt. Somehow my father got hold of it, and I inherited it from him. It's very stately, isn't it?" When the agents didn't respond, he said, "Did Mrs. McCann offer you cof—"

"Councilman, I assume you've heard about the large fire that took place at a restaurant on Ninth Street last week?" Agent Perez would not allow her purpose to be distracted any further by small talk.

"Of course. That was a tragedy," he answered.

"Now, the fire occurred Wednesday evening—actually, it was in the early morning hours on Thursday. Can you tell us where you were on the previous evening? I'm referring to Tuesday evening."

"Are you suggesting I had something to do with that fire?" Townshend asked with a look of shock on his face.

"Right now, we are focusing on what happened on the premises the evening before. Can you tell us where you were Tuesday evening?"

"I'd have to check my schedule book."

Agent Perez assumed there would be nothing embarrassing or incriminating in his book. The entry would be something innocuous like "meet with friends for dinner and card game." It seemed clear to the agents that Townshend was dodging the question.

"Let me try and help you, Councilman. Did you attend a poker game on the premises of Francesca's Restaurant last Tuesday evening?"

"Again, I'd have to double-check my book. I have such a busy schedule I'm not able to remember everything I did or the date I did it."

Agent Perez sighed. "Assuming there was such a game, do you think any of the other poker players could shed any light on the evening?"

Townshend appeared to be puzzled when Perez mentioned other players in a way that implied she knew who they were.

"Look, Agent Perez, I'm a man with a busy schedule. I do get together with friends to play poker from time to time. They are just friendly games—nothing sinister."

"Does the name Diane D'Angelo mean anything to you?" Agent Perez continued her attack.

"The name is familiar. Wait, wasn't she the woman they think was killed in the fire?"

"Did you see her at the game on Tuesday?"

"I'm not sure if I've met her, or if I have, I'm not sure when," Townshend answered as he fiddled with a pen on his desk. "Agent Perez, I don't think I have anything further I can help you with. I really need to get back to some responsibilities I have for the city council."

Ignoring his attempt to dismiss them, Perez looked Townshend straight in the eye. "Councilman, isn't it a fact that you attended a high-stakes poker game that was hosted by Michael D'Angelo's organization?"

Townshend shook his head and stood. "I have no connection with Michael D'Angelo. As I said, I need to get on with my work here."

"One last thing," Agent Perez said as she placed a photograph in front of him. "This is a photo from a security camera. It shows you being dropped off in front of the restaurant shortly after eight Tuesday night. Was it pure coincidence that a big poker game was being played in a room at the back of the restaurant that evening? Or were you dropped off so you could go for an evening stroll in South Philadelphia?"

"I have nothing more to say to you." Townshend walked over to open the door.

Agent Perez handed him a card as she left. "If you remember anything about that evening, please get in touch. I'm sure we'll be talking again."

As they left, Agent Perez turned to her partner. "Did you see the color drain out of his face when I showed him the picture?"

"Yeah. I bet he soiled his pants."

"I think we have him right where we want him now," Perez said.

◆ ◆ ◆

Back in the office, Townshend picked up the phone and dialed a number from his Rolodex. Normally, he would have his assistant place calls for him, but this time he needed the ultimate discretion.

"Richard. It's Henry Townshend. Are you free for lunch today?" Richard Hague, a venerable criminal defense attorney who was a legend in Philadelphia courtrooms, was retired and in his eighties, but was often consulted for advice on criminal matters.

"For you, I'm always free," Hague answered.

"Meet me at my table at the Union League at noon."

CHAPTER 44

Gabe woke up around nine with a pounding headache after his bourbon binge the previous evening. He couldn't sleep any longer, so he roused himself out of bed and downed some pain medication. Soon, the smell of freshly brewed coffee drifted out of the kitchen. As Gabe sat drinking, he dreaded another day of anxiously waiting. No one had asked him to do another trial run today, and he had no plans for the morning. He jumped up from the kitchen table and grabbed the newspaper from his front porch. Thankful there was nothing new about the fire, Gabe threw down the paper and stepped in the shower, mainly to help him wake up.

The hot water felt good as it coursed down over his head. When he felt revived, he turned off the shower and quickly donned his jogging shorts and a lightweight sweatshirt that would block the chill of a spring morning. Outside his door, he took off in a brisk walk. His aching head was not ready for the bumpy ride of running. Gradually, as the caffeine and meds began to kick in, he began a slow trot west. Fifteen minutes later, he turned a corner onto Ninth Street in the direction of what used to be Francesca's.

As he approached and saw piles of rubble and ashes, he was reminded of pictures of London after the blitz. The fire had caused complete devastation, taking out almost a quarter of a city block.

There were still barricades and yellow police tape strung around the perimeter on little posts, designating the whole area as a crime scene. Several people dressed in full firefighting garb, including gas masks, worked inside the tape. They held bags, boxes, and tools, probing through the ashes and picking up samples. The tools were similar to the handheld units people used to pick up trash along a highway. Suddenly, he saw one of the investigators pointing into a pile of the rubble and the others gathering closer. Gabe had no desire to see the charred remains of his cousin, if that's what they found, so he kept moving.

Gabe's heart ached as he realized his cousin Diane was almost certainly buried somewhere beneath the tons of rubble. Her remains might never be recovered. Diane had been involved in the family's gambling operation, but she had been a decent person. She had done nothing to deserve having her young life snuffed out like this. The more he thought about it, the more he felt a sense of rage welling up within him. The people who killed his innocent cousin had to pay for this, and he felt a new sense of determination to complete the mission he had so recently dreaded.

As he continued walking, Gabe pulled out his cell phone and dialed Maria's number.

"Maria, it's Gabe. Is this a bad time?"

"Hi, Gabe. No. I have a free period. I can talk for a few minutes."

Gabe breathed a sigh of relief. He needed something to help him get the images of the burnt rubble where Diane had died out of his mind. The sound of Maria's voice was soothing and provided just what he needed.

"I have something I wanted to drop off for you. Could I meet you at the Starbucks just down the road from your school this afternoon? I promise I won't take more than five minutes if you're busy." Gabe hoped he could stretch the meeting longer.

"Sure. Can I ask what it is?"

"It's a surprise. It's not a big deal, but I think it's something you can use."

"Okay. I'll be done a little after three, and I planned to leave here at three thirty."

"That's perfect. I'll be there. Can I order you something?"

"Normally I don't drink coffee late in the day, but I could handle a decaf latte if they have one."

Gabe smiled. "You got it."

Maria spoke before he could say anything else. "Gabe, I'm sorry, but I've got to go. The kids are starting to come into my room for class."

"No problem, I'll see you this afternoon."

No sooner had Gabe hung up than his phone buzzed.

"Gabe, this is Michael." His boss's voice sounded tired and slightly hoarse.

"Good morning."

"I'd like you to drop by later today. If you can come late this afternoon, I'll ask Lucy to put something out for our dinner. Carmella is at a retreat with her church."

"Sure. Would five be a good time?"

"That's fine. We can have a drink and talk a bit before dinner."

"That sounds good."

"See you then." Michael disconnected.

The nervousness Gabe felt the last time he'd visited Michael's home flashed through his mind, but this time, he had a strong gut feeling there was nothing to worry about with Michael. Now it was the mission that made him nervous.

CHAPTER 45

Gabe walked home by way of his gym and spent about forty-five minutes lifting weights. The physical exercise helped calm his nerves. On his way home, the smell of eggs and bacon drew him into a local diner. He stopped and ordered a late breakfast. It was nearly noon when he finally got home after walking off his breakfast. He looked at his pistol collection and selected his Sig Sauer P365 to carry in his shoulder holster on Friday's mission. The Sig was light, compact, and held ten rounds. Gabe could access his gun quickly by reaching under the windbreaker he planned to wear over his shirt. He had spent many hours practicing his draw.

After stowing his weapon away, Gabe showered again, shaved, and dressed in his best business casual outfit, which included a cotton oxford shirt and a wool houndstooth blazer. At one time, it had been unthinkable to show up at the boss's home on business without a suit and tie. Some of the older capos still followed that practice, but Michael did not expect his younger soldiers to dress like the thugs from South Philadelphia did in the old days.

Gabe set out around two to take a slow drive out of the city to meet Maria. Being busy getting ready to see Maria and the boss helped distract some of the anxiety he felt about the mission, which was just a few days away. He was extremely glad he was not going to be inside the store for the kill. He just wanted to get the whole thing behind him.

Gabe approached the Starbucks where they were to meet a little early, so he continued up the street to Maria's school. Gabe pulled in and drove around to the parking area where he saw Maria's silver-gray Honda. Knowing she was close by filled him with a sense of pleasant anticipation. He pulled back to the front entrance and drove back to Starbucks.

As he entered, coffee, pumpkin spice, vanilla, and other pleasant scents filled the air. He sat down with his coffee in a soft leather chair by a coffee table at just about three thirty and picked up a *New York Times* someone had abandoned on the table. Gabe had ordered Maria's latte but had asked the barista to hold it until she arrived so it would not be cold.

Soon, Maria walked in, smartly dressed in a woman's London Fog–style overcoat. Gabe stood, and they both leaned in for a chaste hug. Gabe took the opportunity to enjoy the smell of her hair and faint scent of perfume. She slipped off the overcoat and hung it over the back of a nearby chair.

She smiled at him. "You look very nice today."

"Thanks. I have a business meeting later today." Gabe regretted saying this as it implied he hadn't dressed up for her.

"Is the meeting with my father?" she asked.

"Ah, yes," Gabe said as he realized the conversation might be heading into an area he couldn't talk about. To change the subject, Gabe beckoned with his hand to the barista and he nodded. "That was for your latte. He's making it now. It's decaf, like you asked for."

"You really know how to take care of a lady, or maybe I should say a sister." Maria laughed. Her grin was infectious, and he couldn't help smiling in return.

After a few moments of banter about the weather and the traffic, the barista brought out a steaming latte.

"Thank you again. This looks great!"

"Well, I promised you a surprise. I think you told me once that you like baseball," Gabe said, a wide grin returning to his face. Any bystander could tell Gabe was enjoying the company of this woman.

"Yes, my dad used to take Raph and me along to Phillies games when we were younger. He always explained what was going on, so I have a pretty good understanding of the game," Maria said with a smirk that suggested she had a hunch what Gabe was about to give her.

Gabe pulled out the tickets from the chest pocket inside his blazer. "Then you'll probably enjoy these! Here are two box seats to the Phillies game this Friday night. The Mets will be in town. I thought maybe you could invite a friend from the convent, or anyone for that matter."

Gabe had been afraid Maria might accept the tickets out of politeness, but he was pleasantly surprised at how Maria's eyes lit up when he handed them to her. "Thank you so much!"

"And please, if for some reason you can't use them, give them to one of your friends. I'd come with you myself, but I know you have some restrictions, and I wouldn't want to put you in an awkward position," Gabe said with a hint of sadness in his eyes.

"Ah, yes. I'm sorry you can't use them," Maria said, pressing her lips together in a slight grimace.

"I have a friend who works at the stadium who can get me tickets almost any time I ask. Maybe I could get a block of tickets, and we could go in a larger group sometime," Gabe said, letting her know he was not going to give up on the idea of seeing a game with her.

"That's a great idea. I'd love that."

Gabe was surprised at how readily she'd agreed to this suggestion. Maybe there was hope for him after all with Maria.

As they sat enjoying their drinks, Gabe looked at his watch several times.

"Are you nervous about the meeting with my father?" she asked.

Such a direct question took Gabe by surprise. He looked up from his drink. "Actually, I have a difficult project coming up in a few days," he said.

"Do you want to talk about it?" Maria asked.

Just then, an older man approached their table. "Do you mind if I have a look at your newspaper?" the man asked as he glanced at the paper Gabe had placed on a little table beside his chair."

"Not at all," Gabe replied, being grateful for the interruption to the conversation.

He leaned in a bit closer as she took a sip of her latte. He spoke softly. "I know you probably don't have a lot of time, so I can't go into details, but it's one of the most difficult projects I've ever had to do."

"Whatever it is, Gabe, I'm sure you'll do well. I know my father has a lot of confidence in you. I'll certainly remember you in my prayers," she said.

"Thanks. That means a lot to me. Just spending a few minutes with you before I start this project is an encouragement to me. I really mean that." Gabe wondered if Maria would pray for his success if she really knew what the project was.

"It's great to see you as well." Maria took a deep breath and continued. "I guess I do need to be getting back. Thanks for the latte." She got up and grabbed her coat. As she walked away, she turned back. "I always remember you in my prayers, Gabe."

He thought he saw a tear on her cheek as she turned and walked away.

CHAPTER 46

Gabe had an hour to kill before he was due at Michael's home. He drove up the street and found a park with some walking paths. He needed to burn off the nervous energy building up inside him. After walking a bit, he returned to his car and drove to Chestnut Hill, arriving at Michael's just before five. Although Gabe was not afraid like he had been on his prior visit, he was still nervous about meeting with the boss right before the deadly project he was about to embark on. He paused and took a few deep breaths before getting out of the car.

Gabe rang the doorbell, and in a few moments, Michael himself opened the massive polished oak door.

"Hi, Gabe. C'mon in."

Gabe immediately caught wind of the pungent spaghetti sauce being prepared by Lucy, the D'Angelos' cook. Michael directed him to a seat in his study. As he took his seat, Gabe couldn't help staring at the framed photo on the wall of Maria playing lacrosse. It was the same one Gabe had noticed the last time he visited.

"I think you admired that photo of Maria the last time you were here," Michael said, as Gabe turned to Michael, his face flushed with embarrassment. "By the way, thanks for making the effort to get to know her."

Gabe didn't expect the subject of Maria to come up. He wasn't going to say anything, but felt he'd better, in case Michael was testing him. "Your wife asked me about my contact with her. I want you to know I didn't tell her anything."

"I know she approached you and I know you didn't tell her anything. But that's not why I asked you to come." Michael walked over to a shelf well-stocked with bottles. "You're a bourbon man if I remember, aren't you?"

"Absolutely."

Michael grabbed a bottle of Blanton's and poured a double. This was a bit of an upgrade from the Jack Daniels on Gabe's home shelf.

Michael didn't waste time getting down to business. "I guess you realize the fire at Francesca's is going to hurt us. That was one of our biggest sources of revenue. Of course, we're all shaken up about Diane."

"Yes, I understand."

"But we'll weather the storm. I figured our casino on South Ninth Street wouldn't last forever. Places like that never do. Sooner or later the authorities get wind, and it becomes too dangerous to operate. We have a lot of other things going on, so I think we'll do okay. The only question I have is whether we try to replace it somewhere else."

"We'd be hard-pressed to find another spot with someone we can trust like Joey in charge. Of course, we'll never be able to replace Diane."

"I agree. One of the reasons I called you here is that the FBI is now involved, and my sources tell me they've questioned Henry Townshend. I think Henry knows better than to talk, but he makes me a little nervous."

"Henry knows we've got photos of him at the poker game with you and Diane." Gabe didn't add the obvious—that it would be scandalous for Townshend to be seen with Michael D'Angelo.

Michael continued, undeterred. "The FBI is still combing through the rubble. There's no telling what they might find. They've also questioned Joey. He hasn't told them anything, but I wonder how long he can hold out if they put pressure on him."

"So, what can we do?"

"Right now, the FBI has no hard evidence on the gambling operation. They certainly don't have any financial records, thanks to your trip to Diane's apartment. But I'm sure they're very suspicious. We need to circle the wagons and lie low for a while. As far as I know, they don't know anything about your involvement."

Gabe sat quietly and sipped his bourbon. After a pause, he spoke. "Are we going to cancel our strike at the Carbones?"

"No. But that leads to the main reason I wanted to talk to you today. I'm going to pull you from the job. I have full confidence you could have done your part, but it's too risky right now."

Gabe's mouth dropped open, and he looked at Michael with panic on his face. "Did I do something wrong?" he asked.

"No, it's nothing like that," Michael answered.

Before Michael could explain, Gabe leaned forward in his chair and spoke. "Doesn't Salerno need a driver who knows the area?"

"He prefers to use his own man. In fact, he usually doesn't allow his client to be present when he works. We wanted you there to help send a message to the Carbones, but I've thought about it, and there's no question that the Carbones will get the message."

"So there's nothing more for me to do on this?"

"No. Just lie low. I really don't want to put you in such a risky position. I know you've been planning this and that lots of precautions were being taken, but you never know what can happen on a job like this. If you ever got arrested, you'd be in a very difficult position. We can avoid that by just letting Salerno do his job. This has nothing to do with your abilities or any lack of confidence. I have as much confidence in you as I have in anybody in our organization right now."

Gabe realized Michael was right. If he ever got arrested, it wouldn't take the police long to figure out he knew a lot about the D'Angelo organization and its operations, both legal and not-so-legal. If they could hold a murder conviction and a life sentence over his head, it would be extremely hard to turn down a deal to cooperate. Gabe took a deep breath, and the panic that had been on his face disappeared.

"Let me guess. You're disappointed and relieved at the same time," said Michael.

Gabe nodded. "That sums it up pretty well."

Michael swirled the bourbon in his glass. "Let me tell you a story that no one knows, not even Carmella, and I'd like to keep it that way," Michael said. Gabe nodded. "Gus knows the story, since he was there, but no one else in our family today knows. When I was your age, in order to become a made man, there was a strict requirement that you participate in a hit sanctioned by your family. There were no exceptions. We had a guy named Danny Di Terlizzi in the organization. He had been a captain for many years. They called him "Danny the Lizard" since it sounded like his name, and he was a slippery character, I guess. Danny's job was to collect money from different rackets that were required to kick money up to the family. This included some bookies on the street, some prostitution rackets, and even some bars and night clubs. Danny handled some large accounts. If someone didn't pay, Danny took action to make sure they did. He had his own group of goons to help him collect. They used to say, 'if you don't pay up, the Lizard will come after you.' Nobody wanted to have to deal with the Lizard in that situation.

"Over a period of time, the family started to suspect Danny was skimming some of the money he collected for himself. Mind you, he didn't keep good records of his collections, but the folks in the family had an idea he was short on the money he was supposed to turn in. They brought him in, and he swore up and down he was turning everything in. So, they watched him, and one day the boss sent some guys to check out the situation, and they found money in the trunk of his car, lots of it that he should have turned over. They figured they'd caught him red-handed. Not only that, but he had also lied to the boss, right to his face. Well, there's only one verdict for that." Michael grabbed the Blanton's and refilled Gabe's glass before resuming the story.

"The next thing you know, they tell Danny the boss wants to speak to him. They're going to drive him to a meeting, so he gets in a car. They told me the boss wanted me at the meeting as well. We all end up at a warehouse, and Danny is hustled inside and tied to a chair. The boss questions him, and Danny denies it at first. Then after being slapped and punched, he admits he borrowed some money and planned to pay it back. 'Do you think I'm an idiot?' the boss asks. By this time, they've beaten him pretty badly, and his face is swollen and bleeding. Then, the boss reaches under his coat and pulls a thirty-eight revolver out. He looks right at me.

"'D'Angelo. You finish him off. I want you to look him in the eye when you do it.' After he hands me the revolver, I'm in a bit of shock. I'd never even fired a gun in my work for the family, much less killed somebody. Everybody was looking at me, and I realize Danny is going to die whether I pull the trigger or not. I'm having some problems with this, since I knew Danny and considered him to be a friend. I liked the guy, but the boss and all his underbosses are there, and they're looking at me. Suddenly, Danny looks right at me and says, 'It's okay, Michael. I don't hold it against you. Just do it and get it over with.'"

Michael paused a moment and slugged back the rest of his bourbon. "So I did. I'll never forget that day as long as I live. I guess they were trying to make it easy for me to do my required hit. They could have told me to go and whack someone sitting in a restaurant. Even so, the shock of that experience changed me. I decided if I ever had the power or influence, I would change this organization to eliminate the violence and the killing, at least as much as is within my power. Six months later, I was inducted into the family. I was a made man. Six years later, I became acting boss. Over time, the 'acting' part was dropped, and I became the real boss. So if you were going to ask if pulling you off this job will hurt your chances, the answer is no. You were willing to step up when we needed you in a rare case when we need to extract blood for blood. As far as I'm concerned, you've met the requirement."

Gabe sat still with wide eyes as he sucked in a quick breath. "I . . . I don't know what to say," he said.

"There's no need to say anything," Michael replied as he refilled his glass. "One more thing. Since we don't know where this is headed, you need to make sure your home is clean—no records or evidence or large stashes of cash. Make sure there are no illegal weapons either. The FBI will run search warrants whenever they can, and they'll use whatever they can find against you."

"Of course." Gabe lifted his bourbon in salute. "Thank you for your confidence in me and thank you for your assurances." Gabe felt an overwhelming sense of relief. "If there's anything I can do to help support the family, please let me know."

"Thank you. I think Lucy has our dinner ready," Michael said as he got up and led the way to the dining room.

Chapter 47

It was the first time Agents Perez and McIntyre had been to the scene of the fire in almost a week. This time, there was no smoke or smoldering ruins, but piles of burnt rubble on the site of what used to be Francesca's Restaurant. A backhoe had cleared debris off the street and sidewalk and moved it into piles along the border of the property. The agents stood and surveyed the scene as a man in a suit walked toward them.

"I'm Detective Clark and I presume you are Agent Perez," he said, looking at her.

"How'd you guess?" she said, offering her hand to shake. "And this is my partner, Special Agent McIntyre." Perez looked at the detective with a deadpan glare. "So what was so important that it required us to drop everything and come over here? I had to leave an important staff meeting," she said, hoping it was not what she was thinking it was.

Detective Clark raised his hand to beckon a man in protective gear who was standing in the rubble. "That's Deputy Fire Chief Greer. He'll show us what they've found."

After getting Perez and McIntyre set up in some protective coveralls, Greer led the way to a path that had been cleared in the rubble from the alley behind the restaurant to near the back of what used to be the building.

"There's no basement under this part of the building so we can walk in on the path that's been cleared."

As they followed, Perez pulled out a handkerchief and covered her face to block the dust and powerful smells of burnt building materials. About a dozen steps in, they approached a pile of debris that had a plastic tarp stretched over it. Greer lifted up the tarp and pointed what looked like a long walking stick with metal appendages that could be operated to grab things by squeezing the handle. He brushed away some ash-like materials to reveal the upper half of a human body. It had skin burned to a dark color that barely stretched over bones. The mouth was wide open in the appearance of a ghastly scream.

Perez sighed and shook her head. She hadn't noticed before, but she was pretty sure she was smelling burnt human flesh, which was now noticeable among the bouquet of foul odors at the scene. She heard a noise and turned to see Agent McIntyre, who had turned away and bent over, retching.

"Are you okay, Dennis?" she asked.

Agent McIntyre coughed a few times and stood up. After taking a breath, he said, "I'll be okay. I guess there's no training that really prepares you for this."

"We're pretty sure this is the missing woman, a Ms. D'Angelo, I believe," Detective Clark said.

"When did you find this?" Perez asked.

"About a half hour before I called you. I knew you'd want to know about this right away," he answered. "We have some techs ready to take some DNA samples so we can confirm the identity."

"Let us know if we can help. We have a top-notch DNA lab at our office," Perez said. She didn't insist on handling the DNA since there were questions about federal jurisdiction over the killing or death of the person who had been found.

"We have some other items we found earlier today that are probably directly relevant to the FBI investigation. One of the main items is right over there," Clark said, pointing to some rubble in which a little yellow flag had been planted. When the group arrived at the flag, Greer removed another covering to reveal a large roulette wheel, partially covered in ashes.

"And Joey Romano said it was nothing more than a friendly card game. I can't wait to question him again," McIntyre said with a look of disgust on his face as he snapped several pictures of the roulette wheel with his phone.

◆   ◆   ◆

That afternoon, Agent Perez addressed a hastily called meeting of the task force, which had expanded beyond the Philadelphia field office.

"Good afternoon," Agent Perez said in front of a screen to show photos taken of the scene of the fire. "We're now working as a multi-state task force, and we have Deputy Director Noel Burke in Washington, DC, Special Agent Donna Marcone in Newark, New Jersey, and of course Special Agents Leon Dempsey, Johnson Reed, Dennis McIntyre, and myself in Philadelphia. We called this meeting to share some important information that's come to light from the scene of the fire."

Agent Perez clicked her controller to display a picture of the scene taken from a distance. You could see several fire department personnel standing about twenty feet in from the rear of the building rubble.

"First off," she said, "I'm sorry to say that the investigation by the fire and police departments has uncovered a body in the rubble." Perez hit the button to show the slide of the body as those in the audience gasped. "We believe that this is Diane D'Angelo, whom we had known was missing since the time of the fire. DNA results are expected imminently. Now that we have a body, this takes the investigation to a new level both in urgency and in terms of the potential charges that will likely come out. In a few moments, you'll see why I say likely charges.

"At this point, I'd like to show some additional evidence the investigators have found," Perez said as she clicked to a close-up photo of the roulette wheel. "The Philadelphia Police Department is in the process of turning this item over to the FBI for our examination. We are already working on identifying the make and model as well as the source where it was likely purchased. Suffice it to say, we've had some folks at Quantico look at this slide, and they believe this is an expensive commercial grade model, of the type you'd find at a major casino."

"So, it wasn't just a poker game, as we thought, there was pretty clearly a casino on-site," Agent Reed said.

"Yes. We have several similar pieces, which are being compiled and evaluated. What I've shown you are the highlights of what we photographed his morning. With the way this is shaping up, we are going to do another round of questioning the owner of the restaurant, Joey Romano. I should add that Romano told us as far as he knew, there was nothing more than a friendly card game going on in the back rooms, which suggests he was lying to us and other law enforcement personnel who questioned him. We also questioned Henry Townshend, a member of city council who was at the restaurant to attend a poker game the night before the fire. Now we've got some very pointed questions for him as well."

"Can we tie the casino to the D'Angelo family?" Agent Reed asked.

"Everything seems to point in that direction, but there's more we need to do. The restaurant, of course, was owned by a close associate of the family and the sole casualty we've discovered is Michael D'Angelo's niece. Hopefully, we'll get some further corroboration from questioning Mr. Romano and maybe even the councilman, but the next point I plan to cover is also indirect evidence against the D'Angelo family."

Agent Perez paused to take a sip from a coffee mug, and the group shuffled through some of the briefing papers that had been handed out before the meeting. "The next slide shows what may be the most telling evidence of all. We've been canvassing security camera footage of the night of the fire in a ten-block radius and got this photo from inside a parking garage about six blocks away."

She clicked to the next slide, which showed a clear image of a front seat passenger in a car leaving the garage about ten minutes after two in the morning—which was just a few minutes after the fire began.

"In case anyone doesn't recognize who this is, it's Bruno Carbone Junior, head of the Mafia in southern New Jersey. And the driver of the car is Tony Bianchi, his consigliere."

Immediately, there was a buzz of murmuring among all members of the group, with a few leaning forward to scrutinize the picture on the screen.

"There's an open deck on top of the garage, which we know provided a direct and unobstructed view of the scene of the fire," Perez continued. "Also, someone disabled the security camera at about one thirty—shortly before the fire—but didn't realize the camera is programmed to resume operation about ten minutes after it's shut off."

Agent Dempsey, the leader of the task force in Philadelphia, spoke. "This is starting to fall into place. I don't think the Carbone family would blow up a restaurant unless they were targeting an operation of the D'Angelo family. It fits what we've been hearing from confidential sources about tension between the families. Does anyone disagree?" The group was silent. "Is anyone tracking the whereabouts of Bruno Carbone right now?" Dempsey asked.

"We just got involved a few days ago in this investigation," Agent Marcone replied. "And we've learned that Carbone flew to San Juan the morning after the fire. The trail seemed to grow cold at that point, but we've been in touch with the field office in San Juan and they strongly suspect that Carbone took off from there on a privately chartered jet to another location in the Caribbean. We've got a team of agents working on this, and we expect to know his probable location pretty quickly."

"Any other information from New Jersey?" Dempsey asked.

"We've seen beefed-up security at casinos and other establishments where the Carbone family has interests."

"I haven't seen anything like this in decades," Agent Dempsey said. "This is not good news. Despite Michael D'Angelo's distaste for violence, he's going to strike back in a big way, and it's only going to escalate from there."

CHAPTER 48

On Thursday evening, an elderly couple approached the check-in desk in the lobby of the Holiday Inn Express on Route 30 near Cherry Hill, New Jersey. They had been dropped off by a nondescript passenger van of the type that shuttled people between airports and hotels.

"Reservation for Hopkins," the elderly man said, presenting his New Jersey driver's license and a credit card. His wife, a short woman with silver-gray hair and sunglasses, stood quietly behind him.

"Would you like a king or two double beds?" asked the clerk behind the desk as she handed Mr. Hopkins a form for his signature.

"Two doubles will be fine."

"Here are two key cards," the clerk said, handing them a little folder. You'll be in room two-oh-seven. Just behind you, turn left, and the elevator is right down the hallway. There is an ice machine by the elevator on each floor. Breakfast is served in the lobby dining area from six to nine every morning. Let us know if you need a wake-up call. Do you need some help with your luggage?"

"No thanks. We're fine."

Mr. Hopkins extended the handle of his large suitcase, allowing him to roll it, and slung a bag with a strap over his shoulder that looked like it might contain a computer or some books. Mrs. Hopkins had a similar suitcase on wheels and a large handbag. They wheeled their luggage to the elevator and took it upstairs. When they arrived in the room and shut the door, Mr. Hopkins hung his coat up and slid off a Hollywood-quality silicone mask that covered his entire head and neck, revealing a thin man in his fifties with a receding hairline and a cheerful smile.

"I'm glad to get rid of this thing, at least for a few hours."

"I don't know. I think it becomes you, Jimmy," Mrs. Hopkins said with a decidedly masculine voice as she removed her wig and sunglasses, revealing she wasn't a woman at all.

"If I may say so, Phil, you look like a rather hot eighty-year-old in your getup!" The two laughed. Phil was one of Jimmy Salerno's most trusted helpers. They had worked together on many jobs, and they knew how the other reacted in different situations. Phil, an extremely useful partner, would be Jimmy's driver for the hit.

Jimmy Salerno was not prone to a lot of small talk and got right down to business. "As soon as we lay out our clothes and gear, I'd like to go over the layout of the gas station and the convenience store." He pulled a large folded sheet from his shoulder bag and spread it on the room's coffee table. The paper looked like a property survey.

"We'll enter the station here, making a right turn off Route 30, and pull up to this door, anywhere along here." They had been over this plan and had driven through the station parking area on several dry runs, but there was never enough planning and practice. "We'll make sure we don't do what that Gabe kid did and park in the wrong spot," Jimmy said.

"How are we going to make sure the spot is available?" Phil asked.

"The chaser car will park in the spot and pull out when we get there."

The chaser was another car that would pull into the lot. If the police arrived or if anyone started to chase Salerno's vehicle, the chaser car would feign engine trouble and block the exit to give Jimmy and Phil a head start driving away.

Jimmy continued. "The target collects cash from the registers every morning, and it takes him about forty-five minutes, between seven thirty and eight fifteen. He should be in an ideal spot for the job, so we'll hit the target between seven forty-five and seven fifty-five. The security guard usually leaves by then. If the guard is still there, we'll have to take him as well."

"We already covered this in our last meeting," Phil said.

"And will keep repeating it until we can say it in our sleep."

"The surveillance said that sometimes the target steps outside to check the pumps," Phil said.

"If he does, we'll take him there. That would make things easier, but we can't count on it."

Just then there was a knock at the door.

"Who is it?" Salerno asked, trying to sound like the old man who checked in. At the same time, he reached for his pistol and slid it into the waistband in the back of his trousers. He pointed to Phil's wig and gestured for him to put it on. Phil slid the wig on and reached for his pistol and placed it in the front pocket of his robe.

"I'm from the front desk," a voice said. "Housekeeping said you were short on towels."

Jimmy got up and looked through the keyhole. He decided that the visitor looked innocent enough and he beckoned Phil to the door, standing behind it with his gun drawn, just to be safe. Phil opened the door a crack just enough to receive the towels and he handed the man a five-dollar tip.

"Never a dull moment, is there? I guess we'd better try and get some rest now," Jimmy said with a smile on his face as the two made ready for bed.

♦ ♦ ♦

The next morning, the two left the hotel a few minutes after six in the same disguises, except for the work clothes underneath their

225

overcoats. Phil grabbed two coffees and two muffins from the break-fast buffet, and they were picked up by the same airport-style limo van that had dropped them off. The limo pulled into a Walmart parking lot about ten minutes up the road and parked in a spot that had relatively few cars or people walking around—except for a large van that blocked the view of Jimmy and Phil from any security cameras on-site.

As soon as they stopped, Jimmy pulled off his old man disguise and changed to a different silicone mask—one that looked like a middle-aged man with red hair. The mask slid on snugly after Jimmy applied a touch of moistening cream to his forehead and face. Next, he stripped down to his T-shirt and slid a protective vest over his torso that was lightweight but would stop most handgun rounds. Next, he put on a business-casual button-down shirt and a special shoulder holster that accommodated his pistol, which was extra-long due to the attached silencer. Jimmy also carried a compact .38 Special revolver in the large pockets of his cargo pants as a backup.

Phil's preparation was much simpler. He took the wig off and put on a baseball cap. He already had his bulletproof vest on, which was custom-made with a flexible strip to hold his compact Glock in place with a few extra magazines. He wore a loose-fitting, canvas button-down shirt over everything. When they were ready, they got out, leaving everything in the van, including their luggage, and slipped into a nondescript gray Toyota parked a couple of spaces away. There was nothing in the car except a burner phone on the passenger seat and a police scanner hooked to a power source in the dashboard so they could monitor police chatter before, during, and after the job.

Jimmy waved, and the limo driver left the parking lot. Everything inside the van would be burned except for the expensive mask and wig. The van would not be found anywhere near the scene of the crime.

Jimmy picked up the burner phone and dialed a number.

"Hello, Hawkeye here."

Hawkeye was the nickname for the lookout who was parked in a lot right next to the service station where the target would be.

"Report?" asked Jimmy.

"Target arrived at six forty-five, right on schedule. He appears to be working by the cash registers."

When they had staked out the area, they'd found Perrelli cleaned out the cash registers every morning with a security guard who had been on duty all night standing by. Typically, the guard would then go off shift a few minutes after Perrelli got started, leaving out a back door.

"Otherwise, traffic is as usual, and no cops are in sight. Only two cars are in the station parking lot," said the lookout.

"Thanks. Give us a call if anything changes." The phones were disconnected.

The car approached the entrance a couple minutes early, and Salerno dialed the lookout.

"Final report?"

"Parking lot is clear and your spot is open. Target is visible in the store. Chaser car is in place by the exit. The guard went in the back at seven thirty. He appears to have left, but I didn't see him drive away."

Salerno did not like the fact that the lookout had not seen the guard drive away, but he made a quick decision to proceed. "We are going forward and will enter the parking lot in less than a minute."

Salerno's car entered the lot and stopped in front of the door. He got out and walked into the store. Perrelli stood by the glass doors of a case containing bottled soft drinks. He turned when Salerno was about eight feet away.

"Can I help you, sir?" Perrelli asked.

Salerno raised his arm and pointed his gun at Perrelli. There were two quick pop sounds from the silenced pistol, which slammed Perrelli back against the beverage cabinet. He sank to the ground in a sitting position with his back leaning against the glass door of the cabinet. Salerno stepped forward, and a third pop left a red dot on the bridge of Perrelli's nose between his eyes.

"What the hell?" someone spoke off to Salerno's side.

He turned and saw the guard standing about ten feet to his left with his gun drawn. Salerno, who had practiced the maneuver hundreds of times, placed two shots in the center of the guard's chest, but not before the guard had fired a shot. Salerno fell backward to the floor. The guard collapsed on the floor and was bleeding, but Salerno managed to pull himself up and walk out of the store, clutching his rib cage with his left hand. He managed to get into the waiting car.

"You okay?" asked Phil.

"I took a shot on my side. I think I have a broken rib," Salerno said with labored breathing. "Let's get out of here." The Kevlar vest Salerno wore had stopped the bullet, but it had been like being hit in the ribs with a sledgehammer.

"The target is dead, but the guard was there. He came out, and I had to take him down as well."

"After he fired a round that hit you in the side," said Phil.

"Something like that."

Salerno reached for the phone and called his lookout. "Report?"

"I can see you are out of there. I can see that the target is down. I saw the other guy come out from the back of the store, but he's down as well. No police yet or other activity. Except someone just pulled up to a pump to get gas. The chaser is standing by."

"We're heading for the rendezvous."

The rendezvous was a location about ten minutes away where a different car would be waiting for Salerno. Salerno dialed one last number on his phone—Michael D'Angelo.

"It's done," he said and disconnected.

CHAPTER 49

Gus was with Michael at the Clubhouse when Michael got the report about the job in New Jersey. A few minutes later, Gus's phone buzzed.

"Hello," Gus said.

"It's Brennan. I've got some news." Brennan was a detective in the Philadelphia Police Department who received payments from the D'Angelo family. In return, he provided information and tip-offs.

"Yeah, what is it?"

"We got a call from the FBI asking if we have any information on Gabriel Rossi. They say he's on security cameras near the fire. They didn't give any more details. As always, you didn't hear this from me."

"How could that be? Gabe wasn't in the area the night of the fire," Gus asked.

"It was the night before the fire when you guys were having a poker game," Brennan answered.

"Of course. Thanks for the heads-up." The phones disconnected. Gus turned to Michael. "The FBI is interested in Gabe."

"I was worried they might be," Michael said.

"Brennan says he was picked up on some security cameras near Francesca's. It was the night of the poker game," Gus added.

"That alone doesn't mean much. They must have something else. I'd bet they're trying to tie him to the gambling. I told him to make sure his house was clean."

"Yeah, but what if they pick him up? Will he talk?" asked Gus.

"I don't think so. But we still need to take precautions."

◆　◆　◆

Gabe's phone rang with a call from his boss. "Hello, Michael. Any news on New Jersey?" Gabe hoped he didn't sound too anxious. He'd been waiting for word on the hit that he came close to participating in.

"Yes, it's done. But that's not why I'm calling. We just heard that the FBI considers you a person of interest related to the fire. I think they're trying to investigate what we were doing there before the fire."

"How can that be? I wasn't there the night of the fire!" Gabe said, almost shouting.

"They've got you on a security camera on the street the night of the poker game."

"Well, if that's all they have, it can't be a big deal. There's no law against going for a walk at night."

"They must have something else. The FBI was asking the Philadelphia police about you. They don't do that for no reason."

"I didn't go anywhere near the poker game. I did go to Diane's apartment after the fire, but I kept my head down and I made sure any security cameras wouldn't get a shot of my face."

"Look, I don't know what they may have, but we gotta take this seriously since the tip came from one of my guys inside the police department," Michael said.

"Okay, so what do I need to do?"

"Is your house clean like I asked?"

"Clean as a whistle."

"What about your guns?" Michael knew Gabe had a collection of guns, most legal but some not-so-legal.

"I moved everything to a locker under a fake ID, including ammo. All I kept was my carry pistol and a small backup pistol. I have both on me."

"I'm sorry, but you need to disappear for a while. You know your options. Call the boys at the Clubhouse, and they'll fix you up with a car." If the FBI or the police were looking for Gabe, they would have only a description of the car registered in his name. "Where are you now?"

"I'm home."

"You need to leave right away. They could be on the way right now to pick you up for questioning. Report back in when you're settled."

"I'll go right now." Gabe began to sweat as he thought about the very real possibility he could be questioned by the police. As the call ended, Gabe took a deep breath and immediately went to his closet to grab the bugout bag he had packed for situations like this. The bag contained clothes, a razor, some extra shoes, and various items he might need if he had to stay away for a few days, including a burner phone. Gabe immediately disconnected the battery on his smartphone and headed out the door. For good measure, he left several brochures in his trash basket on extended-stay hotels in Las Vegas to throw anyone looking for him off the trail.

At the Clubhouse, a Honda CR-V that had seen better days waited for him. He hoped it'd get him where he needed to go.

Now Gabe needed to decide where to go. The hideout of choice was a safe house the family maintained on Lake Arrowpoint in the Pocono Mountains. The spot was in a small resort community where everyone minded their own business. There was food and supplies in the house, and it was not far from several casinos where the family had interests. There were also several assets close by he could call on for help—men who worked for the family and could provide protection if needed. It was an ideal spot to lie low for a while, but something bothered Gabe about leaving town just now. Maybe it was an intuition or maybe it was just Gabe's affection for Maria, but he didn't want to go too far from her. But where could he go? Then he thought of something Maria had told him.

CHAPTER 50

Gabe began driving toward the suburbs in the direction of the convent where Maria lived. At around eleven o'clock, Gabe pulled over into a fast-food restaurant parking lot and dialed her number.

"Maria," Gabe said when she picked up. "Do you have a moment?"

"Yes, I just sent the kids to lunch, and then they have recess. I'm free until about twelve forty-five."

"I'm sorry to bother you, but I need your help."

"Of course, what can I do for you?"

"I should tell you this in person, but I know that's not practical. There are some crazy things happening in my work, and I'm in danger and need a place where I can lie low for a day or two. I can't give you all the details right now, but I promise I'll explain more when I can."

There was silence for a moment. Gabe felt bad about not being straight with Maria, but if he got picked up by the FBI, he could be threatened with a prison sentence. If he cooperated, he would be in danger from the family. So as far as he was concerned, he was in danger.

"I don't understand, Gabe. What kind of danger? Is someone looking for you?"

"Yes. Please trust me. I know it's a lot to ask for, but I really need your help."

"I don't know what I can do to help you."

"When I was with you and the kids by the lake, you showed me around the grounds. We didn't go inside, but you told me there are apartments in the dormitory on the third floor for guests."

"Yes, but those apartments are for visiting clergy and official guests of the archdiocese."

"Is anyone using them now?"

"No, but I can't just let anyone use them. Besides, I can't bring a man into the building unless he's a priest."

"If there is a way you could sneak me into one of those apartments, I would only need to stay a day or two until I can figure some things out. I can keep quiet and stay inside the apartment."

"Oh, Gabe, I don't know. I'd love to help you, but I could get thrown out if I got caught letting you into the building. I'm really sorry. Isn't there some other way I could help?"

"No. That's okay. I knew I was out of line asking you for this. Look, I have to go. I'll talk to you soon." He disconnected.

♦   ♦   ♦

Maria went to the break room and stared out the window, thinking about Gabe. *What if something happened to Gabe that I could have prevented? My only concern is about breaking the rules. Could I live with myself if Gabe got hurt?*

She hurried out of the building, got in her car, picked up her phone, and dialed the number Gabe had used to call her.

When he answered, she said, "Gabe, how far are you from the convent?"

"Fifteen minutes tops."

"Okay, pull into the parking lot by the lake, and park at the far end. The trees block the view from the main building. Anyone who sees you drive in will think you're a fisherman."

"Maria, are you sure you want to do this? I don't want you to get in trouble."

"Yes, I'm sure. There's a path around the far side of the lake. If you follow it, it will take you to the back of the dormitory. Is there any way you could look like a service technician? There's a large AC unit out there. If anyone sees you, just tell them you're there to check the heating and AC system. I'll see you there in fifteen to twenty minutes." After a brief pause, Maria spoke again. "Gabe, one more thing. Does my father know about this? Is he all right?"

"Yes, your father is fine. I'm the only one who needs to lie low for a little bit. Your father knows I need to keep a low profile, but he doesn't know I'm asking you for help."

"Good. You'd tell me if he were in danger, wouldn't you?"

"Of course. But could I ask you not to tell him I contacted you?"

"I don't think there's any reason I'd need to tell him," she said.

◆　◆　◆

Gabe pulled over and got in the back seat of his SUV. He wore a casual pair of tan pants and a canvas shirt that was almost the same color. Together, the shirt and pants would look like a technician's uniform. There was a Walmart across the street, and he ran in and found a small toolbox in the hardware department. Fortunately the store wasn't busy in the midmorning. In less than fifteen minutes, Gabe was carrying the toolbox on the path. He also juggled a small duffel bag, which had his necessities for an overnight stay, and he had added a baseball cap for effect. When he arrived, he began puttering around the large AC unit by the side of the building. He hadn't yet been there five minutes when the back utility door swung open.

"Hello, how does the AC unit look?" Maria asked in case anyone could hear.

"So far so good, but I think I need to check the vents inside."

"Come right this way," she said, holding the door open for him.

They quickly ascended the back stairwell to the third floor. Maria opened an apartment with windows facing the front. Gabe noticed he could see anyone approaching the front as well as most of the parking lot by the lake.

"The refrigerator is stocked to hold you over a few days," Maria said as she closed the shades on the windows. "There's a coffee maker here, and the coffee is in the cupboard. No one is in the building right now, but just the same, you shouldn't leave the apartment. If you need to leave, you can call me or text me. The women will start returning to the building around four this afternoon."

"Of course." Gabe thought for a moment. "What about the landline?" There was a phone on the wall in the kitchen.

"I suggest you not answer it, but if it rings twice and stops and rings again in a minute, it will be me. So that can be a backup for you."

"Can I call your landline if I can't get through on your cell?"

"Yes. No one will know if I pick up my phone downstairs. You can also put the TV on if you keep the volume low. I won't be able to visit for obvious reasons, but I can come up in a pinch if there is something you need."

"Tonight, after you're done with dinner and services, can we check in by phone?" Gabe asked.

"Sure. In fact, I think I'm going to call the school and ask someone to substitute this afternoon. I'm getting a bit of a headache. So I'll be around if you need me."

"I'm sorry. I probably caused your headache."

"No, I get them from time to time. I'll talk to you soon," Maria said as she closed the door and returned downstairs.

CHAPTER 51

A call was placed to Bruno Carbone's villa in Martinique.

"Bruno. It's Tony, and I'm here with Hank." Tony, the consigliere, got right to the point. "I've got some bad news. Your cousin Nickie was killed this morning."

"What, was it a car accident or something?" Bruno asked.

"No. He was whacked right in his store at the gas station."

"You sure it was a hit and not a robbery?"

"No question it was a hit. It was a professional job all the way. Guy walks in and puts two in Nickie's chest and one in his head. Then, the guard comes out. The guard and the professional both shoot. The pro gets up and walks out—he must have been wearing a vest. The guard is shot dead."

"The shooter. Was it anybody we know?"

"No. We got it on the security camera. If you look closely, the guy is probably wearing a mask, one of those realistic ones they use in the movies."

"Damn!" Bruno said, pounding the desk with his hand. He took a deep breath. "Nickie was a good man. I tell you what. It don't take a rocket scientist to figure out who's behind this. Michael D'Angelo is so good, and he's against violence, and he gives so much to the church, blah blah blah. Then he goes and kills my cousin in cold blood. I'm not gonna let go of this. No way."

"The woman who decided to sleep in her office that night was D'Angelo's niece or something," Hank added.

"Yeah. That's why they targeted one of my relatives. Well, this ain't over yet. Tony, you've got the scoop on D'Angelo's daughter. She's a nun, right?"

"Yeah, she lives in a convent right outside of Philadelphia. We've got the details," Tony said. Hank looked downward and shook his head, as if he knew what was coming.

"Okay. Listen to this. We're done being a sleeping dragon. I want that woman. Don't kill her. I want her taken alive. Then we'll see if D'Angelo has any balls to deal with us."

"Bruno, hitting your cousin who's in our business is bad. I agree we should do something about it. But going after a boss's daughter who's not in the business at all? And she's a nun! Are you sure you want to do that?" Hank asked.

"Hank, I'm the boss of this family. I've told you guys what to do, and now you better do it. If you're getting too soft for the job, maybe we should retire you."

When Bruno disconnected the call, Hank sighed and shook his head again. "This isn't gonna end well."

"We'd better obey the boss, Hank, or it definitely won't," Tony said, glaring at Hank.

◆　◆　◆

A half hour later, Gus Nasuti's phone buzzed.

"Gus, it's Hank. I got something for you that's important. I'm doing this for old time's sake, okay? And you didn't hear this from me." Hank and Gus had been friends before the New Jersey operation split off from Philadelphia.

"Yeah, Hank. I'm listening."

"After what happened today, Junior is royally pissed off."

"I can see that."

"He knows about Michael's daughter, the one who's a nun."

"Yeah, that's his only daughter, and she's preparing to be a nun."

"Bruno is going to have her kidnapped."

Gus's mouth fell open. "Are you fuckin' kidding me?"

"No. I just got off the call where he told his consigliere to get it done."

"I hope you didn't go along with it."

"Of course not. I argued against it but got shot down. That's why I'm calling you."

"Thanks for the heads-up. I owe you one," Gus said.

"No problem. Gus, how are we going to end all this craziness?"

"I think you know the answer to that, Hank. Sometimes, when you see a snake, you gotta cut off the head. Nice talking to you, Hank."

◆ ◆ ◆

Ten minutes later, Gabe took a call on his phone.

"Gabe, it's Michael. Are you anywhere near Maria?"

"I'm in a friend's apartment. Not far at all."

"You need to get Maria and take her to Lake Arrowpoint. I mean right away."

"What's wrong? Is she in danger?"

"We just got tipped off that Carbone is going to have her kidnapped. I guess it's payback for what we did this morning."

Gabe's face turned ashen. "What should I tell her?" he asked as he began to realize how dangerous the situation had become. The Carbones would kill Gabe in a heartbeat if he tried to protect Maria.

"Just tell her there are some bad people we do business with, and she's not safe there."

"Michael, I'm on it. I'll get her out of there right away."

CHAPTER 52

Gabe grabbed his phone, praying that Maria had not gone to dinner yet in the main building of the convent.

"Hello, Gabe?"

"Yes, it's me. Look, I just had a call from your father. We need to leave here right away."

"What? I was just getting ready to go to dinner and then I have to be at the vespers service."

"No, we don't have time. Please, listen to me. Throw some clothes in a bag. I'll explain when we get in the car. We can take my car. Just trust me on this."

"Gabe, you need to tell me right now why I have to leave," Maria said with a firmness in her voice that Gabe had not heard previously.

Gabe did some quick thinking—he didn't want to scare her with talk about kidnapping. "They might know that I'm here and that puts you in danger as well. You won't be safe even if I leave."

"Okay, but what about school?"

"Maybe you can tell them you have a family emergency, which is sort of true. We really need to leave now. Where should I meet you?"

"I'll come up for you. Can you wear your repairman outfit?"

"I still have it on. Can you be here in five or ten minutes?"

"See you then."

Gabe stood, staring out the window impatiently, watching the parking lot and the driveway into the convent. After about ten minutes, he saw a full-size black SUV pull into the entrance—not the type of vehicle anyone from the convent would drive. Gabe was about to charge out of the apartment to get Maria when he heard her open the door with her key. Gabe hurried toward the door.

"We've got company, and we need to go out the back right away."

"Who is here and what do they want?" she asked, almost screaming.

"They are bad people. We need to get out of here now. We'll talk when we get in the car," Gabe said.

Maria began to cry, but Gabe gently took her arm and guided her out of the apartment. They hurried down the steps as quickly as they could with their bags. As they passed the rear door into the lobby, Gabe glanced through the little glass pane and saw two men wearing dark windbreakers standing at the front door. Gabe pushed Maria forward and they left out the rear door and hurried down the path through the woods toward the lake.

"There are two of them," Gabe said. "Can they get in the front door?"

"The door is locked, and they can't get in without a key fob. They'll have to hit the intercom button, which goes to my apartment. I guess they'll be out of luck."

"I wouldn't count on it. Those guys are experts at getting into buildings. They'll check the back and pick the lock of the door we just left through if they have to," Gabe said as they were about one hundred feet down the path. "Let's hope it takes them a while to figure out that we left through the back."

As the path came out of the woods by the lake, Maria stopped. "I think I left my phone in the apartment."

"We can't go back for it now. Besides, they probably can use your phone to find your location. I've got a phone you can use that can't be traced."

They walked a little way and entered the far end of the parking lot where Gabe's car sat. They loaded their bags in the back seat.

Gabe tried to start the car. The engine turned over but didn't start. He tried again with the same result.

"Shit! This is no good. Please pardon my language," Gabe said.

"We can take my car. It's parked up at the other end of the lot."

Unfortunately, Maria's car was in plain view of the main building and the nuns' dormitory.

Gabe tried again, but the car wouldn't start. "Okay, let's go. I'll drive us."

They grabbed their things and walked briskly to the front of the lot, hoping they would not be seen.

"The problem is I'm sure they have the make, model, and color of your car."

"Where are we going?" Maria asked.

"North," Gabe said as he slinked low to the driver's side of Maria's car and got in. She got in the other side and handed Gabe the keys.

"I can get us to Route 309 by some back streets. That will take us north."

Gabe had memorized the directions to the safe house but didn't know the local roads very well. "Can we get to the Pennsylvania Turnpike from here?"

"Yes, from Route 309."

Gabe put the car into gear and nodded. "Good, let's do it."

"You still didn't tell me where we're going."

"Your father's business has a place up in the Poconos. It's near one of the hotels our company owns." Gabe avoided using the term "safe house" for now.

"That's news to me. I guess there's a lot I don't know about the business."

♦　♦　♦

While the two Carbone operatives were trying to enter Maria's building, the driver, a man named Lenny, remained in the black SUV. He clicked a few buttons on his laptop, hoping to get a signal from the GPS tracking device they had placed on Maria's car several weeks ago. When the tracker blipped, he immediately grabbed a handheld radio and called his colleagues.

"Are you guys in the building yet?" Lenny asked.

"No. The front door is locked. Frank's going around back to check for other doors," a man named Max replied.

"Don't waste any more time. I just turned on the tracker, and she's on the move."

"How did she get to her car? We just saw it in the lot a few minutes ago."

"Don't know." Lenny watched as the blip moved farther away from their location. "I'll get Bianchi on the phone and see what we're supposed to do."

"If we can get into the building, we should still check her apartment. We can find her with the tracker if she's driving away," Max said.

Frank, who had gone around the back and easily picked the lock to the back door, let Max in the front. As they were standing in the lobby, the elevator doors opened, and a young woman wearing a nun's habit walked out. Frank and Max instinctively turned away so she would not see their faces.

"May I help you?" the young woman asked.

"We're here to see Ms. D'Angelo about a plumbing problem," Max said. Their jeans and windbreakers made them look like they could be plumbers.

"That's the door to her apartment right over there, but I'm not sure if she's in. If she's away, who should I tell her was here?"

"Just tell her the plumbers got here early. We can come back later," Frank said.

The young woman continued out the front door, and the two men knocked on Maria's door, not expecting an answer. After a moment, Frank pulled out some tools and picked the lock. They entered and gave the apartment a quick look. Nothing seemed out of order, but there was a cell phone sitting on the countertop.

"Looks like she forgot her phone. Maybe she won't be gone long," said Max.

"Or maybe she left in a big hurry," said Frank.

Just then, the radio in Max's pocket crackled to life. "Let's go," said the driver. "Bianchi told us to follow her from a safe distance and not let her see us. She's heading toward the turnpike, so she may be leaving town."

"I wonder if someone tipped her off," said Frank.

CHAPTER 53

Gabe and Maria got on the ramp and entered the Pennsylvania Turnpike, heading west toward the Northeast Extension, a branch of the turnpike that headed north.

Maria noticed Gabe kept looking in the rearview mirror. "Do you think they're following us?"

"If they were, I think we lost them," Gabe said.

Maria took a deep breath. "Gabe, I'm scared. What if they're still looking for us?" she asked with a trembling voice.

"Don't worry. We'll be safe where we're going."

"Does my father know where we're going?" Maria asked.

"Yes. I'm sure he'll have some of his people around to help us if we need it."

"None of this makes any sense to me. Why are they coming after us? I don't even know who these people are."

Gabe knew he would need to choose his words carefully. "In our businesses, sometimes we have to deal with some unsavory characters. If these people think you've crossed them, they can get pretty angry. Does that make sense?" Gabe asked.

"No, it doesn't. I guess I knew less than I thought I did about my father's business." Maria stared straight ahead and took a tissue from her purse. "What kind of business is he involved in?"

"We have interests in casinos and resorts with casinos," Gabe said.

"Okay, but that doesn't really tell me anything," she said.

"As I said, in that business, you sometimes have to deal with people who aren't very nice."

"You mean the kind of people who might hurt or kill you?"

Gabe placed his hand on Maria's arm. "They were probably just there to scare us."

"How long do we need to be away?" she asked.

"I promise I'll try and get you back as soon as possible, but we might need to stay away a few days," Gabe said.

Maria turned toward Gabe and glared at him. "A few days? I've got school to teach and responsibilities at the convent."

"Maria, please trust me. I'll do the best I can to get you back to your life at the convent."

Maria shook her head. "Can't we just call the police?"

"I don't think that would be a good idea," Gabe said. "Your father is aware of the whole situation and he's taking steps to fix it. We'll call him when we get there."

The two rode in silence for several minutes. After looking in the rearview mirror, Gabe sped up and entered the passing lane to overtake several cars.

"Is something wrong?" Maria asked.

"I thought I saw something, but I'm sure it was nothing. I just want to get us to our destination as soon as possible," Gabe said.

Maria folded her arms across her chest. "So, my father is involved in gambling businesses with people bad enough to send a crew out to hurt us?"

Gabe stumbled to answer the question. "Maria, there are all kinds of people in the casino business. Some are good and some aren't so good."

Maria stared straight ahead with a troubled look on her face. "Is my father one of the good ones or one who's not so good?"

"Your father can be aggressive in business, but he's a good man," Gabe said as he put his blinker on to change lanes and pass a slow car ahead.

"I know he does a lot of good. He supports the church and he gives a lot to charity. He's always been a kind and generous father to me. But I guess I've been kept in the dark about a lot of things." Maria paused a moment. "What about my mother and my brother? Are they in danger too?"

"I'm sure your father has taken steps to protect your mother, and Raph knows how to take care of himself. He can handle situations like this." Gabe glanced at Maria. "Listen to me, Maria. You're lucky to have Michael D'Angelo as your father. He helps more people than you realize."

Gabe gripped the steering wheel tighter. He had been essentially truthful up to now, even if a little misleading, but what if she dug further? He could rationalize his answers with the thought that even the old-school Cosa Nostra leaders were beloved by many. That was why thousands of people, including celebrities and politicians, had gone to their funerals, even after they had been assassinated in a mob hit.

Maria wiped her eyes with a tissue. "If those men at the convent were there to scare us, what would they have done?" she asked with a tremor in her voice.

"I don't know, Maria. But we couldn't wait around to find out."

"But I've had nothing to do with the business. Why would they come after me?"

"I guess they know how important you are to your father and they figure they can intimidate your father by scaring us," Gabe said.

Maria bit her lip and turned toward Gabe. "So, what do we do now? I'm supposed to teach school Monday morning."

"Let's get to the cabin and we'll call your father and see what he wants us to do. Can you call the school Monday if we can't make it back in time?"

"I'll be in big trouble if I don't call the convent soon. But what am I going to tell them—that I had to leave because some thugs came to get me?" she said, shaking her head.

"Can you tell them you had to leave suddenly for a family emergency? That's actually a true statement."

"I don't want to have to run away like this!" Maria began to cry. "And I'm scared. Why couldn't we just go to my parents' home?"

Gabe reached out a hand and patted hers. "Maria, everything will be okay. I promise I'll keep you safe. I'm sure your father is working on this, and when things calm down a little, I can take you home. But we need to wait for instructions. Your father told me to take you to the cabin, so I'm sure that's the best thing."

Gabe didn't explain Michael was also concerned that if the FBI picked him up for questioning, there would be no one to protect her at her parents' home.

Maria began to calm down, and they sat in silence for a while. Then she spoke again. "I feel like such an idiot knowing so little about my family's business. And now I've got to run away and leave town because of it. All I can say is even if my father is a good man, he must have a dark side to get involved with people like this."

Gabe let her last statement go unanswered.

◆　　◆　　◆

Maria stared out the car window and wondered if the leaders in the church who expressed gratitude for Michael's support knew more than they would admit. Life was relatively simple in the convent. She worked, prayed, and did her best to treat everyone with respect. Not everyone in the convent, or in the church, for that matter, had a character worthy of respect, but she could always turn her doubts and cares over to God. Maybe the only answer was to turn her present anxieties over to God. Now that she was about to spend a weekend at a remote cabin with a man she was attracted to, she wondered how that fit into her ongoing efforts to qualify to become a nun. Was this a test, or was it a sign from God that she should consider another type of vocation?

CHAPTER 54

The black SUV caught up with Maria's car on the turnpike but followed from a mile back. Max's phone buzzed.

"Max, it's Tony. What's the situation?"

"We're following her north on the turnpike, about a mile behind."

"Have you gotten a look at her? Is she alone?"

"No. We'd have to get real close. Do you want us to?" Max asked.

"Don't get too close," Tony said. "I'm concerned she was warned or that you got made in the parking lot at the convent. So, keep a little distance. I don't want to risk the operation by having her see you guys and get scared. Let's see where she goes. Maybe tonight you'll have a chance to get close and grab her."

"Got it," said Max. "But what if she's not alone in the car?"

"I'm sure you guys will do what you have to do to bring her back," Bianchi said as he disconnected.

"Bring us up a little closer," Max said as he looked through a pair of binoculars. "I still can't tell if anyone else is with her."

As they drove on, he lost the signal for Maria's car as she entered the Lehigh Tunnel, which travels under a mountain for nearly a mile. Moments later, the SUV was in the tunnel as well, and Max lost his wi-fi signal. When they exited, Max's screen showed the location of

Maria's car. She had gained a little ground and was a mile-and-a-half ahead.

After about twenty minutes, Max blurted out, "Get ready. They just got off the White Haven exit." They made an abrupt turn on the ramp as the exit came on them quickly. "Slow down. They're stopped at the toll booth. Okay, the toll booth is clear. Looks like they're heading east on Route nine forty. Let's get through the booth and turn right at the end of the ramp."

Members of crime families never liked to linger at toll booths. There were often security cameras, and of course, it was hard to forget the horrific shooting of Sonny Corleone at a toll booth in *The Godfather*. Even now, it wasn't inconceivable that they were being lured into a trap by following Maria's car. In a few moments, however, they were past the booth and heading east on 940.

"I wonder where she's going?" said Frank. "We're out in the middle of nowhere."

They followed Maria's car through the town of Blakeslee, which wasn't much more than a crossroads with a couple of gas stations, a food market, and a few shops. After a couple of miles, her car turned north on a two-lane road that didn't display a road name or route number, and she continued for about six miles when the GPS tracker showed her car turn off onto an area where no road was marked. Max stared at the screen, as it appeared she was driving into the woods. The SUV was still a mile back, and they approached where Maria's car turned off.

There was a sign that said "Arrowpoint Lake, Private Community," and there was a gravel road leading into the woods. Max told the driver to pull over to the side of the road. About a mile in from the gate, a body of water was depicted on the GPS map. Max and Frank watched the red dot that represented Maria's car move across the map around the south side of the lake until it stopped on the far side.

"It's getting dark, and I don't want to drive in there blind. We need some better info on this place." Max called one of the Carbone soldiers who worked on computers. "What can you tell me about Arrowpoint Lake? We're at the gate, and it's dark."

Jake, the computer guy, answered, "Hold on while I pull it up." After they waited a few minutes, he said, "It's a private community of homes around the lake. There appears to be a gravel road that goes in from the gate and forks when it comes to the lake. The lake is a little more than a mile in."

"I'm pretty sure our target took the fork to the right," Max said.

"The road doesn't go all the way around the lake. Both branches reach a dead end. So, if you go in, there's probably only one way out," Jake said. "It looks like a pretty quiet place back there. If you drive up to the driveway, they'll hear you coming."

"How far are the police?" Frank asked.

"Hold on." A minute later, Jake answered, "There's a police barracks about ten miles from where you are. Unless they happen to be cruising in the area, it would take at least twenty minutes to get there. That doesn't include driving down the gravel road. I just found some information on the lake. The cabins are privately owned, and it's mostly weekend traffic this time of year."

At Jake's suggestion, Max pulled up Google Maps and zeroed in on the satellite view of the lake. According to the location of Maria's car on the GPS tracker, she was at one of the last cabins on the road that wound around the southeast side of the lake. It might have been the very last cabin before the dead end.

"If there is a little traffic, that might work in our favor. There won't be too many people around, but it won't be unusual to hear some vehicle traffic on the road," Max said.

"I just looked up the property in the county records. It appears to be owned by Angelcrest Properties, LLC. That's a Pennsylvania LLC, but there's no information in the record about owners of the company."

"That sounds like something the D'Angelo family might own," Frank said.

"I see some open space by the lake about a quarter mile before the end of the road. Can you see what that is?" Max asked.

"I've enlarged the screen, and it looks like a boat ramp and a little parking area. I think if you park around the right side of the lot, there will be some trees between you and the road. You'll see what I mean when you get there. Maybe you can park there and walk the rest of the way," Jake said.

"Yeah, that's a good idea. After we grab the girl, we can call Lenny, and he can drive over and pick us up. But let's keep an eye on the property for a few hours and make our move later tonight. We don't want to go in blind if we can help it."

CHAPTER 55

Gabe and Maria pulled into the cabin's driveway just before sunset. It was a well-appointed one-story log cabin with a front porch and overhanging roof supported by log pillars. Entering through the front door, Gabe quickly disarmed the burglar alarm—of which he'd been briefed—and admired the large foyer leading to a great room with a cathedral ceiling and large glass windows overlooking the lake and mountains. In the center of the rear wall, sliding glass doors led to a wooden deck. Around the corner to the left, there was a modern kitchen with granite countertops and a hallway leading to three bedrooms.

"This would be a wonderful place for a vacation. I just wish we could be here under different circumstances." Maria crossed her arms as she spoke.

"Why don't you pick out a bedroom for yourself," Gabe said as he carried the bags into the great room.

"Sure. Where will you sleep?"

"Tonight, I'll sleep out here on the couch, where I can keep an eye on things," Gabe said. "While you're doing that, I'll take a look and see if there is something to eat."

He rummaged in the freezer, finding several frozen options. He turned as Maria reentered the room. "Shall I heat up this frozen pizza?"

"That's fine. Are we going to call my father now?"

Gabe slid the pizza into the oven and grabbed his burner phone, noticing there was very little signal at this location. He tried dialing Michael's number but couldn't get through. "There's no signal here. First thing in the morning, we can ride back to town and see if we can make the call there."

"Why don't you try the landline? I'd really like you to make the call."

"Okay." Gabe went to the landline and dialed one of Michael's burner phones, which he replaced at least once a week. Someone answered, but Gabe spoke first. "We're at the cabin but there's no cell phone signal here."

"Good. Is Maria okay?" he asked.

"She's here with me, safe and sound," Gabe said. Maria put out her hand, signaling she wanted to speak to her father and Gabe held up a finger.

"Any sign of trouble along the way?"

"No. It was smooth sailing."

"Why don't you try to find a signal, and I'll call in the morning about nine. Keep safe," Michael said and disconnected. He obviously didn't want to take the chance that the landline was being monitored. Michael would initiate the call tomorrow since he would use a new burner phone.

"He said he couldn't talk now but he'll speak to you in the morning. He'll call us first thing, so we'll need to drive to town and find a better signal," Gabe said, embellishing the message to help calm Maria.

"Gabe, I'm so scared. What if those people in the black car find us?"

Gabe gently wrapped his arms around her, and she rested her head on his shoulder. Maria returned the embrace and held on.

"We're safe here, Maria. I care about you, and I promise I'll keep you safe," Gabe said as Maria gripped him even tighter. They held their embrace for several minutes, and Gabe stroked her back in a comforting way. Finally, they relaxed their grips on one another. Maria looked Gabe in the eye with a sad but affectionate gaze. He brushed aside a strand of her hair that had fallen in her face and put his two hands on her shoulders.

"Why don't you take a seat on that couch by the fireplace, and I'll start a fire."

The fireplace was ready with kindling and small logs in place and a large box of matches on the raised stone floor in front of the grate. Gabe lit the fire, then went to the kitchen and poured two glasses of chardonnay from a bottle in the refrigerator. When the oven's timer dinged, he went and returned with slices of pizza on two plates. As they sat enjoying their simple meal, warmth from the crackling fire filled the room on the cool mountain evening. After they put their plates down, Maria moved over slightly and rested her head on Gabe's shoulder. When he put his hand over top of hers, a warmth filled him as he snuggled the woman he had come to love.

"Thank you, Gabe, for keeping me safe," Maria whispered. He turned to her, and she lifted her head and gazed again into his eyes. Gabe gently stroked her cheek and returned the gaze. After a brief pause, he leaned forward to kiss her, but she pulled back, hesitating. Then she breathed deeply, took Gabe's face in her hands, and aggressively pulled him in for a kiss. It wasn't a long kiss, but it was passionate.

When their kiss ended, Maria continued to sit close to Gabe with her head on his shoulder. Gabe sensed something had changed in Maria on a deep level. He reached his arm over and ran his fingers through her hair. "Are you okay with all of this? I mean with what we just did?"

"Yes."

Maria sat in silence, staring straight ahead for a few moments as if pondering his question. "I haven't taken permanent vows, and I think I've come to a decision. I've been praying for God to guide me and I think I can see things more clearly now."

"You mean you're not going to become a nun?" Gabe asked.

"I don't think I can go back to living in the convent."

"When did you decide on this?"

"I've had this feeling growing inside me for some time, but tonight it's like a light went on in my head," she said, beginning to blush. "Actually, the light went on in my heart."

"So does that mean we can be together?" Gabe looked into her eyes with a hopeful smile.

"Yes. We won't need to sneak around anymore. But I think we need to take things one step at a time. For one thing, we need to figure out how we can get home safely."

"Don't worry. We'll be home soon. I promise you." Despite his confident words, Gabe was deeply perplexed about how he could get Maria back to the safety of her parents' home. He was sure the police or the FBI would be watching, and he needed to stay under the radar for a while.

"Thanks, Gabe." Maria took his hand. "It was really scary today, but I feel safe with you."

After a pause, Gabe spoke. "So how will it work with the convent?"

"As soon as we get back, I need to speak to my superiors and tell them I've made a decision not to continue my training."

"Will they be upset?"

"They told all of us that if we seek God's will and reach a prayerful decision to leave, we can go with the blessing of the church."

"What about your parents?" Gabe knew he had to tread cautiously here. He didn't know how they would feel about Maria leaving the convent, and he didn't want to be blamed for pulling her away from the church.

"I don't think that will be a problem. They've supported me at the convent, but I'm sure if they had the choice, they'd want me to settle down and give them grandchildren."

"That sounds good to me," Gabe said.

Maria sat up and turned toward him. "Gabe, you need to be patient with me. After a year training to be a nun, it's going to take a while for me to adjust to life outside the convent."

"I understand."

Maria sat back and put her head on Gabe's shoulder again.

"It's been a long day and we should probably try to get some rest," Gabe said.

"Can we just sit here for a while? I'm tired but I'm not sure I'll be able to sleep."

"Sure thing." Gabe pulled her in closer on the couch and put his arm around her.

After a time, Maria rose. "I guess you're right. I should probably try to get some sleep." She kissed him on the forehead.

After Maria had retired for the night, Gabe grabbed a blanket and some pillows from one of the rooms and made his bed on the couch. He stayed dressed as he was, so he would be ready if he needed to get up in the night. He left his gun on the coffee table next to the couch. As Gabe stretched out, it occurred to him that his current predicament provided a unique opportunity to run away with Maria if she were willing. As far as he knew, nobody was aware of this cabin except for Michael and a few of his underbosses. He and Maria would be expected to lie low for a while, and it would be days before anyone knew they were gone. Gabe had more than enough money stashed away to buy new identities, although he'd probably need to make a risky trip into Philadelphia to access the funds. He could make a fresh start with the woman he loved. But would Maria be willing to cut herself off from her family and everything else in the life she knew? And how safe could they be with not only the FBI, but two Mafia families hunting for them? Gabe realized he needed to put these thoughts out of his mind and devote all his effort to the task at hand—protecting Maria from the very real danger they faced.

CHAPTER 56

Max and Frank crouched behind some trees, looking across the street toward the lake house with Maria's car parked out front. Max surveyed the scene through a small pair of binoculars.

"I can't really see much. It looks like the rooms on the front of the house are bedrooms," Max said. "Did you see anything around the back?"

"No, there are some sliding glass doors, and I can see some shadows, but the space directly behind the doors is open, and I didn't want anyone to see me. The lights were dim, but I think there was a fire in the fireplace," Frank answered.

"I can smell the smoke."

Max's walkie-talkie beeped. "What is it?"

"Just reporting in. No traffic down here. How does it look at the house?" Lenny asked.

"Only one car. We're going in about midnight. I'll check in with you first. You may need to come for us quickly after that. Let us know right away if any cars pass by."

"Got it."

Max turned to Frank. "You got all the stuff to tie her up?"

"Yeah, and I got a sedative to knock her out if she doesn't cooperate. I also got a rag to stick in her mouth to stop her from screaming if we need it."

"Remember, the boss wants her alive. That doesn't apply to anyone else who might be in the house."

At five minutes before midnight, Max called Lenny on his walkie-talkie.

"Yeah?" said Lenny.

"We're going in now. Is all clear?"

"Quiet as a graveyard here."

"Be ready to come get us in a hurry. Also, drive over here if you hear any shooting," Max said.

"Got it."

Max turned to Frank. "You go around the back and make sure she doesn't try to run out the back door. I'll signal you when I've got her secure."

The two walked briskly across the street. Max crossed the small front lawn to a flagstone pathway that extended from the driveway to the front porch, and Frank continued through the side of the property around to the back. Just before reaching the front steps, a bright set of lights switched on, illuminating the front porch and yard. Max froze.

CHAPTER 57

Gabe was tired, but the restless energy of the day had kept him from falling asleep. As he lay quietly considering their next moves, the front porch lights switched on. He grabbed his gun and tiptoed over to the door to Maria's room, which was right around the corner from the front hallway.

"Maria, are you awake?" Gabe said as he knocked gently.

Maria answered from inside the bedroom. "Yes. What's going on? Why did you turn the porch lights on?"

"I didn't. They come on from a motion detector. I think someone may be outside."

"What?"

"Stay in the bedroom and keep down low."

"I want to come with you!"

"Maria, please. I'll check out front and be back in just a minute."

Just then, there was a loud crashing sound.

"Gabe, don't leave me!" Maria screamed.

Gabe took a step sideways into the front foyer, pointing his gun toward the front door as a large man, who had obviously kicked the door down, entered. The man immediately fired his pistol at Gabe.

Gabe felt the bullet hit but remained standing and fired off three rounds at the man. All three shots hit the intruder in the chest and knocked him to the floor. Gabe looked down and saw a red stain on his T-shirt on the upper left side of his chest. His breathing became difficult as he felt a sharp biting pain in his back from the bullet's exit wound. Gabe felt faint and dropped to the floor, landing on his back. The moment seemed eerily quiet until Maria started screaming.

"Gabe! Are you okay?" She came out of the door and screamed again when she saw him on the floor. She knelt and gently cradled his head. "Gabe, Gabe, can you hear me?"

He was wheezing and gasping for breath. Gabe opened his eyes and looked at her. He tried to speak but was barely able to whisper.

"I . . . love . . . you," Gabe said as the dark red stain on his shirt continued to grow. Gabe tried raise his head and reach for her hand but then his arm went limp and dropped to the floor.

"Gabe, please stay with me! I'll call an ambulance," Maria cried and prayed out loud, looking toward heaven. "Dear God, please, help Gabe! Please, save him." She glanced at the man lying in front of the door, motionless. As she rose to go to the phone, she heard a rattling sound toward the back of the cabin. She glanced up and saw a dark figure standing on the porch, trying to work the outside door handle.

Maria began to tremble. She wanted to kneel and help Gabe, but he had grown still. She looked down to see his eyes open in a blank stare. His shirt was covered in blood and had started to puddle on the floor. She wanted to run to the phone and call 911, but it was as though her muscles wouldn't obey her. Suddenly, she saw the figure on the porch turn to his left and raise his hands in front of him. He was aiming a pistol off to the side of the house. Multiple shots rang out, and the man fell on the porch. That meant there were more people with guns outside.

Maria stood in a daze. She closed her eyes and began to whisper silently. "Our Father, who art in heaven, hallowed be thy name. Thy kingdom come . . ."

Just then, two men dressed in black tactical fatigues stormed the front door, aiming rifles at her. "Freeze!" they said. "Get on your knees and put your hands on your head!"

Maria continued to stand, still paralyzed with fear as the two men continued to point their rifles at her. Then a third man walked forward, holstered his weapon, and walked behind her, pulling her arms back. She offered no resistance as he handcuffed her. He grabbed her arm and pulled her over to one of the chairs in the great room.

"You need to sit here for a moment, ma'am."

Next, a woman entered the room, wearing a vest that looked like a black life jacket with "FBI" in large white letters.

"Ma'am, I'm Agent Perez with the FBI." A second agent checked the necks of the bodies for a pulse. "Mac, what's going on with the bodies?"

"Gunshot wounds in all three. No pulse from the big guy by the door or from the guy on the back porch. Weapons are on the floor beside all three of them." Next, the agent kneeled to check on Gabe and felt his neck. "This one has a weak pulse."

"Get a trauma kit for the one with a pulse and get an ambulance here right away. We'll need the coroner for the big guy and the guy on the porch, along with the crime scene people," Perez said. She turned to Maria. "What is your name, ma'am?"

Maria paused as tears streamed down her face. "Maria," she said so softly it was barely audible.

"Did you say Maria?"

Maria glanced at Gabe on the floor and began to cry. "Are you going to get help for Gabe?" she asked, barely able to get the words out.

"Yes, an ambulance will be here in a few minutes," Perez said, glancing over at the bodies on the floor. She turned back to Maria. "Do you have a last name?"

"D'Angelo," she whispered.

"Ms. D'Angelo, do you know who any of these people are?" she asked, pointing to the men on the floor and on the back porch. "Take your time, but it's very important we find out who was involved here," Perez added.

Maria turned and looked at Gabe and broke down again. Perez handed her a tissue. Maria continued to cry for a moment before she spoke.

"That's Gabe. I mean Gabriel Rossi," Maria said, fighting back tears. "I don't know who the other people are, but I think that one broke into the cabin." Maria pointed to the man lying in front of the door.

Agent Perez spoke with a gentler tone. "Ms. D'Angelo, are you okay? I mean, did you get hurt in any way here tonight? If so, we can take you to the hospital to be checked."

"I guess I'm okay, but is Gabe going to be okay? Can I go to the hospital with him?" she asked.

"As I said, an ambulance will be here in a few minutes, and they'll do what they can for him. When they get here, I'll have the EMT take a quick look at you. If you're okay, we'd like to take you to somewhere where we can talk for a little bit. I promise you it will be a safe place. We will have lots of FBI agents and police with us." She paused, seeming to mentally switch gears. "Mac, can you do a gunshot residue wipe on Ms. D'Angelo? You can uncuff her in the process." She looked at Maria. "It's just a little tissue we'll use to wipe your hands to eliminate you as a suspect."

Mac put on plastic gloves and did a swipe on each of Maria's hands. The EMTs arrived and took over the scene to work on Gabe. After they put him on a stretcher to carry him out, Perez called one of the EMTs to come over and have a look at Maria.

"She's obviously upset, but her vitals are good," the technician said.

Perez nodded and turned again to Maria. "Ms. D'Angelo, we're going to the car and we'll take you somewhere safe. I'll ride with you to make sure you are all right. Is that okay?" she asked, and Maria nodded.

Maria noticed the other agent look at Agent Perez and point at the kitchen table where there was an open laptop. Perez nodded as he prepared to put the computer in an evidence container.

Maria realized she was still in her nightgown and robe. "Can I get dressed?"

Perez nodded and sent a female agent into Maria's bedroom. After the room was cleared, Maria got dressed, but the crime scene technicians arrived, and Perez got involved describing what she knew about the scene. By the time they left, it was almost two in the morning, and Maria had not slept in nearly twenty-four hours.

Agent Perez said, "I don't think any further questioning is needed now. I see no grounds to place you in lockup tonight, Maria. We've rented rooms near the Regional Police Department for you to stay in for tonight. Local law enforcement personnel will guard your room."

Maria felt too tired to raise any objections as she let the woman lead her from the lake house.

CHAPTER 58

By nine the next morning, Maria had been brought back to the Regional Police Office. Perez had gotten an extensive report back on her, and despite her familial connections, Perez was convinced Maria was not a player in the crime family. Also, the gunshot residue tests on Maria's hands had come back negative, so she was not involved in the shootout at the cabin, other than as a bystander. But why was she at the cabin with someone who appeared to be a soldier in the D'Angelo crime family? Perez wanted to find out the answer and understand what had really happened yesterday. Maria, Perez, and Mac sat in a conference room.

"Good morning, Maria. I hope you got some rest," Perez said.

Maria looked pale and exhausted. At first, she acted like she didn't hear Perez's question until she looked at the agent and spoke. "Is Gabe going to be okay? And can I go and see him?"

"I'm sure they're doing all they can for him at the hospital," Perez answered. "And no, it won't be possible to see him yet." Perez made a note on her pad to check on the status of Gabriel Rossi. At this moment, she didn't know whether he was dead or alive—she hoped he would survive and become a witness.

"Maria, I want you to know right up front that you are not in trouble and you are not a suspect, but you seem to be the only witness to what happened last evening at the cabin. So, we'd like to ask you a few questions."

"Fine, but will I be able to go home soon? And can I make a call to my parents?"

"We'll arrange to let you make some calls and get you out of here as soon as possible, but let's just go over some things first."

Maria nodded and Perez switched on a recorder.

"Why don't we start at the beginning? How did you come to be at the cabin on Arrowpoint Lake?"

"Yesterday afternoon, Gabe got a call from my father," Maria said as she began to choke up. "He told Gabe I was in danger and asked him to take me away from the convent."

"Okay, and your father is Michael D'Angelo, correct?"

"Yes."

"And so, Gabe contacted you when you were at the convent?" Perez asked.

"Yes. He was already at the convent."

Perez widened her eyes and jotted something down in her notebook.

"Gabe had called me early in the day and asked if he could hide in one of the apartments in our dormitory. I'm just training to be a nun, but I'm also the residential manager."

"Why did he want to hide?"

"He told me he was in danger."

"So you took him in and let him stay there. Did he stay in your apartment?"

"No. Of course not. I put him in a vacant apartment on the third floor. My rooms are on the first floor. He has never been in my apartment. I admit I bent the rules, but he told me he was in danger and that he would explain later."

Perez noticed Maria did not seem comfortable talking about the fact that she had allowed Gabe into the nuns' dormitory.

"Did he tell you why he needed to hide?"

Maria shook her head. "No. Not at that time."

"So, when did he mention you were in danger?"

"Late that afternoon. He called me from the apartment and told me I was in danger and we both needed to leave right away. So I packed a few things, and we went out the back because Gabe said he'd looked out the window and saw a suspicious-looking car in the parking lot and some men walking toward the dorm."

At this point, Maria was breathing heavily and began to weep, placing her head in her hands. Perez handed her a box of tissues and gave her a moment to regain her composure before continuing.

"Maria, I realize this is very difficult for you. I just have a few more questions," she said, pausing to let Maria wipe her tears. After Maria had finished, Perez spoke softly. "So, you were able to get away?"

"Gabe's car wouldn't start, so we got in my car and left."

Perez made a note to check the convent parking areas for the car. "Did you get a look at the men who were walking toward your dorm?"

"No, but Gabe said they were in a black SUV."

"Then what happened?"

"We drove out of there and got on the turnpike, heading north. Gabe said he was taking me to a place my father's company owned in the Poconos. He said we'd be safe there," Maria said, and she began to break down again.

"Had you ever been there before?"

"No. I didn't even know my father's company had such a place."

"Obviously you knew Gabe before all this happened."

"Yes, he's a distant relative. I had seen him a few times over the years, but I got to know Gabe a lot better after we got reacquainted a few months ago." Maria began to cry again at the mention of Gabe, and she reached for the box of tissues.

"Do you need a break?" Perez asked.

Maria took several deep breaths. "No. I'd like to get this over with if we can."

"Were you close to Gabe?"

"Yes, he was a good friend," Maria answered.

"Were you lovers?"

"No. Absolutely not. We were good friends. We got together when we could. When you live in a convent, you can't go on dates."

Perez knew she had hit a sensitive spot. Even if they were not technically lovers, Perez could sense Maria had feelings for Gabe. "Now, we understand Mr. Rossi worked in your father's organization. Is that correct?"

"Yes."

"What did he do for the organization?"

"I don't know exactly. He told me the business owned casinos and resorts and he worked on managing them. That's all I knew," Maria said, beginning to regain her composure.

"Did he tell you why you were in danger?"

"He said that in the casino business you sometimes deal with some unsavory people and that if you get on their wrong side, it could get dangerous."

"Did he tell you what specifically happened that put you in danger?"

"No. I asked, but he couldn't or wouldn't give me the details."

"Did that bother you?"

"I suppose. But you have to realize that, in families like mine, the women aren't supposed to press the men for details about their work. I've lived with that all my life."

"What do you know about your father's businesses?"

"As I said, I know he's involved with casinos, resorts, and some other types of businesses, maybe some construction companies. I know he's very successful and he also does a lot of good. He's involved with charities. He gave a lot to the children's hospital. He supports the church as well."

"Does the name Gus Nasuti mean anything to you?"

"I think he's a friend of my father's, but I don't really know him."

"How about your brother?"

"Raph? He works for my father as well. He lives in the city, so I don't see him much. I'm probably closer to his wife, Rose, than I am to him."

Perez took more notes. "So, do you know anything about what your brother does for the family business?"

"No," Maria said, crossing her arms and looking down toward the floor. "Look, I'm embarrassed to tell you this, but I don't know a lot about my father's business. I guess I was sheltered or kept away from it. What I know is my father was always kind and loving with me. I love him, but I don't know more than I've told you."

"I understand. So, let's go back to what happened yesterday. Take your time. I know it's not easy to talk about."

"I think we got there early evening, when it was starting to get dark."

"Did anything unusual happen on the way?"

"No. It took about two hours to drive there. We didn't see the black SUV or any suspicious cars. We thought we got away from them. Do you know how they found us?"

"We're looking into that. Some people are very good at following you. They can do it without you even realizing they are there," Perez said, making a note on her pad. "What happened after you arrived at the cabin?"

"I put my stuff in one of the bedrooms. Gabe put a pizza in the oven. Later, he lit a fire in the fireplace, and we sat, talking in the living room and eating our pizza. I guess around ten, I went to bed. Gabe slept on the sofa, I guess so he could keep watch over the cabin better."

Perez had seen the blanket and pillows on the sofa, so Maria's story seemed to fit the known facts. "Did you fall asleep?"

"I think I dozed in and out of a light sleep. I wasn't asleep when Gabe knocked on my door." Tears sprang again to Maria's eyes, and this time, she agreed to take a break and went to the ladies' room. She was back in a few minutes.

Perez waited until she was seated and began again. "Maria, as best you can, tell me what happened before the shooting."

"I guess it was around midnight. I saw the porch lights go on. They were very bright and shined in my room. Then, Gabe knocked on my door, and I asked him what was going on. He said the lights went on because someone was outside. I was terrified and wanted to go out to Gabe, but he told me to stay in the room."

"Try the best you can to tell me what happened next."

"There was a crashing sound and then a bunch of gunshots, and then it was quiet. I called for Gabe, but he didn't answer. I looked out my door and saw him on the floor, bleeding. I saw another man on the back porch trying to get in, and I screamed. Then, there were more gunshots, and you guys came in."

"Was Gabe alert when you first came out of your room?"

"Yes, but he couldn't say much." Maria put her head in her hands and began to sob uncontrollably.

Perez realized Maria was too upset to continue. After what she had been through, it was not surprising.

"Maria, thanks for your help. I'm going to leave you for a few moments. Is there anything I can get you, coffee or a soda?"

"No, thanks. I'd just like to call home."

"Okay, I'll go and find a place where you can make the call. I'll be right back."

◆　◆　◆

Perez placed a call to Agent Dempsey in Philadelphia and gave him the details of the interview with Maria.

"It seems hard to believe," Dempsey said. "I mean, she's twenty-three years old and didn't know her father was a Mafia boss?"

"It seems she was very sheltered. Remember that ninety-nine percent of the public in Philadelphia doesn't even know that D'Angelo is a Mafia boss, and most people her age know little or nothing about the Mafia. He's done a great job of living under the radar. I don't think she or Rossi had any idea the Carbone guys followed them all the way to Arrowpoint Lake."

"In case you didn't know, we picked up the driver of the black SUV. So far, he's not talking. The US Attorney's office is preparing conspiracy charges against him, so maybe he'll see the light and co-operate," Dempsey said.

"That's good."

"Well, our plan worked. The Carbone guys led us right to the safe house. Too bad we couldn't have prevented the shooting."

"Yeah. I guess that's the way it goes," Perez said.

CHAPTER 59

"Mom?" Maria said after she had placed a call home from the room where Perez had left her.

"Maria, where are you? I've been worried sick. The convent doesn't know where you are."

"I'm at a police station in the Pocono Mountains," Maria said, her voice starting to quiver.

"Why are you at a police station? Are you all right?"

"I'm okay but Gabe . . ." Maria's voice broke.

"Maria, what about Gabe?"

"Some men broke into the cabin where we were staying and they shot Gabe. I don't even know for sure if he's alive right now."

"Oh no! Why were you at a cabin?" Carmella's voice sounded panicked.

"Dad told Gabe I was in danger, and he took me to a cabin up here. Then these men broke in last night and . . ." Maria's voice trailed off as she started to weep.

"Don't worry, I'll come and get you," Carmella said, almost in tears herself.

"I don't know if you can right now. I think I can go now, but I need to speak to the lady who brought me here. She's an FBI agent. Is Dad there? Can I speak to him?"

"Honey, I tried to call you but couldn't get through. The FBI came early this morning and took your dad away. I called your father's lawyer, Mr. Sandone, and he's on his way to help him."

"Did they arrest Dad?" she asked.

"No, as far as I know they just took him for questioning."

"Mom, what kind of people is he dealing with who come after Gabe and me with guns?" she said, almost screaming.

"I'm sure your father can explain everything to you. You know he's a good man. The main thing is that you're safe." Carmella said.

"Mom, I don't know what to do. Can I come home when they let me leave?"

"Of course."

"Yesterday, Dad said I was in danger. What are we going to do?"

"I'll call Gus Nasuti. He'll know what to do. Maybe we can get some people from your father's business to keep an eye on our house."

Maria was now beginning to understand more about the character of her father's business. Would these be guys in a big black SUV, just like the ones who had come after her?

"Okay, Mom. I better hang up. I'll see when I can leave and I'll let you know."

After the call, Maria stepped outside of the office, looking for Agent Perez. She found her back in the conference room, working on a laptop.

Maria looked at Perez with a cold, flinty look in her eyes. "You didn't tell me you had arrested my father," she said.

"He's not under arrest. We just brought him in for questioning. With all that's happened, you can understand why we'd want to talk to him."

Maria began to regain her composure. She sighed and shook her head. "Can I leave now?"

"Yes. But you need to be careful. Do you have somewhere safe to go?"

"I'd like to go to my parents' home in Chestnut Hill."

"Look, I'm going back to Philadelphia this afternoon," Perez said. "I can have a driver take us both and drop you off at home."

"Can't you just take me to my car?"

"I'm sorry, but your vehicle was part of the crime scene. We can have it delivered to you in a few days." Perez offered a small smile. "Just let me know. I'll be leaving around one. In the meantime, we can have lunch brought in for you if you'd like."

"Thanks, but I'm not hungry. Maybe just a bottle of water," Maria said.

"That's fine. Just so you can feel safe, we'll have some agents keep an eye on your parents' home after you are dropped off."

◆　◆　◆

Maria hardly said a word as she rode in the back seat of the FBI vehicle. Agent Perez, sitting beside her, did not try to get her to answer more questions. Maria stared out the car window as the shock of the past day began to take hold. The man she loved was shot trying to protect her, and her father was in FBI custody. During the past several days, Maria had learned her father was not just a successful businessman. He was involved with bad people, and she was wondering how deep those connections went. Maria thought back on the feelings that led to her telling Gabe she intended to leave the convent last night. Now she wondered how she could even consider becoming a nun if her name was linked with the kind of people who shot and killed one another.

When the car pulled into the street where Maria's parents lived, there were dozens of reporters standing in her front yard. It wasn't clear to her if they were waiting for Maria or for the return of her father.

"Pull up as close to the front door as you can," Perez shouted to the driver over the increasingly loud yelling of the reporters. Then she turned to Maria. "Let me walk you to the door. Keep your head down. You don't need to say anything."

Maria didn't answer but complied.

"Stay back! Get out of the way!" Perez shouted as she hustled Maria through the crowd up the front steps. Reporters started shouting questions.

"Ms. D'Angelo, what's it like being the daughter of a Mafia leader?"

"Are you still planning to become a nun?"

"Why were you spending a weekend in a cabin with a man?"

Maria's mother was waiting and quickly opened the door. Perez handed her a card. "Please call me if you need anything. We'll have cars stationed out front to make sure you are safe," Perez added as Maria slipped inside.

Maria grabbed her mother with a firm embrace.

"I was so worried about you! Are you okay now?" asked Carmella.

"I was so afraid. They were coming after us, and they broke in. They shot Gabe when he was protecting me!" Maria began to cry.

"It's okay, dear," Carmella said as she continued to embrace her daughter tightly.

"The FBI said they are watching the house to protect me." Maria was barely able to utter the words.

"I'm sure they are, Maria."

"When is Dad coming home?"

"Your father's lawyer says they can't hold him much longer unless they charge him, and they haven't charged him with anything."

"Is he going to prison?"

"No, darling, he'll be home soon. Can I get you something to eat or a warm drink?" Carmella asked.

Maria shook her head and wondered if her life would ever be the same again.

CHAPTER 60

Bruno answered a phone call early Saturday morning in Martinique.

"Bruno, it's Tony and Hank." It was Tony's voice speaking.

"Yeah, so, do you have her?"

"No."

"What do you mean no?" Bruno screamed. "I thought you guys were right on her tail."

"They followed her to a lake house in the Poconos." Tony took a deep breath and continued. "There was only one car in the driveway, the woman's car. Max and Frank went in at midnight. Lenny was parked in the car a quarter mile down the road, out of sight. Right after they went in, Lenny lost contact and couldn't reach them. Then he heard gunshots. Lots of them. Lenny got closer to see what happened, and the place was crawling with FBI agents. That's the last we heard from Lenny. We think they picked him up."

"What? How did the FBI get there? Did they pick up Max and Frank?"

"We don't know how they got there. There was a lot of gunfire. I doubt they're alive."

"Well, it sounds like our guys led the FBI right to a D'Angelo safe house and got killed in the process. This is a royal screwup." Tony and

Hank remained silent as Junior raged. "I better get back. I need to get to the bottom of this."

"I'm not sure it's safe," Tony said.

"I don't care. I can't sit over here while the whole organization goes to hell. I'll plan on flying back tomorrow, or sooner if I can get a plane."

"I'd stay away from the Newark airport. The FBI will be there. I'd pick a smaller airport. Let me know so we can have your driver there to pick you up," Hank said.

Bruno slammed down the phone.

◆　◆　◆

Later that day, Hank received a message that Bruno had moved up his return flight and was coming in on a charter flight from San Juan into the private Signature aviation terminal at Atlantic City International Airport. His flight was scheduled to land at nine thirty that evening. Hank immediately went to work on his plan. He didn't have much time to put all the pieces in place, but he had the support from the older underbosses of the Carbone family, and an evening arrival was better than daytime. Tony Bianchi was left out of the loop. Fortunately, Tony felt that arranging travel logistics was beneath him, so his lack of awareness didn't raise any concerns on his part.

Bruno arrived on a twin-engine Merlin turboprop that landed right on time. The airline charter service was one the Carbone family had worked with in the past, and they could be relied on to keep the flight from San Juan to Atlantic City as discreet as possible. After the charter landed, a black Lincoln Town Car with tinted windows sat immediately in front of the doors to the terminal with an open trunk. After a porter placed his luggage in the trunk, Bruno opened the right rear door of the car and got in. Bruno's usual driver was a middle-aged man who was bald and weighed about two hundred pounds.

Instead, a slim younger man with a thick head of hair sat behind the wheel.

"Where's Vinny?" Bruno asked.

"He's sick in bed with the flu. I'm filling in for him. If you like, we can call Mr. Maranzano, and you can talk to him," the driver said.

"That won't be necessary. Let's get the show on the road."

The private aviation terminal had a separate entrance from the main airport terminal. The driver drove down the driveway to the exit. It was quiet at this hour. The airport was surrounded by a chain-link fence, and the gate at the entrance to the private terminal was left open most of the time. When the car got to the gate, it stopped, as if to look for traffic. However, the driver abruptly put the car in park, hit the button to open the windows, and got out. He began walking away from the car quickly, in front of the car and toward the highway.

"What the hell is going on?" Bruno screamed.

In an instant, two dark-clad figures emerged from the hedge along the road wearing ski masks, each carrying a submachine gun. The first stopped about ten feet from the car on the side where Bruno was seated and pointed the machine gun toward the rear window. Bruno tried in vain to duck down, but the gunman stepped closer and opened fire into the car, hitting his target with multiple rounds until his thirty-round magazine was empty. The second gunman approached the car and fired an additional volley of rounds for good measure into Bruno's body, which was almost certainly dead already. He glanced in and saw his target was sprawled sideways on the seat with dozens of bloody wounds all over his body. The shooters and driver of the car disappeared into the night.

The car and Carbone's shot-up body were discovered five minutes later, when a member of airport security was making his rounds and stopped to see why an apparently empty car had stopped at the gate. Within minutes, multiple Egg Harbor Township police vehicles, ambulances, and vehicles from the New York and New Jersey Port Authority had surrounded the scene. In less than a half hour, the

New Jersey State Police Crime Scene Investigation Unit was present and took over the investigation. Not surprisingly, there were also numerous reporters from the major news outlets present, some giving live broadcasts from the scene, and most attempting to obtain statements from the police personnel present.

The private aviation terminal closed as investigators combed the area for clues and security footage. Incoming charter flights were diverted to the main terminal. Soon investigators identified the victim of the shooting. It was not clear who first contacted the FBI, but when the victim was identified as Bruno Carbone Jr., the FBI was on the case.

By the time the FBI arrived, the scene was pandemonium. Agent Donna Marcone got there in record time, having commandeered a helicopter from Newark. Within minutes of arriving, she managed to track down Deputy Chief Ron Gonzoles of the New Jersey State Police.

"Tell me what you got so far, Officer Gonzoles," she said.

"Looks like Bruno Carbone was the victim. He was shot in a limo that's parked at the exit," the officer said as he pointed to the car in the distance. "No sign of the driver or the perps, so it must have been a well-planned job."

"Is that ID one-hundred-percent certain?" Agent Marcone asked.

"We're pretty certain, but maybe your guys can help us verify that."

"Sure thing. How did it go down?"

"We've got security cameras showing an aircraft landing here about nine twenty-five coming in from San Juan. Carbone was the sole passenger. He got off, walked through the terminal, and got in the car by the front door."

"I've got our crime scene team coming in. By the way, you've got way too many people walking around here. We're not sure what the boundaries of the crime scene are, and I strongly suggest you clear the area so the FBI can investigate. In fact, the FBI is assuming the lead on this case," Agent Marcone said with her head cocked to one side.

"Ah, I don't have authority to relinquish the scene," Officer Gonzoles said.

"Call your boss. The US Attorney is probably speaking to him right now. The FBI is involved in a multistate investigation of the crime families in Pennsylvania and New Jersey. Can you get me the security camera footage?" Marcone asked.

Officer Gonzoles smirked. "Sure thing," he said.

CHAPTER 61

Deputy Director Noel Burke, on video from Washington DC, called a special meeting of the task force from Pennsylvania and New Jersey on Sunday morning. Sunday-morning meetings were rare.

"I'm going to begin by asking Agent Marcone to brief us on yesterday's events and any additional information she believes is relevant," the deputy director said.

"As you know, the shooting of Bruno Carbone took place last evening around nine forty-five at the private terminal at Atlantic City International Airport. Carbone came in from San Juan on a private charter. We had no advance warning he was coming. It looks like someone stalled filing the flight plan until it was too late for us to know about it. This is important, since it probably means no one outside of the Carbone organization knew he was coming in, and the shooting was very carefully timed and choreographed. Carbone took more than two dozen nine-millimeter rounds. If that sounds like overkill, it was. Whoever did this wanted to make sure Carbone was dead. We've examined security footage and canvassed the airport personnel, and there is no evidence of any involvement by the D'Angelo family. Our tentative conclusion is this was an inside job by someone in the Carbone family. Agent Perez has some additional information that bears on that as well. At this point, I should mention that early Friday morning, a service station owner in Cherry Hill, New Jersey, with known ties to the Carbone mob was also gunned down. The victim, Nicolas Perrelli, was a relative of Bruno Carbone Jr. It was a professional hit with no evidence left by the shooter except some shell casings that were wiped clean." Agent Marcone ended by giving the floor to Agent Perez. "We are working on any connections between the shootings. Agent Perez has some information that might shed some light on a possible connection."

Agent Perez stood up and addressed the group. "We have worked up a timeline, and we've never seen this much violent activity take place in such a short time, assuming that the events are connected. Perrelli was shot just before eight Friday morning at his service station. On Friday evening, there was a shootout at a cabin at Lake Arrowpoint near Blakeslee in the Poconos at which Gabriel Rossi, a soldier in the D'Angelo organization, was gunned down. Apparently he's still alive and hanging on by a thread. Two members of the Carbone family were killed in the shootout. By the time our team arrived, one of the Carbone soldiers was dead inside the cabin, presumably shot by Rossi. The other Carbone soldier was outside the cabin and was shot by our team when he drew his gun. It appears the cabin was a safe house operated by the D'Angelo family."

"It sounds like it wasn't very safe for a safe house," Agent Reed said. "How did our team come to be there at the time of the shootout?"

"I was coming to that. We got a tip-off that the Carbone operatives were traveling to the location and we followed them. It turns out the Carbone vehicle was following a car containing Rossi and Michael D'Angelo's daughter, Maria. We picked up Maria, who was unharmed and not part of the shootout. I interviewed her, and she revealed Rossi had been told by her father to bring her to the safe house. We found a GPS tracker on her car. As you may have read in the briefing materials, Ms. D'Angelo was training to be a nun at St. Helen's Convent in Lindenwood."

"If the Carbones had a tracker on her car, they must have been watching her," Agent Reed said.

"Yes, that is likely," Agent Perez answered.

"So, maybe the Carbone family planned to kidnap her in retaliation for hitting Bruno's cousin at the service station?" Agent Reed asked.

"That is a very possible scenario. What is unusual is how quickly they were able to act. If our theories are correct, the Carbones must have had a plan in place that they were ready to implement on short notice," Agent Perez added. "It also fits our theory that the restaurant fire was the work of the Carbone family. So we have a series of 'tit for tat' events, if you will pardon the expression."

"If the two presumed kidnappers are dead, was there anyone else in the Carbone car?" the deputy director asked.

"There was a driver and he's now in custody. We picked him up trying to flee the scene of the shooting. His name is Leonard Vinetti. So far, he's not talking, but we have enough to charge him with conspiracy to commit kidnapping and felony murder. I think he'll cave before too long. He's looking at life without parole at the very least," Agent Perez said.

"Who's likely to become the new boss in New Jersey?" asked the deputy director.

"The senior member of the family now is Henry 'Hank' Maranzano. Ironically, Maranzano still has some ties to older members of the Philadelphia mob. He will also probably have the support of the Gambino family in New York, what's left of it anyway," Agent Marcone said. "Bruno was close to his consigliere, Tony Bianchi. Right now, Bianchi is hiding and we don't know if he's dead or alive. My guess is his future in the organization is not so bright with Bruno off the scene," Marcone added.

Agent Dempsey spoke up. "None of the people in these crime families are Eagle Scouts, to be sure, but they do have a code of honor, especially the older ones. I have a hunch that Bruno Carbone Jr.

was a bit too reckless for their taste. He was a hothead, and he had pretty much started a war between the families. If Bruno ordered the kidnapping of Ms. D'Angelo, that may have been too much for guys like Maranzano to swallow. They may have decided a change was needed."

"You may be right," Burke said. "Agents Marcone and Perez, you've done a great job on a shooting that occurred less than twenty-four hours ago. I know identifying the shooter won't be easy, but please keep us posted. Now, while you are all here, I'd like Agent Perez to provide an update on the wider investigation into the D'Angelo family in Philadelphia."

Agent Perez nodded. "We've had Michael D'Angelo in custody since yesterday, but he'll be released today. At the moment, we don't have enough to connect him specifically to the shooting at the lake house or to the killing of Carbone. He's lawyered up and not talking. We are holding off bringing charges for now, since we're on the verge of getting a lot more evidence that could support a very substantial indictment under federal anti-racketeering laws. First, we now have a deal with Joey Romano, the restaurant owner, after confronting him with the evidence of the gambling operation at his location, including the gambling equipment found in the rubble of the fire. We've offered the witness protection program, and I think he'll take it. He'll testify about the gambling operation, how it worked, and who the players were. He can even place Michael D'Angelo at the poker game the night before the fire. Apparently D'Angelo had a practice of welcoming new guests so the security cameras could record pictures of him getting all chummy with them.

"Second, we, I mean the US Attorney's office, are on the verge of a deal with Henry Townshend. He can corroborate the evidence of the gambling operation and provide testimony that he received a substantial bribe in the form of free poker chips on his first and only visit to the D'Angelo poker game. Third, we got an unexpected benefit when the DEA arrested Benjamin Geller under the Drug Kingpin Act a few weeks ago. He has been a major importer of cocaine and meth from Mexican cartels. Geller is close to a deal with the US Attorney, and would be able to testify he was the victim of an extortion scheme by the D'Angelo family. Last but not least, when we arrived at the scene of the shootings at Arrowpoint Lake, we found Gabriel Rossi's laptop computer in plain sight. We've only had the computer since Friday night, so it's in our forensics lab for analysis. Rossi's home was clean when we searched it yesterday, but we suspect we will find lots of useful evidence in the computer."

"It's impressive that you have been able to bring all this together so quickly," Burke said. "How long before you think the US Attorney will be ready to indict?"

"I won't speak for the attorney's office, but I think it could be a matter of weeks, not months," Perez answered. "Of course, they are not only targeting Michael D'Angelo, but also other key players in the organization. That's where we need to fill in some more details in the evidence."

"I agree they should get their ducks in a row. It's like the story of the young bull and the old bull, if you'll pardon the analogy," the deputy director said.

CHAPTER 62

Michael D'Angelo was released from FBI custody Sunday morning, and his lawyer, Robert Sandone, drove him home to Chestnut Hill. When Michael was in custody, Sandone had been given a chance to consult privately with him and had briefed him on the shootout at the cabin, assuring Michael that Maria had been present but was unharmed. Sandone also told Michael that Gabe had been shot, although they didn't have any up-to-date information on his condition. As Michael got into the passenger's seat of his lawyer's S500 Mercedes Benz, he had to pick up several newspapers lying on the seat.

"I picked those up for you when I went to get the car," Sandone said. "Take a look at the headlines."

Michael stared at the front page of the *Philadelphia Inquirer,* which featured the headline: "New Jersey Mob Leader Gunned Down at Atlantic City Airport." Michael's mouth dropped open and he gasped. "It didn't take long for the news reporters to get all over this thing," he said.

"Read down a few paragraphs," Sandone said.

Michael skimmed the article, shaking his head until he came to the paragraph with a smaller caption that stated, "Reputed Head of Philadelphia Mafia in Custody." Michael threw the newspaper down on the floor. "Holy shit! They make it sound like I was behind this,"

Michael stated. "I didn't even know about Carbone until you brought me up to date after the FBI took me in."

"I know you weren't involved with Carbone's killing," said Sandone. "They didn't even have any evidence to hold you for questioning relating to Carbone or the shootout at the lake house. The reporters must have got wind that you were taken in and they figured they could sell some newspapers by making you look guilty."

"Any news on Gabe?" Michael asked with a worried look on his face.

"Keep reading," Sandone said as Michael picked up the papers he had thrown down.

Sandone had briefed Michael about Gabe, but they didn't know anything about his condition. The article went on to report on the shootout at the lake house and the fact that "sources" said the FBI was investigating possible connections between the lake house shooting and the shooting of Carbone. When Michael came to the part about Gabe—"an alleged soldier in the D'Angelo family in critical condition"—he laid the paper down. "Can I go and visit Gabe in the hospital?"

"Technically Gabe is in police custody, so they won't let you anywhere near him. Did you see the part about Maria?" Sandone asked.

Michael picked up the newspaper and continued reading until he came to the place where it said, "Maria D'Angelo, daughter of Michael D'Angelo and resident of St. Helen's Convent in Lindenwood, Pennsylvania, was in the vicinity of the shootout in the Pocono Mountains. She was reported to be unharmed and was questioned by the FBI."

Michael shook his head. "Maria's connection to me and our business is out in the open now. I guess I was naïve to think we could keep this secret forever. Her mother is not going to be happy about this."

"I'd be more worried about Gabe," Sandone said.

"Yeah. I hate to put it like this, but if Gabe lives, it could be a real problem for us."

◆ ◆ ◆

Sandone pulled the car into the D'Angelos' driveway and stopped in front of the door. By this time, the reporters who had been present when Maria arrived at home were gone. Carmella opened the door before he walked up the front steps as though she had been waiting.

"Is Maria home?" Michael asked as he stepped into the foyer.

"Yes, she's in her room. The FBI dropped her off yesterday."

"Sandone told me about it."

Carmella took a step backward and looked at Michael with a cold, flinty stare. "Michael, how could you put her in danger like that?"

"I had Gabe take her to the cabin to keep her *out* of danger."

"And what about Gabe? Maria told me some men came to the cabin and shot him. Is he going to live?"

"I don't know. You probably know as much as I do," Michael said. He looked down and shook his head. "I have no idea how they found her."

"Well, they obviously followed Maria's car. Why didn't you send help before they got there?"

"I had assets on the way, but they didn't get there in time. There wasn't much I could do. I spoke to Gabe after they arrived early Friday evening. He knows how to spot a tail and he didn't see anything. He's a good man, and I trusted him to take care of Maria."

"What about now? Is Maria safe? Are we safe?"

"There's no more danger. The guy who put Maria in danger is dead."

"What do you mean?"

"Didn't you read the news? Bruno Carbone was killed at the Atlantic City Airport."

"Michael, why did he want to hurt Gabe or Maria? Did you have him killed?"

Michael moved into the living room and collapsed in a chair. "No, I didn't have him killed. It was his own people. They killed him because he was out of control. He's the one who burned down Joey's restaurant."

Carmella shook her head in apparent disbelief. "My God, how can we live like this, with burning and shooting and killing?"

"Carmella, it's over now. The guy who caused it all is gone. Hank Maranzano is now in charge in New Jersey. He's a friend."

Carmella stood over her husband, hands on hips. "And what about you? Why did they question you? Are you in trouble now?"

"There's been a lot going on related to the family." Michael rubbed his brow. "They obviously wanted to pump me for information."

"What did you tell them?"

"Of course Bobby Sandone wouldn't allow me to answer any questions. If they had enough to charge me, they would have charged me, and I'd be down in lockup."

Carmella's stance softened. "Well, if everything is okay now, you had better go upstairs and talk to your daughter. She's been afraid to leave her room since yesterday. I haven't been able to get her to eat anything. Maybe you can make her feel better."

Michael paused and thought for a moment how to approach Maria before he quietly tip-toed up the stairs and gently knocked on her bedroom door. She didn't answer. He opened the door and peeked in. She was lying on her side in a fetal position, facing away from the door, wearing a sweatshirt and gym shorts. Michael couldn't see her face but noticed her hair was rumpled.

"Maria, it's me," Michael said as he sat on her bed and gently placed his hand on her shoulder.

She didn't move from her position or speak but put her hands up to cover her face. Michael spoke again. "Maria, it's all right. You're safe now."

He sat stroking her hair, waiting for her to respond. After what seemed like a long time, although it was only a few minutes, he began to worry. "Maria, please. Speak to me and tell me you're okay." He tried gently to move her hands away from her face.

Finally, she spoke, almost in a whisper. "Daddy, I'm so scared. Is Gabe going to die?"

"I don't know, dear. I'm so sorry about what happened to him. I know Gabe is a close friend of yours. He's a close friend of mine as well. But you're safe now. The danger is gone."

"How do you know?" she asked.

"The man who was responsible is gone." Michael didn't know whether Maria had seen the newspapers, but based on the state she was in, he guessed she had not.

"I'm here now, Maria. You don't have to be afraid. I love you and will keep you safe."

"The men who came after us . . . why do you deal with people like that?"

"I'm sorry, Maria. You don't always get to choose the people you have to deal with."

"You're not leaving again, are you?"

"No, sweetheart. I'm not going anywhere."

"Please don't leave again."

"I won't. I'll be right here. Are you going to get up soon?"

"I just need to rest. I'm not ready to get up yet."

"Will you promise to come down for dinner tonight? I'd really love it if you joined your mother and me."

"I'll see if I feel better."

"Okay dear, just get some rest. I'll be right downstairs if you need me. Your mother is there too." Michael sat for a moment, and neither spoke before he got up and left.

CHAPTER 63

Maria came downstairs at dinnertime wearing the sweatshirt she had been wearing in bed, although she had put on a pair of jeans. She looked pale, and her hair was not brushed. Lucy had made lasagna, one of Maria's favorite dishes. She picked at it for a few minutes before excusing herself to go back upstairs.

"I'm very worried about her," Michael said. "I could hardly get her to talk when I went to her room."

"Yes, we should be worried after what she's been through," Carmella said sternly.

"Does the convent know where she is? And isn't she expected at the school tomorrow morning?" Michael asked.

"I called Father Pierce. He's taking care of the notifications. They'll find a substitute at the school, but that's not the main problem. She's not well, and I can fully understand that after what she's been through. We need to get help for her."

"You're right, as usual."

"I spoke to Father Pierce about that as well, and he'll help us find the right kind of help. He's pretty good at things like that."

Michael dropped his fork on his plate. "Carmella, I'm sorry about everything. I did my best to try and protect her but I obviously didn't do enough. At least she's safe at home now."

"Safe? After being attacked by some thugs sent by Carbone and seeing Gabe get shot?" After speaking, Carmella rose abruptly and left the dining room.

◆   ◆   ◆

After about two weeks, most of which she spent in bed, Maria felt well enough to receive a visitor from the convent. Sister Margaret had phoned and asked if she could drop in, and Maria received her in the living room. The sister brought a bouquet of flowers.

"Good morning, Maria. It's so good to see you. How are you feeling?"

"I guess I'm doing better," she said with a quiver in her voice. Since coming home, Maria had tried to block out of her mind the horrible night at the cabin, and much of the experience was a blur. Still, she could not help visualizing Gabe on the floor in a pool of blood, gasping for breath. She had heard Gabe was alive and out of danger, but she knew nothing more.

"That's good," the sister said.

"I'm sorry I haven't been able to take care of my responsibilities," Maria said.

"Don't you worry about that. We've all missed you at St. Helen's. We know you've been through a lot, and our priority is to make sure you get well."

Maria was silent and sat with her arms crossed as if she was experiencing a chill.

The sister continued. "So, if there is any way we can help with the healing process, we want to be there for you. You're in our prayers every day. And that leads to an important point. We've discussed this at the convent and with the archdiocese, and we've decided it's best for you and best for the convent to give you a leave of absence from the novice program."

Maria thought this was odd since she had not yet taken her preliminary vows to become a novice. Regardless, she figured the convent had been watching the news carefully and probably wanted nothing to do with such negative publicity.

"What does that mean?" she asked.

"It means that, for now, you are relieved from all responsibilities. You won't stay in the dormitory—we think it's best for you to stay home, where you are, and where you can receive the care and attention you need."

Maria thought back to the brief moments of happiness she had experienced with Gabe at the cabin before the carnage began. She still felt the same way she did when she told Gabe she didn't want to return to the convent. But that was a big decision, and so for the moment, she decided to hear what the sister had to say. "How long will my leave of absence last?" Maria asked.

"We don't want to put a time limit on it. We want to make sure you are well and that it's the right time before we discuss any steps to bring you back." Maria sat back against her chair and crossed her arms. After an awkward silence, the sister spoke again. "Do you have any other questions? Or is there anything we can do for you?"

After thinking for a few moments, it seemed clear to Maria the convent was going to keep her out of the program indefinitely, and the most the sister could promise was that they would "discuss" bringing her back when the time was right. Maria was skeptical about the sister's words. If they had effectively suspended her from the program after a few relatively innocent encounters with Gabe, would they ever let her back now that she was openly associated with her father's unsavory business? Despite the flowers and the show of compassion, Maria quickly concluded the convent had no intention of bringing her back and was just sugarcoating their decision to get rid of her. Not only that, she sensed Sister Margaret wanted to be the one to determine Maria's future. With a mental clarity she had not had in weeks, Maria felt a sense of resolve to take control of the decision about her future.

"Thank you for your concern and willingness to help," Maria said, "but I think I can make the process even easier for both of us. As you know, I have been thinking and praying a lot over the past months about my future. I had a number of counseling sessions with Sister Anna that were very helpful. I remember, at the beginning of my time as a novice, you told me that if I should come to discern it's not God's will for me to take final vows, I would be released from my preliminary vows and sent off with the blessing of the church. That's the situation I am in now. This wasn't a hasty decision by any means, but I've come to a firm conclusion that God's plan for me is not to pursue a religious vocation. So there's no need for a leave of absence."

"I see," Sister Margaret said with a grimace.

Maria could see the sister seemed to be taken aback by her statement.

"Then I'll have to bring this to the leadership of the convent. They may wish to conduct a further interview." Sister Margaret rose from her chair abruptly to leave. "Maria, I hope you are feeling better, and we will be in touch. I'll see myself out."

Maria felt a sense of relief. After Sister Margaret left, Carmella entered the living room, where Maria was still seated on a sofa.

"I saw Sister Margaret leave. She seemed a little put out. Is everything okay?"

"Yes. I just told Sister Margaret I'm leaving the convent," Maria said with a hint of a smile. It was the first time she'd smiled since coming home.

"Oh, Maria!" her mother said as she sat down and hugged her daughter. "You're sure that's what you want?" she asked.

"It's not only what I want, but I believe it's God's will."

"I hope your father and I didn't do anything to spoil your experience at the convent. I know sometimes it might have seemed like we weren't in favor of it, but we always wanted you to be happy, whatever you decided," Carmella said, her eyes beginning to tear up.

"No, I've been thinking and praying about this for a long time. I'm still in shock after what happened to me, but one good thing is it brought my thoughts into focus, and it's clear to me now that I'm not cut out to be a nun. I'm still committed to serving God, but not as a nun," Maria said.

Carmella continued to hug Maria and the tears began to flow. "I can't tell you how relieved I am. I was proud you were training to be a nun, but I was afraid we'd lose you as part of our family. If there's anything we can do to help you, just let us know. And of course, you're welcome to stay here as long as you want."

Maria pulled back from the hug. "Tell me something, Mom. You must have known all about Dad's business dealings. Why was I kept in the dark?"

"Maria, your father is a good man. A lot of people don't understand our lifestyle. We just wanted you to have a chance to live a different life."

"Is Dad home now?" Maria asked.

"No, he had to go out."

"I really need to talk to him about this."

CHAPTER 64

A year later, Maria boarded a plane to fly to El Paso, Texas, to visit her father. Michael had been indicted under the federal racketeering laws a few weeks after the incident at Arrowpoint Lake and had been in custody ever since. Now he was serving a long prison sentence. After landing, Maria stood just outside the baggage area to wait for the Uber she had ordered to take her on the half-hour drive to the La Tuna minimum security prison. She had missed her father but dreaded this meeting. She didn't want to wait any longer to get answers.

After clearing security at the prison, which involved metal detectors and a search of her purse, she was taken to a large room with numerous small tables. There was no need to speak through a glass window by phone in a minimum-security facility. Michael was standing by one of the tables. When Maria saw him, she walked briskly over, and they embraced tightly, holding on until a guard warned them about the rule against physical contact. When she pulled away, she saw something she had never seen before—tears in the eyes of her father.

"How are you, dear?" Michael asked.

"I'm fine. I'm more concerned about how you are right now," she said as they took their seats.

"I can't complain, but it's not a luxury hotel. I have to work a few hours a day in the laundry, but I might be getting reassigned to work in the library since the laundry is causing problems for my allergies. Of course, they don't have a chef like Lucy here either, but you get used to it." Michael paused and spoke again. "How's your mother doing?"

"She's well. She started going to the opera. She says she used to love doing that when she was younger."

"Whatever makes her happy is fine with me. You do know I made sure she was well taken care of, don't you?" Maria nodded. Michael continued. "You can ask Mr. Sandone if you have any questions. He can put you in touch with the lawyers who handle the trust I set up."

Suddenly, the look on Maria's face turned somber. "Dad, I need to ask you about some things. After the FBI brought me home from the cabin, I was too shocked to talk for a while. When I was feeling better, I didn't have much of a chance to talk to you. Then you were arrested," Maria said as she began to lose her composure. "How did you get into all this trouble? I had no idea . . ."

"They said a lot of things about me in the trial that weren't true, especially Uncle Joey. He betrayed me and told lies about our family just to save his own neck from going to prison," Michael said, biting his lip and starting to shake. "Then the big drug dealer, Geller, and that crooked politician, Townshend, made up their stories just to save their own skins."

Maria shook her head and sighed. She had sat in on parts of the trial and realized there was too much incriminating evidence about her father for him to brush it off in such a cavalier manner. "And what about Gabe?" she asked. Maria had attended the day Gabe took the stand.

◆　◆　◆

Maria remembered when Gabe was sworn in, and the prosecutor began questioning him. "Mr. Rossi, what were your responsibilities working for the D'Angelo organization?"

"I was in charge of gambling operations in southeastern Pennsylvania," Gabe answered.

"Were these legal gambling operations?" the prosecutor asked.

"Most were not. There was sports betting in Philadelphia, and a gambling operation in a space connected to Francesca's Restaurant in South Philadelphia."

"Could you describe the operations at the restaurant?"

"There was a small casino in the back of the restaurant with blackjack, roulette, and slot machines."

"Was this casino open to the public?" the prosecutor asked.

"You could get in by invitation only," Gabe said.

"Are you familiar with the finances of this casino?"

"Yes. I was in charge of the finances and familiar with the money we were making."

"Who did you report to in your job?" the prosecutor asked.

"I reported to Michael D'Angelo. He was the boss of the whole organization."

"Was Mr. D'Angelo present during the poker games?"

"He usually paid a visit sometime during the night."

"Besides the casino, was there any other gambling at the location?"

"Yes, there were high-stakes poker games twice a week. The games were run by Diane D'Angelo, the niece of Michael D'Angelo." Gabe looked down and grimaced at the mention of Diane. "Diane set up and managed the games. She also had a bookkeeping system to record revenues and expenses," he said.

"Mr. Rossi, isn't it true that the casino—the whole restaurant in fact—was burned down in a fire last year?"

"Yes. That's correct."

"And unfortunately, Ms. D'Angelo died in that fire?"

"Yes," Gabe said, looking down.

"Did you have copies of Ms. D'Angelo's records?" the prosecution asked.

"Yes. After the fire, I copied her records onto my computer."

"Was that the computer that was found in the cabin at the time you were taken into custody?"

"Yes," Gabe said. He looked down, biting his lip.

"Mr. Rossi, we'll come back to the time you were taken into custody, but now I'd like to ask some more questions about the poker games at the restaurant. Were these just friendly games of poker that happened to occur on the restaurant premises?"

"They were high-stakes games, with a minimum stake of twenty-five thousand dollars for each player. We had some top poker players from the area. They included business leaders and leaders from city government." After taking a drink of water from a bottle he held, he said, "The house took a rake out of the pot during each round of play."

"What's a rake?" the prosecutor asked.

"The dealer took chips from the pot which amounted to about five percent. If the pot was ten thousand dollars before everyone folded, he would 'rake in,' or take, five hundred dollars' worth of chips from the pot," Gabe said. "Sometimes the pot was much larger."

"You're aware, Mr. Rossi, that the casino and poker games were not licensed or in any way sanctioned by the government?"

"Yes. This was not a legal gambling operation."

"In the course of an evening, how much money did the D'Angelo organization make on the poker games?"

"It varied, but it was usually many thousands of dollars. If you add in the receipts from the casino, from the blackjack, the roulette, and the slot machines, the organization could make over a hundred thousand dollars in a good week."

"Again, was Michael D'Angelo present during the poker games?"

"He would come in most nights to say hello to regulars and welcome visitors. We had hidden cameras that took photos of Michael interacting with the guests."

Maria recalled how at this point in the trial, she began to cry and had to walk out. She was not only shocked at the gambling operation her father's organization ran, but also shocked at Gabe himself. She had trusted him. Maria was relieved to learn he had recovered from his gunshot wounds, but she couldn't believe her ears when she heard the details of Gabe's work for her father. Maria did not attend any more of the trial until her father was sentenced after being convicted. Mr. Sandone had asked that she and her mother attend the sentencing hearing to help portray Michael D'Angelo as a husband and father. Based on the length of the sentence, it didn't really help.

CHAPTER 65

Maria and her father continued to talk during her visit. "I trusted Gabe, and he betrayed me," Michael said.

"In a way, I feel like he betrayed me as well," Maria said as she reached into her purse for a tissue to wipe the tears from her eyes. "You're not going to hurt him, are you?"

"No. My whole time in the business I've tried to get away from violence. Besides, I'm not really in a position to do anything here."

"I had no idea about the things he was involved in. But I can say he was very good to me; he was there as a friend when I needed one, and we were growing close to one another. I guess I should just say it—I was falling in love with him. As far as I could tell, he was always very loyal to you. I don't think he had much of a choice after they arrested him," she said.

Eventually, Michael sighed and looked around the room and shook his head. "It hurt when Gabe turned on us, but I guess I can't really blame him. He was in critical condition, and they had his computer. He's young and he was facing a long prison term, maybe enough to put him away for the rest of his life. They'll put him in witness protection, and I doubt we'll ever see or hear from him again."

"But what about you, Dad? I feel like you and Mom kept me in the dark about your business, and it got you in enough trouble to send you to prison. How could you do that?"

"When you were still a baby, your mother made me promise I would do everything I could to keep you away from the business. We both worked hard to do that and I guess we were successful, at least until recently. We wanted you to have the chance to lead a different life."

"But why did you stay in the business? You're a smart man. I'm sure you could have been successful in a legal business."

"Maria, I need to be careful what I say. I have appeals and we don't know if someone's listening. But from the day I became a leader, I worked to change the business I inherited. I wanted to make it legitimate, and I didn't want any more violence."

"Then what about the casino and the sports betting? At the trial, the witnesses said you started them," Maria said, shaking her head.

"I guess I couldn't change things as quickly as I wanted to," Michael said, turning his head to the side with a look of disgust, as if realizing he was violating his lawyer's instructions to keep quiet about the things that came out in the trial. Michael looked into Maria's eyes. "You must think I'm a terrible father, but I've always tried to be an honorable man, and I've tried to do some good in the world."

"I know, Dad. And I know you've always been good to me. I appreciate that. It's just that my whole world has been shaken up. I'm praying for God to help me forgive you, but I'm having a hard time with all this."

Michael was about to speak, but she held up her hand to stop him. "That's not all. From now on, wherever I go, when people see me they'll think, 'There's the daughter of Michael D'Angelo, head of the Mafia in Philadelphia.' How am I supposed to deal with that?"

"I'm sorry," Michael said with a quiet voice.

"What are you sorry for? A moment ago you said Uncle Joey and the others made up things about you at the trial." The two were silent.

Michael sighed and shook his head, looking upward. He kept silent for a few moments more before speaking. "I guess I'm sorry for everything. You were put in danger because of the life I led and the life I made for our family. Not only that, we also kept you in the dark about the kind of life we were really living. I remember your christening. You were such a beautiful baby. When I looked at you, I thought I sensed a voice calling me to a different life. I didn't listen. In a way, I spent my entire career fighting that voice. Sure, I helped clean up the organization a little bit, but I think I'm here in prison because I didn't really listen to that voice. I'm so sorry."

"Thank you for that. I appreciate you were finally able to say that to me."

"I've done a lot of bad things. You don't know the half," Michael said.

Maria interrupted him. "You can stop. You've said enough about your past."

Michael ignored her. "My parents named me after an angel, but I guess I'm a fallen angel."

"Dad, I think we're all fallen angels in our own way. Look at me. I was all set to give my life to God as a nun, and I fell out of the program. Yes, in the end I resigned, but I knew in my heart all along I was leading a double life. I don't know if it was apparent to you, but at the same time I was training to be a nun, I wanted to spend time alone with Gabe, and I found any way I could to see him without the convent knowing about it."

Michael lowered his head. "I have something else to confess. I asked Gabe to befriend you. I thought if you spent time with him, you might have second thoughts about your vows. Your mother figured this out. Even though she was hoping you'd leave the convent, she was furious at me for meddling in your life. I'm really sorry about that."

"I guess I should be upset about that, but at the time, I was really happy getting to know him." Maria paused. "One thing I learned from my time at the convent is the meaning of grace. There is forgiveness for all of us if we are truly sorry, and I believe you are. I want you to know I still love you, and nothing you've said or done can change that. God's love is like that, maybe even more so."

"I know it's a lot to ask, but can you come back sometime?"

"Of course," Maria answered. "Can I give you some good news?"

"I need all I can get."

"I got a teaching job. It's at St. Bart's Catholic School over in Maple Grove. I'll be the sixth-grade teacher. I start at the end of August."

Michael smiled. "That's great news. I know how much you love teaching. You know there used to be a big amusement park over there? My parents took me there when I was a kid. I don't think it's there any longer. I believe they tore it down and built a mall. But I think you'll like the area."

"I'm looking forward to it," she said.

CHAPTER 66

Several months later, Maria reported to work in Maple Grove. The school was an impressive stone building that stood on one of the main thoroughfares through the town, at the top of a hill. The parish church was next door.

Maria worked in her classroom, bringing in supplies, taking stock of the books and teaching materials, and generally settling in before the children would arrive a few days later. Later that morning, there would be a special orientation for the new teachers and a staff meeting for all the teachers.

As she placed a stack of books onto a shelf, she heard a knock on the classroom door even though it was wide open. She turned and saw a tall, handsome man standing in the doorway. Maria's mouth dropped open, and she stared incredulously. "Brian! Is that you?" she asked.

"Yes, it's me." It was Brian Murphy, the former captain of the Villanova University football team, whom she had dated.

"You haven't changed a bit!" she said, although she noticed he was just a bit thinner, and his curly locks had been trimmed and neatly combed. "What are you doing here?"

"Well, you may be surprised to learn that I work here. I'm the eighth-grade teacher. I was hired about two weeks ago to fill a slot that opened unexpectedly at the end of the summer."

That explained why Maria had not seen his name on any of the memos to the teachers that came out earlier in the summer.

"I'm also going to be the assistant headmaster. But more importantly, what are you doing here?" he asked.

"I'm the new sixth-grade teacher," she said with a wide grin on her face. For some time, Maria had felt both sadness and anger over Gabe. There was sadness since she had felt growing affection for him and now she was not likely ever to see him again; there was anger when she thought about all Gabe had kept from her about his role in her father's organization. She didn't hold any grudge against him for testifying against her father, as it was clear the FBI had lots of damning evidence from Gabe's own computer. At Gabe's age, the prospect of a lengthy prison term was truly horrifying, and she didn't blame him for cooperating with the government. Maybe he would turn his life around as a result. Now Maria began to sense a warm feeling about the prospect of getting reacquainted with Brian. She glanced at his hands and took note that there was no wedding ring.

"So what have you been doing?" Maria asked.

"I took some time off right after graduating from Villanova and did some traveling, mostly in Europe. It was kind of a 'self-discovery' trip. I had some injuries in my senior year that pretty much put an end to my football aspirations. Then, I got a job teaching in Baltimore for a year, while I attended graduate classes at night. After I got my master's degree, I wanted to find a position teaching in a Catholic school where I could grow in my career, and here I am."

Maria hoped he'd not heard of her troubled history from reading the news. Fortunately, the publicity had ended, and the news of Maria's troubles had mostly faded away.

"I'm so glad you're here. It's nice to see a familiar face on the staff."

"You're no longer at the convent, are you?" Brian asked. Unless he was just trying to make conversation, Maria felt reassured Brian had lived away from Philadelphia and did not seem to know she had left the convent or the circumstances that led her to leave.

"No. That's over and done with. It's a long story. I'm staying with my mother in Chestnut Hill for now, but I'd like to be closer. So, I'm probably going to get an apartment nearby."

"I've had my eye on this school for a long time. You probably know it's one of the best. I'm really happy to see you as well. By the way, they've asked me to coach the boys' soccer team, so I'll really have my work cut out for me this year."

"Well, I guess we're both in the orientation meeting later this morning."

"That's right. Look, I'd really love to catch up with you, and we have a short day tomorrow. Would you like to get coffee with me after work? There's a Starbucks around the corner near the mall."

Maria felt a surge of contentment. She had been afraid she'd be a stranger with no friends at the school. Now she was off to a good start, seeing someone she had been close to in college.

"Sure, that would be great."

Maria knew she had broken Brian's heart in college, but he showed no sign of holding it against her now. Nor did Maria have any negative feelings about Brian's impatience and how that contributed to their breakup.

Chapter 67

Three years after Maria started work at St. Bart's School, she sat at her desk on a Friday after the school day ended, entering grades in a book. She had a busy weekend planned, including a birthday party at the D'Angelo homestead in Chestnut Hill on Saturday evening for her niece, Tessa, who would be seven years old. After Michael was sentenced to prison for most likely the rest of his life, Carmella moved out and the house passed to Raph, who became the head of the family. Raph claimed he wanted to continue the legacy of his father and make the family businesses legitimate, although this would take time. Maria had heard this before, and she took it with a grain of salt. Maria did not approve of Raph's lifestyle, but he was family, and they got along fine on the few occasions when they got together. Plus, Maria was very fond of Tessa, and the feeling was mutual.

Maria would attend Tessa's party with Brian, whom she had been dating now for two years. As much as Maria was looking forward to the party, she was even more excited about tonight. Brian was taking her to Rizzo's Pizzeria in Glenside, not far from her home in Maple Grove. Rizzo's was not a fancy restaurant, but it held special meaning for the couple, since they had gone there on their first date. The two were getting very serious about the relationship, and Maria sensed something in the air. Going to the spot they went on their first date reinforced the feeling. Would tonight be the night Brian popped the question? It would be just like Brian to ask her at Rizzo's. Maria had flutters in her stomach thinking about it and she knew she would say yes if Brian proposed.

Suddenly, Maria was startled by a figure standing in the shadows in the hallway. A chill ran up her spine since most of the faculty had left by this time, and she knew she was probably alone in the building. Maria had always been taught to avoid danger, but there was nowhere to retreat to. She did her best to put on a courageous face and spoke. "May I help you?" she said with trembling lips. The dark figure remained silent but entered the room where Maria could see him in the light.

Maria gasped and her mouth fell open. "Gabe, what are you doing here?" she asked, breathing heavily. Gabe was thinner, and the immaculately groomed hair Maria remembered had grown out and covered his ears, with locks of hair covering most of his forehead. He wore a light stubble on his face, giving him a ruddy, handsome look.

"I had to see you," he said. As Maria gazed at him, memories flooded her mind, including the times she spent with Gabe, and their first and only kiss in the cabin at Lake Arrowpoint. She also thought of Gabe's testimony at the trial, and a sick feeling formed in her stomach.

"I thought you were in prison," Maria said, nearly at a loss for words.

"I was, but I was released into witness protection."

"You shouldn't be here," she said.

"You're right. I'm not supposed to be here. I'm supposed to stay in my new location, but I traveled a long way to see you. Please don't tell anyone I'm here," Gabe said.

"You should go," Maria said with her brows furrowed.

"Please just let me speak to you for a few minutes."

"Your few minutes is almost up. I was in the dark about what you and my father were doing, and I almost got killed because of the people you were dealing with," Maria said sternly.

"You're right. I'm sorry."

"Sorry isn't really enough," she said, tears forming in her eyes. "I was falling in love with you, and you lied to me about your life."

"I never lied to you. I just covered over what I was really doing for your father."

"That's just like lying."

"I'm different from who I was then. I only cooperated because they had evidence on my computer I couldn't deny. I was looking at a long prison sentence," Gabe said.

"I know. I don't blame you for that," she said. "I'm actually glad you came clean."

"Maria, I'm really changed, and I want to do something better with my life. I can leave the witness protection plan if I want."

"Is that safe for you to do?" Maria asked as she grabbed a tissue to wipe the tears now starting to stream out of her eyes.

"Could you talk to Raph and see if he'll leave me alone?" Gabe asked.

"Maybe, I mean . . ." Maria said as she struggled for words. "I'm pretty sure they're not going to bother you."

"Thank you," he said, and he stood staring at Maria for a few moments. "Can I see you again?" Gabe stepped forward and took one of Maria's hands into both of his. She didn't resist.

"I don't know, Gabe," she said, fighting back the tears.

"I thought about you every day during the last few years. I never gave up on my hopes that I'd see you again and I'm not giving up now," Gabe said, and he turned and left the room.

Maria sat for a few minutes with her head in her hands. Finally she picked up her phone and dialed Brian's number. "Hello, Brian," she said when he picked up. "I'm really sorry, but I don't think I can go tonight. I have a terrible headache. I'll call you tomorrow," she said and disconnected.

Acknowledgements

After practicing law for more than thirty years, drafting briefs, contracts, and legal opinions, I wondered if I could use my skills to create something more interesting. The result was *Among Fallen Angels*. When I began working on this novel, I had no idea what I was getting into. I soon realized a novel is not a solo performance, but requires a team of helpers to serve as beta readers, editors, proofreaders, and people of other skill sets to ready the book for publication. If I tried to list everyone by name, I'm sure I would forget someone.

First, I'm grateful to all my beta readers for their encouragement and often cogent suggestions. You know who you are! Second, among a number of editors I worked with, I'm especially grateful to Alexa Nazarro of the Aaxel Author Group for her tireless work to help me shape the characters and plot and to express it in language that befits the story. Many thanks are also due to Mary Hall and Rich Carnahan of Publish Pros, who helped me put the final touches on the book to make it ready to publish.

About the Author

Tom Morris grew up in Huntingdon Valley, Pennsylvania, a suburb of Philadelphia. He received his BA in Philosophy from Kings College in London, and his law degree from the Dickinson School of Law at Penn State. He practiced law in Philadelphia for seven years and was acquainted with a few lawyers who represented organized crime figures.

He later moved to Florida, where he served as general counsel for Armstrong Global Holdings and was on their executive committee before retiring. He now resides in the Chicago area with his wife, Gwen, and their golden retriever. When he isn't writing, Tom enjoys hiking, fishing, hunting, and reading.